Mr. Carstairs of the CIA had been searching intently for the right person to smuggle those vital documents out of Mexico. He would have to find just the kind of person who could get away with ferrying state secrets across international borders . . .

Mr. Carstairs caught his first glimpse of Mrs. Pollifax, who was seated alone in the waiting room. He could scarcely believe his eyes. The first thing that struck him was that really absurd hat—it was difficult to overlook —with a single fuchsia-colored rose completely askew. His gaze traveled over the wisps of her white hair that refused to be confined, and marked the cheerful glance that was as interested and curious as his own. Very ladylike. Very un-spylike.

So very un-spylike. So perfectly innocent. The image of everyone's grandmother . . . and who would suspect his own grandmother of being a secret courier?

"I'm Carstairs," he said warmly, taking her hand. "Tell me, have you ever been to Mexico?"

Fawcett Crest Books
by Dorothy Gilman:

THE AMAZING MRS. POLLIFAX

THE CLAIRVOYANT COUNTESS

A NUN IN THE CLOSET

A PALM FOR MRS. POLLIFAX

THE ELUSIVE MRS. POLLIFAX

THE UNEXPECTED MRS. POLLIFAX

MRS. POLLIFAX ON SAFARI

The
Unexpected
Mrs. Pollifax

by Dorothy Gilman

FAWCETT CREST • NEW YORK

To Dr. Robert Vidor, with thanks

ISBN 0-449-20674-2

Reader's Digest Condensation, October, 1970

Printed in Canada

First Fawcett Crest Edition: November 1970

20   19   18   17   16   15   14   13   12   11

The nurse walked out of the room, closing the door behind her, and Mrs. Pollifax looked at the doctor and he in turn looked at her. He was a very *nice* young man, with black hair, very white teeth and horn-rimmed glasses that he removed now, placing the stem of the earpiece between his teeth. "Well, Mrs. Pollifax," he said pleasantly, "I don't know how you manage it, but for a woman of your age you're in fantastically good health. I congratulate you."

"Oh," said Mrs. Pollifax flatly, and the doctor glanced at her with such a peculiar expression that she added brightly, for his benefit, "Oh!"

He smiled and returned his glasses to his nose. "Which brings me to the fact that, although I find you in excellent health physically, I do note certain signs of depression. You're not quite the same Mrs. Pollifax I saw last year. Anything in particular troubling you?"

She hesitated, wondering if he could possibly understand. He looked so absurdly young—he *was* young.

He added pointedly, "I had the distinct feeling that you were disappointed at being in such excellent health."

She said guardedly, "I don't believe I've ever cared about outliving my contemporaries, you know. I've never regarded life as a competition to see who can hold out the longest. I think one can sometimes have too *much* time." She paused and then added recklessly, "I daresay it sounds terribly frivolous when people are starving in India, but I can't help feeling I've outlived my usefulness." There, she thought firmly, she had said it, the words were out and curdling the air.

"I see. Your children, Mrs. Pollifax, are . . . ?"

"Grown and far away. And visits aren't the same, you know. One can never *enter* their lives."

He was listening attentively—yes, he was a very nice young doctor. "I think you said you do a great deal of volunteer work?"

In a precise voice she ticked off the list of charities to which she gave her time; it was a long and sensible list.

The doctor nodded. "Yes, but do you enjoy volunteer work?"

Mrs. Pollifax blinked at the unexpectedness of his question. "That's odd," she said, and suddenly smiled at him. "Actually I suppose I loathe it."

He could not help smiling back at her; there was something contagious about her smile, something conspiratorial and twinkling. "Then perhaps it's time you looked for more congenial outlets," he suggested.

Mrs. Pollifax said slowly, with a little frown, "I enjoy meeting the people, you know, it's just that so often nothing more is needed for volunteer work than a good set of teeth."

"I beg your pardon?"

"Teeth—for smiling. There are rules, too. You can't imagine how regimented some of the volunteer work can be. It's very impersonal—not yours, somehow, because of all the restrictions."

"Do you feel you're a particularly creative person?"

Mrs. Pollifax smiled. "Goodness, I don't know. I'm just— me."

He ignored that, saying very seriously, "It's terribly important for everyone, at any age, to live to his full potential. Otherwise a kind of dry rot sets in, a rust, a disintegration of personality."

"Yes," she said simply. "Yes, I agree with you wholeheartedly on that, but what is one to do? After my husband died I set out to make a very sensible life for myself—I always intended to, you see—so that I would never be a nuisance to my children. It's just that—"

"It's too sensible, perhaps?" Caught by something in her eyes that did not match the light mockery of her voice, he said, "But isn't there something you've always longed to do, something you've never had either the time or the freedom for until now?"

Mrs. Pollifax looked at him. "When I was growing up— oh for years—I planned to become a spy," she admitted.

The doctor threw back his head and laughed, and Mrs. Pollifax wondered why, when she was being her most serious, people found her so amusing. She supposed that her tastes always had been somewhat peculiar. Her husband's favorite form of endearment for her had been "lovable little goose," which was his way of forgiving the odd bent in her that he didn't quite understand, and as they grew older the children, too, had acquired the habit of thinking her just a little absurd.

She could hear Jane now: "But mother, why on earth— why on *earth*—a dozen antimacassars? Nobody's used antimacassars since Queen Victoria died!" How futile it had seemed even to explain the woman selling crochetwork at the door that morning, a dear, mangy little woman with a most fascinating story of being abandoned six years earlier on McGovern Street. With no husband and four babies to support she had turned in desperation to the handwork learned as a child at a convent, and Mrs. Pollifax had listened with rapt attention, enjoying every minute of it. After buying the antimacassars, however, she had felt it only kind to make a suggestion. "When you go to the next house," she had said tactfully, "it would be much wiser to call it McGivern Street, not McGovern. Strangers invariably make this mistake, but there has never been a McGovern Street here, and if you'd lived on it for six years you'd have known this. Although otherwise," she added warmly, "it's a terribly good story. The tears came to my eyes, they really did."

The woman had looked astonished, then confused, then badly frightened until she saw the twinkle in Mrs. Pollifax's eye. "Well, if you aren't the surprise," she said, beginning to laugh. "I certainly had you down as an easy mark."

They'd had a lovely talk over a cup of tea in the kitchen, and the woman's real story had proven even more fascinating than her false one, and just to prove her basic honesty the woman had offered to sell Mrs. Pollifax the antimacassars at list price—they'd been made in Japan. But Mrs. Pollifax had firmly refused, feeling the morning was well worth the price. Jane would never have understood, however; Jane had sensible Pollifax blood flowing in her veins and Jane would have been deeply shocked. "What, you didn't call the police?" she would have demanded. "Mother, honestly! That would have been the sensible thing to do."

Mrs. Pollifax thought with astonishment, "I don't suppose that I *am* a very sensible person actually. Perhaps the doctor's right, I can't be happy trying to be what I'm not."

The doctor was still chuckling, his glasses off again as he polished them with his handkerchief, but the mood of confessional had ended with his roar of laughter and was not to be recaptured. He wrote out a prescription for antidepressant pills, they chatted a few minutes longer but without further rapport, and Mrs. Pollifax left his office.

"But I wasn't joking," she thought indignantly as she walked down the street. "I really was going to be a spy." She had worked hard at it, too, going to the town dump every Saturday morning with her cousin John to watch him shoot rats, and proving such a persistent tag-along that he had condescended to show her how guns worked. On several glorious occasions he had allowed her to shoot with him. There were the maps, too, that she had pored over in her room year after year, and with such scholarly devotion that when the second world war began she was able instantly to announce the longitude and latitude of obscure little islands nobody else had ever heard of. What a funny child she had been, she thought with affection, a lonely but very happy child. She was lonely now but so—so *unused,* so *purposeless,* she realized; and at the back of her mind lay the memory of last Monday when she had carried her geraniums to the roof of the apartment building and had stood at the edge of the parapet looking down, her mind searching for one good reason why she should not take a step forward into oblivion. And she had found none. Even now she was not sure what would have happened if young Mr. Garbor hadn't seen her and called out, "Mrs. Pollifax! For heaven's sake step back!" When she obeyed him she saw that he was trembling.

She hadn't told the doctor this. Obviously she must find a way to instill novelty into her life or she would be afraid to carry her geraniums to the roof, and she was very fond of geraniums.

She walked up the steps to her apartment house and pushed aside the heavy glass door. Her mailbox produced an assortment of circulars, but no letters today. She stuffed them into her purse and unlocked the inner door to discover that Miss Hartshorne had preceded her to the elevator and was standing guard beside it. Immediately Mrs. Pollifax felt herself and her intentions shrivel. It was not Miss Hartshorne's fault that she reminded Mrs. Pollifax of the algebra teacher who had nearly blighted her life at thirteen, but Mrs. Pollifax illogically blamed her for it nevertheless.

"Mrs. Pollifax," boomed Miss Hartshorne in her quartermaster's voice.

"Lovely day, isn't it?" said Mrs. Pollifax, trembling a little. The elevator arrived and they stepped inside. Thoroughly cowed, Mrs. Pollifax let Miss Hartshorne press the floor button and received a pitying glance in return. ("You have forgotten pi again, Emily").

"It's warm," Miss Hartshorne announced as the elevator began to rise.

"Yes, warm. Quite humid, too," contributed Mrs. Pollifax, and pulling herself together added, "Planning a trip this summer, Miss Hartshorne?" It was not so much a question as an exploratory statement, because Miss Hartshorne was always planning a trip and when she was not planning one she was showing colored slides of previous trips. Sometimes Mrs. Pollifax felt that her neighbor did not really see the countries through which she traveled until she came home to view them on a screen in her living room.

"In September," said Miss Hartshorne crisply. "It's the only month for the knowledgeable traveler."

"Oh, I see," replied Mrs. Pollifax humbly.

The door opened and Miss Hartshorne moved toward apartment 4-C and Mrs. Pollifax to 4-A. "Good day," Miss Hartshorne said dismissingly.

"Yes—that is, to you, too," mumbled Mrs. Pollifax, and opened the door of her apartment with a feeling of escape.

Nothing had changed in her three rooms except the slant of the sun, and Mrs. Pollifax adjusted the venetian blinds before removing her hat. As she passed the desk the engagement calendar caught her eye and she stopped to glance at it with a sense of *ennui*. This was Monday; on Tuesday she wheeled the bookcart at the hospital, on Wednesday she rolled bandages, on Thursday morning there was a meeting of the Art Association and in the afternoon she worked in the gift shop of the hospital. On Friday the Garden Club met, on Saturday morning she would have her hair trimmed, and in the afternoon Elise Wiggin would come for tea—but Elise talked of nothing but her grandchildren and how joyously they embraced toilet training.

The doctor had said, "Isn't there something you've always wanted to do but never had the time or freedom for?"

Mrs. Pollifax tossed the day's newspaper on the couch, and then on second thought picked it up and leafed through its pages because it was important to be well informed and in touch with the world. On page three the photograph of a woman caught her eye. FINDS CAREER AT 63, said the words over the photograph, and Mrs. Pollifax, captured, immediately sat down to read. It was about a woman named Magda Carroll who had turned to "Little Theater" groups after her children married, and following only two plays she had been discovered by a Broadway casting director. Now she was performing in a play that had opened to rave reviews in New York. "I owe it all to my age," she told the interviewer.

"The theater world is teeming with bright and talented young things, but there is a dearth of sixty-three-year-old character actresses. They needed me—I was unexpected."

Mrs. Pollifax let the paper slide to the floor. " 'They needed me—I was unexpected.' How perfectly wonderful," she whispered, but the words made her wistful. She stood up and walked to the mirror in the hall and stared at the woman reflected there: small, feminine, somewhat cushiony in figure, hair nearly white, eyes blue, a nice little woman unsuited for almost everything practical. But wasn't there any area at all, she wondered, in which she, too, might be unexpected?

Nonsense, she told herself; what she was thinking was absolutely out of the question.

"You could always try," she reminded herself timidly. "After all, nothing ventured, nothing gained—and you're a taxpayer, aren't you?"

Preposterous. Unthinkable.

But at the back of her mind there remained the rooftop and how very nearly her right foot had moved into space.

"Isn't there something you've always longed to do?" the doctor had asked.

"Of course it wouldn't hurt to ask," she began again, feeling her way cautiously toward the idea once more. "Just looking into the idea would be a nice little vacation from volunteer work."

Now she was rationalizing because it was insane, utterly.

"But I haven't visited Washington, D.C., since I was eleven years old," she thought. "Think of the new buildings I've not seen except in pictures. Everyone should remain in touch with their own Capitol."

She would go. "I'll go!" she announced out loud, and feeling positively giddy at her recklessness she walked to the closet and pulled down her suitcase.

On the following morning Mrs. Pollifax left by train for Washington. The first thing she did after registering at a hotel was to go by taxi to the Capitol building and visit her congressman. The next day was spent in sight-seeing and in restoring her courage, which had a tendency to rise in her like a tide and then ebb, leaving behind tattered weeds of doubt. But on Thursday, after lunch, she resolutely boarded the bus for the twenty-minute ride to Langley, Virginia, where the new headquarters of the Central Intelligence Agency had been built. Its address and location had been discovered by

Mrs. Pollifax in the public library, where she had exercised a great deal of discretion, even glancing over her shoulder several times as she copied it into her memo pad. Now she was astonished—even shocked—to see sign after sign along the road directing everyone, presumably Russians, too, to the Central Intelligence Agency. Nor was there anything discreet about the building itself. It was enormous—"covers nine acres," growled the bus driver—and with its towers, penthouses and floors of glass it fairly screamed for attention. Mrs. Pollifax realized that she ought to feel intimidated, but her courage was on the rise today—she was here now, and in such a glorious mood that only Miss Hartshorne could have squashed her, and Miss Hartshorne was several hundred miles away. Mrs. Pollifax walked through the gates and approached the guards inside with her head high. "I would like," she said, consulting her memo pad, "to see Mr. Jaspar Mason."

She was given a form to fill out on which she listed her name, her address and the name of Mr. Mason, and then a guard in uniform escorted her down the corridor. Mrs. Pollifax walked slowly, reading all the signs posted on how classified wastepaper should be prepared for disposal, and at what hours it would be collected, and she decided that at the very least this was something that would impress Miss Hartshorne.

The room into which Mrs. Pollifax was ushered proved to be small, bright and impersonal. It was empty of Mr. Mason, however, and from its contents—several chairs, a striped couch and a mosaic coffee table—Mrs. Pollifax deduced that it was a repository for those visitors who penetrated the walls of the citadel without invitation. Mr. Mason contributed further to this impression when he joined her. He carried himself like a man capable of classifying and disposing of people as well as wastepaper but with tact, skill and efficiency. He briskly shook her hand, glanced at his watch and motioned her to a chair. "I'm afraid I can give you only ten minutes," he said. "This room is needed at two o'clock. But tell me how I can help you."

With equal efficiency Mrs. Pollifax handed him the introduction that she had extracted from her congressman; she had not told the congressman her real reason for wishing to interview someone in this building, but she had been compelling. The young man read the note, frowned, glanced at Mrs. Pollifax and frowned again. He seemed particularly disapproving when he looked at her hat, and Mrs. Pollifax guessed that the single fuchsia-pink rose that adorned it must be leaning again like a broken reed.

"Ah—yes, Mrs. Politflack," he murmured, obviously baffled by the contents of the introduction—which sounded in awe of Mrs. Pollifax—and by Mrs. Pollifax herself, who did not strike him as awesome at all.

"Pollifax," she pointed out gently.

"Oh—sorry. Now just what is it I can do for you, Mrs. Pollifax? It says here that you are a member of a garden club of your city, and are gathering facts and information—"

Mrs. Pollifax brushed this aside impatiently. "No, no, not really," she confided, and glancing around to be sure that the door was closed, she leaned toward him. In a low voice she said, "Actually I've come to inquire about your spies."

The young man's jaw dropped. "I beg your pardon?"

Mrs. Pollifax nodded. "I was wondering if you needed any."

He continued staring at her and she wished that he would close his mouth. Apparently he was very obtuse—perhaps he was hard of hearing. Taking care to enunciate clearly, she said in a louder voice, "I would like to apply for work as a spy. That's why I'm here, you see."

The young man closed his mouth. "You can't possibly— you're not serious," he said blankly.

"Yes, of course," she told him warmly. "I've come to volunteer. I'm quite alone, you see, with no encumbrances or responsibilities. It's true that my only qualifications are those of character, but when you reach my age character is what you have the most of. I've raised two children and run a home, I drive a car and know first aid, I never shrink from the sight of blood and I'm very good in emergencies."

Mr. Mason looked oddly stricken. He said in a dazed voice, "But really, you know, spying these days is not bloody at all, Mrs.—Mrs.—"

"Pollifax," she reminded him. "I'm terribly relieved to hear that, Mr. Mason. But still I hoped that you might find use for someone—someone expendable, you know—if only to preserve the lives of your younger, better-trained people. I don't mean to sound melodramatic, but I am quite prepared to offer you my life or I would not have come."

Mr. Mason looked shocked. "But Mrs. Politick," he protested, "this is simply not the way in which spies are recruited. Not at *all*. I appreciate the spirit in which you—"

"Then how?" asked Mrs. Pollifax reasonably. "Where do I present myself?"

"It's—well, it's not a matter of *presenting* oneself, it's a matter of your country looking for *you*."

Mrs. Pollifax's glance was gently reproving. "That's all very well," she said, "but how on earth could my country find me in New Brunswick, New Jersey? And have they tried?"

Mr. Mason looked wan. "No, I don't suppose—"

"There, you see?"

Someone tapped on the door and a young woman appeared, smiled at them both and said, "Mr. Mason, I'm sorry to interrupt, but there's an urgent telephone call for you in your office. It's Miss Webster."

"Miss Webster," murmured Mr. Mason dazedly, and then, "Good heavens yes, Miss Webster. Where *is* Miss Webster?" He jumped to his feet and said hastily, "I must excuse myself, I'm so sorry, Mrs. Politick."

"Pollifax," she reminded him forgivingly, and leaned back in her chair to wait for his return.

Two

Carstairs was lean, tall, with a crew-cut head of gray hair and a tanned, weather-beaten face. He looked an outdoor man although his secretary, Bishop, had no idea how he managed to maintain such a façade. He spent long hours in his office, which was a very special room equipped to bring him into contact with any part of the world in only a few seconds time. He often worked until midnight, and when something unusual was going on he would stay the night. Bishop didn't envy him his job. He knew that Carstairs was OSS-trained, and that presumably his nerves had long ago been hammered into steel, but it was inhuman the way he kept his calm—Bishop was apt to hit the ceiling if his pencil point broke.

"Anything from Tirpak?" asked Carstairs right away, as Bishop handed him reports that had been filtering in since midnight.

"Nothing from him since Nicaragua."

"That was two days ago. No word from Costa Rica, either?"

Bishop shook his head.

"Damn." Carstairs leaned back in his chair and thought about it, not liking it very much. "Well, business as usual," he told Bishop. "It's time I made arrangements for Tirpak at the Mexico City end. One must be optimistic. I'll be in Higgins' office."

"Right."

"And keep the wires open for any news from Tirpak; he's overdue and if there's any word I want to hear immediately."

Carstairs opened and closed the door of his soundproof office and joined the life of the humming building. Higgins was in charge of what Carstairs—humorously but never aloud —called "Personnel": those thousands of paper faces locked up in top-secret steel files and presided over by Higgins of the cherubic face and fantastic memory. "Good morning," said Carstairs, peering into Higgins' room.

"Actually it's cloudy outside," Higgins said mildly. "That's the trouble with this modern architecture. But come in anyway, Bill. Coffee?"

"You're saving my life."

Higgins looked doubtful. "You'd better taste the swill before you say that, and you'll have to manage your own carton, I've already lost a fingernail prying open the lid of mine. What can I do for you?"

"I need a tourist."

"Well, name your type," Higgins said dolefully, and lifting his coffee high murmured, *"Skoal."*

"I want," said Carstairs, "a very particular type of tourist."

Higgins put down his coffee and sighed. "I was afraid of that. Tourists I can supply by the droves, but a particular type—well, go ahead, I'm free for half an hour."

"He or she will have to come from your inactive list. This tourist must be someone absolutely unknown, Higgins, and that's vital."

"Go on. For what type of job, by the way?"

Carstairs hesitated. He always hated divulging information, a feeling bred into him during the war years, but Higgins was not likely to meet with torture during the next twenty-four hours. "There's a package coming into Mexico City. This particular tourist is to be nothing but a tourist for several weeks but on a certain date stop in at a specified place and pick up said package—rendered innocuous for customs, of course—and bring it into the United States."

Higgins lifted an eyebrow. "A regular courier won't do?"

"Couriers are pretty well known to them," pointed out Carstairs gently.

"And to mail it . . . ?"

"Far, far too risky."

Higgins' gaze grew speculative. "I see. I gather, then, that this package of yours is dynamite—not literally, of course, but figuratively—and that you are therefore reduced to being terribly ingenious and circumspect, but that the job is not dangerous so long as said tourist is utterly unknown to *them.*"

"Bless you for saving us both precious minutes," said Carstairs fondly.

"Have you considered someone not inactive but absolutely new—a fresh face?"

Surprised, Carstairs said, "No I hadn't—that would mean someone totally unseasoned, wouldn't it?"

Higgins shrugged. "If there's no point of contact would it matter?"

"Mmmm," murmured Carstairs thoughtfully.

"One has to sacrifice something for said tourist's being unknown to anyone. I mean, that's what you want to avoid, isn't it—someone met in Vienna in 1935 suddenly popping up in Mexico City years later?"

Carstairs smiled faintly—he doubted if Higgins had even been born in 1935. "Suppose you show me the possibilities," he suggested. "Very little is demanded of my tourist except accuracy, but he or she must look exactly right."

They walked back into the files where photograph after photograph was drawn out, sometimes to be instantly withdrawn with a "Oh dear no, he won't do, he broke his tibia in the Balkans," or "Oops, sorry, this lady's been loaned to the Orient." When Carstairs left it was with five photographs and a soggy carton of cold coffee.

"Nothing yet," said Bishop, glancing up from his typewriter.

"Damn," said Carstairs again, checked his watch—it was just half-past nine—and went into the office. Bishop, bless his heart, had left a fresh carton of coffee on his desk and Carstairs peeled it open, brought a cube of sugar from his desk drawer and dropped it into the coffee. He reminded himself that Tirpak was good, one of his best men, but if Tirpak had reported from Nicaragua two days ago he should have been

in Costa Rica by now. For eight months Tirpak had been on
this job, and from the bits and pieces he'd sent out of South
America by wireless and coded mail his eight months had
been extremely fruitful. Visually Tirpak was only a photograph in the top-secret files, but Carstairs knew his mind
very well—it was that of a computer, a statistician, a jurist.
Months ago he had been fed all the tips, stories and rumors
that reached the department and from these he was bringing back neat, cold, irrefutable facts on all of Castro's secret
operations in the hemisphere. But alone the facts were nothing; what was most vital of all was the proof that Tirpak was
carrying with him out of South America, proof so concrete
and detailed that each nation in the Alliance for Progress
would know once and for all the face of its enemy and in
exactly what form the Trojan horse of communism would
appear in its country.

Coffee in hand Carstairs walked to the ceiling-high map
on the wall and stared at it moodily. One might say that Tirpak's job of work was finished now, and so it was in the literal
sense, but actually it was only beginning. This was "phase
two," the most difficult of all, the getting of the proof into
the right hands, moving it north, country by country, until it
would arrive here on Carstairs' desk to be forwarded upstairs. That was the difference between this particular job
and the others, that it entailed quantities of documents, photographs, dossiers and descriptions of operating methods. It
could only be expected that eventually the wrong people
would get wind of Tirpak's job, and it was no coincidence
that several of Tirpak's informants had begun disappearing.
The wonder of it was that Tirpak had worked for so long in
secrecy. Now time was against him and Carstairs realized
that he was worried. He knew the shape that phase two ought
to take if everything went off perfectly . . . the shabby
photographic studio in Costa Rica where Tirpak's bulky
packages of material would be reduced to microfilm, and
then the trip into Mexico to leave the microfilm with De-
Gamez, for Tirpak was *persona non grata* in the United
States, a myth that had to be perpetuated for his safety. Once
the microfilm reached Mexico City it would be out of Tirpak's hands and the rest would be up to Carstairs and his
tourist—but Tirpak ought to have reached Costa Rica before
now.

Restlessly, Carstairs lit a cigarette. This was when he
sweated, this was when his own war experience went against

him because he knew what it was like to be on the run. He wondered where Tirpak was on this humid July morning, whether he was running scared or still had the situation well in hand. If he couldn't reach Costa Rica would he try to push through to Mexico? Was he being followed? Had he been killed, and all that documentation scattered and lost? This had happened before too.

The door opened and Carstairs immediately rearranged his features into their habitual mask. "Yes, Bishop," he said.

Bishop was smiling. "Tirpak has reached Costa Rica."

Carstairs' reaction was fervent and brief. "Thank God," he said, and then added savagely, "What took him so long?"

"They're decoding the message now," Bishop said. "It'll be here in exactly five minutes."

Five minutes later Carstairs was frowning over the message from Tirpak. It was the longest one that Tirpak had permitted himself, but Costa Rica was the safest place he had visited in eight months. In essence Tirpak said that it was Castro's Red Chinese friends who were interested in him, and he had decided it was time for him to go into hiding. All the documents were being processed as planned, and would be forwarded to Mexico City, suitably camouflaged. Tirpak planned to throw them off the scent by remaining in Costa Rica for a week or two. Carstairs could absolutely (repeat, *absolutely*) count on the microfilms arriving in Mexico City between August 12 and August 18.

When he had finished reading the decoded words a third time Carstairs put down the sheet and lit a cigarette. Tirpak had obviously been having a rough time or he wouldn't be planning to stay in Costa Rica to "throw them off the scent." In a word, things were getting very hot for him. He must have been closely watched and followed, so closely that for him to travel any further would jeopardize both the documents and any other agents he contacted.

But Tirpak was a seasoned man, and not a giver of reckless promises. Carstairs had unalterable faith in Tirpak's ingenuity, and if Tirpak said the microfilms would arrive in Mexico City between the twelfth and the eighteenth then the microfilms would be there. It was time for Carstairs to get his tourist moving.

"Bishop," he said, arranging the five photographs on his desk, "Bishop, you know the setup. Which one?"

Bishop sat down and carefully scrutinized the five photos.

"I'm afraid I lack your imagination, you know. They all look like authentic, true-blue American tourists to me."

Carstairs sighed. "Heaven knows that nobody should be judged by face alone, but this chap's expression is too damn eager for me. Retired businessman, excellent background, but personality a bit—ingratiating, shall we say? Might get carried away in a foreign country and do some bragging—it's amazing the loss of identity some people suffer in a strange country. This man might do except that he was in on some behind-the-line work in China during World War Two. If it's the Red Chinese that have been hotly pursuing Tirpak we certainly can't risk him."

"And the woman?" Bishop asked only from curiosity. Carstairs had an uncanny knack for assessing people; he was astonishingly perceptive and of course he was a perfectionist or he would never have gotten away with the outrageous operations he launched.

"Too young. I want someone over forty-five for this, especially if they're inexperienced. This tourist must be absolutely *right*."

Bishop stabbed the fourth picture with a finger. "How about this woman?"

"Mmm." Carstairs studied the face. "Humorless, but not bad. Compulsive type. She'll do the job, won't mix, probably won't talk to a soul." His glance dropped to the data beneath the photo. "Charlotte Webster, age fifty-eight—" He frowned. "She's not precisely what I had in mind, but she's passable. Bishop, I'd like to take a look at Miss Webster without committing myself. Is there some way in which I could see her without being seen, so to speak?"

Bishop said promptly, "Yes, sir. I can ask Mason downstairs to set up an appointment to review her credentials. He can meet her in his first-floor interviewing room and you can stop in and look her over."

"Absolutely inspired, Bishop. Excellent. Contact Mason and ask him to take over. Tell him he's to handle it completely and without involving me. Tell him I'd like to see her today if it's possible. I've a hectic afternoon ahead but I'm free for a few minutes at two o'clock. See if he can set up an appointment with her for two this afternoon."

"Right, sir."

When Bishop had gone Carstairs took a last look at the photograph, frowned, sighed heavily and then resolutely put it aside.

Carstairs went to lunch at forty minutes past one. The table-service rooms were filled and so he walked on to the cafeteria and picked up a tray instead. He finished eating at two, and after consulting his watch he hurried toward the first-floor interviewing room. To the guard stationed outside he said briefly, "Mason's appointment in there?"

"Yes, sir. A woman."

"Good."

Carstairs opened the door. The woman was seated alone in the room, waiting, and she was at once so utterly and astonishingly right for the job that Carstairs could scarcely believe his eyes. He had always been extremely intuitive about his people: it was almost a psychic quality that enabled him to separate pretense from authenticity. His glance first noted the really absurd hat—it was difficult to overlook—with one fuchsia-colored rose completely askew; it then traveled over the wisps of white hair that refused to be confined, marked the cheerful mouth, and when it met a glance that was as interested and curious as his own he felt the triumph of a casting director who discovers the perfect actress for a pivotal role. He strode across the room with hand outstretched. "I'm Carstairs," he said warmly. "I wanted to meet you while you're here. We're not really interested in your qualifications, you see, we want you for a job. Have you been talking with Mason?"

"Mr. Mason?" For just a moment she appeared bewildered. "Oh yes, but he was called to the telephone, and—"

"It doesn't matter, I'll take over now." He sat down beside her on the couch. "I realize that you're inexperienced but this is the very simplest of jobs. The important thing from the very beginning has been that I find someone absolutely right. I think you'll do. I think you'll do very well indeed."

"I will?" Her cheeks turned pink with pleasure.

"Yes. Are you free to work for us from August 3 to August 22?"

"Why—oh yes," she gasped. "Yes, I'm quite free—I'd be delighted!"

"Excellent. Have you ever visited Mexico?"

"Mexico!" She looked positively radiant. "No, never. You'd like me to go to Mexico?"

He appreciated the quick response; there had been no hesitation at all. "Yes. You'll be paid the usual fee for courier work, and of course all your expenses will be taken care of while you are there. It's quite simple. You'll be an American tourist and use your own name. The job consists of visiting a specific place in Mexico City at a specific date, and for the rest of the time you'll be on your own." She was listening with a look of wonder, as if she could not believe her good fortune. He reflected that an extremely bad photographer had taken her picture; Miss Webster was not only right but perfect. "You can handle this?" he added with a smile.

She drew a deep breath and nodded. "That's why I came, you see—because I thought I could." She added quickly, "Yes, I'm sure I can handle it. I will do my very, *very* best."

"I think you will, too," he said. "Look here, do you mind coming up to my office for a moment? I won't have time to brief you this afternoon, and only my secretary can tell me when I'm free, but I'll want to arrange an appointment with you as soon as possible." With a nod Carstairs dismissed the guard outside the door and guided his companion toward the bank of elevators. "I'd like to wrap this up without delay. I'll need you for at least an hour and my schedule this afternoon is quite hopeless. I could see you this evening but I think tomorrow morning would be better. Would that be convenient?"

"It would be perfect," she assured him, beaming. As they entered the elevator she had been fumbling in her purse; now she extracted a small white card and held it out to him. "I don't believe you know my name," she told him. "I always carry these with me."

Carstairs was amused, but he dropped the card into his pocket. The doors slid open at his floor and he grasped the woman's arm to escort her down the hall. "Here we are," he said. "Bishop? Ah, there you are. Am I free tomorrow from nine to ten?"

Bishop sighed. "Are you ever? Yes, technically you're free."

"Good. Nine it is then." He held out his hand. "I'm terribly sorry to bring you back again but I always insist on very thorough briefings."

"I think you should," she told him approvingly. "And really, you have been so kind. So *unexpectedly* kind. Thank you."

"Kind," echoed Carstairs when she had gone. "She's not only perfect but she appreciates my finer qualities. Well, Bishop, what do you think? I found my innocent tourist, didn't I? In fact one so congenitally innocent that she'd baffle Mao Tse-tung himself."

Bishop's jaw dropped. He said in a hollow voice, "Sir—"

"What is it, Bishop, are you feeling ill?"

"That was your *tourist?*"

"Yes, isn't she marvelous?"

Bishop swallowed. He said, "As you entered this office, sir, I was just putting down the receiver of the telephone. It was Mason calling to tell you that Miss Webster has just arrived."

Carstairs frowned. "Webster? Webster?"

"He sent a message up earlier, telling of Miss Webster's delay. I forwarded it to the table-service room."

"I ate in the cafeteria."

"Now Miss Webster is here."

"Nonsense," said Carstairs, "Miss Webster has just left."

"No, sir, Miss Webster has just arrived."

Carstairs began, softly and vehemently, to swear. "Then will you do me the kindness, Bishop, of asking Mason just who the hell was waiting for me down there in his interviewing room at two o'clock, and who the devil I've just engaged for this job? On the double, Bishop. I'll be in my office."

He strode into his office and sat down. Gingerly, reluctantly, he drew from his pocket the calling card that he had been given and placed it on the desk before him. He read it and frowned. He read it again and reached for the photograph of Miss Webster. There was a very superficial physical resemblance between her and his tourist but he knew now that Miss Webster was not going to do at all. Miss Webster was a dehydrated and flavorless copy of the original. "Well?" he growled as Bishop returned.

"Her name was Politick or Politflack, Mason can't remember which, but they'd know in the lobby."

"Pollifax," said Carstairs. "Go on. What brought her here?"

Without expression Bishop said carefully, "Mason says that she came here to apply for work as a secret agent."

Carstairs opened his mouth, closed it and stared incredulously at Bishop. "Impossible," he said at last. "Nobody just walks in asking to be an agent."

"Mason was most emphatic—and still quite shaken by the incident."

A full minute passed, and then the corners of Carstairs' mouth began to twitch and he threw back his head and roared. When his laughter had subsided to a chuckle he said, "Unbelievable. Preposterous." But he had reached a decision and he knew it. "Bishop," he said, "it's unorthodox even for this unorthodox department, but damn it—order an immediate, top-priority security check run on"—he consulted the chaste white card on his desk—"on Mrs. Virgil Pollifax of the Hemlock Apartments in New Brunswick, New Jersey. I want the results before eight o'clock tomorrow morning. And when you've done that, Bishop, start praying."

"Praying, sir?"

"Yes, Bishop. Pray that she's never unwittingly contributed to subversive organizations, voted Socialist or entertained a Red bishop for dinner. After that," he added flatly, "you can tell Mason to send Miss Webster home."

Three

"Flight Number 51 loading at Gate Four. . . . Flight Number 51 . . . to Mexico City loading at Gate Four. . . ."

Mrs. Pollifax found her seat on the plane and sat down feeling suffused with an almost unbearable excitement. For days she had been practicing the inscrutable look of a secret agent, but now she found it impossible to sustain; she was far too enraptured by the thought of her first visit to Mexico and her first trip anywhere by jet. And it was just as well, she told herself sternly, for Mr. Carstairs had emphasized that she was not a secret agent but an American tourist. "You are to be yourself," he had told her firmly, and had added, with a faint smile, "If I thought you capable of being anyone else I would never have given you this job to do."

Mrs. Pollifax had listened to him with shining eyes.

"You will arrive in Mexico City on the third of August and you will check in at the Hotel Reforma Intercontinental. The reservations were made an hour ago, in your name. You will be Mrs. Virgil Pollifax, visiting Mexico for three weeks, and you will behave like any other tourist. Where you go is entirely up to you. You will be on your own completely, and I assume you'll visit the usual tourist places, Taxco, Xochimilco, Acapulco, and so on—whatever is of interest to Mrs. Virgil Pollifax. But on August 19, without fail, you will visit this book store on the Calle el Siglo in Mexico City."

He had handed Mrs. Pollifax a slip of paper. "I want you

to memorize this address before you leave the building," he said quietly, and Mrs. Pollifax's heart beat a little faster.

"You will not see me again but you will be visited once before you leave by one of the men in my department who will make certain you've forgotten nothing."

Mrs. Pollifax had looked at the words on the piece of paper.

El Papagayo Librerí (The Parrot Bookstore)
Calle el Siglo 14,
Mexico City

Senor R. DeGamez, Proprietor—Fine Books Bought & Sold

Carstairs had continued. "On the nineteenth of August you will walk into the bookshop and ask for Dickens' *A Tale of Two Cities.*"

"The nineteenth," Mrs. Pollifax repeated eagerly.

"The gentleman there, whose name as you can see is Senor DeGamez, will say with regret that he is very sorry but he does not have a copy at the moment."

Mrs. Pollifax waited breathlessly.

"Whereupon you will tell him—with the proper apology for contradicting him—that there is a copy in his window. You will then go to the window with him and he will find the book there and you will say, 'I think Madame Defarge is simply gruesome, don't you?' "

Mrs. Pollifax repeated the words under her breath.

"These identifying phrases are a nuisance," Carstairs told her. "The gentleman will be expecting you about ten o'clock in the morning, but it is always wiser to have a double check set up for you both. Your asking for *A Tale of Two Cities* and your reference to Madame Defarge are the important things to remember."

Mrs. Pollifax nodded. "And that's all?"

"That is all."

"And whatever I'm to bring you will be in the book?" she asked, and instantly covered her mouth with her hand. "Oh dear, I should never have asked that, should I."

Carstairs smiled. "No, and I would not in any case tell you. Although actually," he added dryly, "I can in all honesty say at this particular moment that I don't know myself what he will give you. You will of course—as soon as you have paid for the book—leave and not return again. There will be nothing more asked of you but to continue your sight-seeing for two more days and return by jet on the twenty-first. You will receive your tickets and reservations by mail within the next few days, as well as the tourist card necessary for entering Mexico."

She nodded. "What happens when I come home? What about Customs?"

Carstairs smiled, saying gently, "That need not concern you. Let's just say that we will be aware of your arrival in this country, and there will be no problems for you. None at all."

"Oh."

"In the meantime I must emphasize that you are a tourist who happens merely to be dropping in at the Parrot Bookstore. I want you to think of it that way."

"Oh," Mrs. Pollifax said sadly, and as Carstairs lifted his brows inquiringly she added, "It doesn't sound dangerous in the least."

Carstairs looked shocked. "My dear Mrs. Pollifax, there is always risk—we discussed that—but if there was the slightest element of real danger involved I can assure you that I would never allow an amateur to be sitting here in my office. This is what we call simple courier work, and in this case your amateur status is especially useful. I know that I can trust you to follow directions intelligently—"

"Oh yes," gasped Mrs. Pollifax.

"And out of it you will have a very nice little vacation in Mexico. We will both be satisfied." He stood up, smiling lest he might have sounded reproving, and added, "Bishop will now show you to a quiet corner where you can memorize that address. I hope you weren't insulted at taking a lie detector test?"

"Oh no, it was terribly interesting," she told him, beaming.

"Good. Nothing personal, you understand, it's routine for everyone, even our clerks." He had held out his hand and shaken hers. "I won't be seeing you again, Mrs. Pollifax—have lots of fun."

She shrewdly suspected that he had used the word *fun* deliberately, to rid her of any lingering fancies concerning her trip. Well, she didn't mind; she was going to have fun. Her suitcase was fairly bursting with tourist literature on Mexico City and its environs, and Miss Hartshorne had insisted upon giving her three rolls of color film. "As a bon voyage gift," she explained, "because you will just adore having slides of your trip, they're the perfect souvenir for your Memory Book." Miss Hartshorne had insisted also upon coming to her apartment to instruct her, and had left telling Mrs. Pollifax she just knew she would come home with perfectly marvelous pictures of Mexico that everyone in the apartment house would enjoy viewing.

Mrs. Pollifax's daughter had received the news with dismay. "But Mother," Jane had wailed over the long-distance wires, "if you wanted to do some traveling why didn't you tell us? You could have come out here to Arizona. I've hired Mrs. Blair to take care of the children while John and I are in Canada. If I'd only known—we'd feel so much better if it could be you, and the children just love it when you come."

"It's just a little trip I thought I'd take for myself," Mrs. Pollifax told her gently, and wished her daughter a happy vacation in Canada.

Her son, Roger, on the other hand, had visited Mexico in his student days, and he told her that she must eat no green stuff and be terribly careful about the water. But there was a great deal more of his mother in him than in Jane, and he had added, "I was getting worried about you, Mother, you haven't erupted in years. Godspeed and all that. See you at Christmas and if you get in a jam send me a wire."

Dear Roger, she thought as she fastened her seat belt. She leaned forward to glance out of the window and saw a great many hands waving from the deck, and she fluttered her own with animation. As the plane began to taxi toward the runway Mrs. Pollifax thought with jarring abruptness, "I do hope I'm going to like this." Sunlight caught a wing of the plane and the glare momentarily blinded her; then with a nearly overwhelming burst of sound the landscape beyond Mrs. Pollifax's window began to move with dizzying speed, it blurred into a streak and dropped away. We're in the air, she realized, and felt an enormous and very personal feeling of accomplishment.

"We're airborne," said the man sitting next to her.

Airborne . . . she must remember that. People like Miss Hartshorne knew these things without being told, and, after all, nothing was an experience unless there was a name for it. She smiled and nodded and brought out the latest copy of *Ladies Home Journal* and placed it in her lap. Presently, because she had not slept at all well the night before, Mrs. Pollifax dozed. . . .

As the plane banked and turned over Mexico City, Mrs. Pollifax peered down at its glittering whiteness and thought how flat the city looked, horizontal rather than vertical, and so different from New York with its skyscrapers rising like cliffs out of the shadows. A moment later Mrs. Pollifax was infinitely relieved to discover that landings were more comfortable than takeoffs, and presently she was breathing Mexico City's thin, rarefied mountain air. All the way to the hotel she kept her face pressed to the window of the taxi, but when she spied her first sombrero she gave a sigh of contentment and leaned back. Never mind if most of the women looked sleek and Parisian and the men dressed exactly like Americans—this was Mexico because she had seen a sombrero.

The hotel proved luxurious beyond Mrs. Pollifax's dreams —almost too much so, thought Mrs. Pollifax, who would personally have preferred something native, but she recalled that the choice was not hers, and that this was where tourists stayed. "And I am a tourist," she reminded herself.

Mrs. Pollifax had arrived in the late afternoon. She dined early at the hotel, had a lukewarm bath and, sensibly, retired at nine. The next morning she was first in line for the tour bus that promised to introduce her to Mexico City. On the tour she fell into conversation with two American schoolteachers, Miss Lambert and Mrs. Donahue, but in spite of exchanging pleasantries during the trip she was careful to note each street sign they passed. When the tour ended Mrs. Pollifax had learned the location of the Paseo de la Reforma, the Palacio de Bellas Artes, the Palace of Justice, the National Pawnshop and the Zocalo; she had made two new friends and learned a great deal of Mexico's history, but she had not discovered the whereabouts of the Calle el Siglo. Both Miss Lambert and Mrs. Donahue warned her of the change in altitude and the necessity of adjusting gradually to it. She therefore went no further than Sanborne's that evening, where she ate dinner, admired the lavish gifts in their showcases, and went to bed early again.

The next day Mrs. Pollifax bought a map and after an hour's study set out to find the Calle el Siglo and the Parrot Bookstore, for she was conscientious by nature and did not feel she could relax and really enjoy herself until she knew precisely where she must present herself on August 19. To her surprise she discovered that the street was in walking distance of the hotel, and that it was a perfectly respectable side street already found by the tourists, whom she could identify by the cameras strung about their necks on leather thongs. She wandered almost the length of it, and when she saw the Parrot Bookstore across the street she blushed and quickly averted her eyes. But that one swift glance told her that it was neither shabby nor neglected, as she had somewhat romantically imagined, but a very smart and modern store, small and narrow in width but with a very striking mosaic of a parrot set into its glittering cement façade.

On the following afternoon, returning to the hotel with her two friends after a visit to the National Palace, they found themselves momentarily lost and Mrs. Pollifax steered them all up the Calle el Siglo, saying with a ruthless lack of conscience that it was a direct route to the hotel. This time they passed the door of the Parrot, and Mrs. Pollifax glanced inside and took note of the man behind the counter. She thought he looked very pleasant: about her age, with white hair and a white moustache that was very striking against the Spanish swarthiness of his skin. Like a grandee, she decided.

During the week that Mrs. Pollifax spent sight-seeing in Mexico City she found the opportunity nearly every day to pass the Parrot Bookstore. She did not seek it out deliberately, but if it proved a convenient way to return to her hotel—and it often did—she did not avoid it. Once she passed it in the evening, when it was closed, in the company of Miss Lambert and Mrs. Donahue. Once she and Miss Lambert passed it in the morning when Senor DeGamez was just inserting the key in the door, and twice Mrs. Pollifax passed on the other side without giving it more than a glance. She realized that she was beginning to think of it as *her* shop, and to feel a proprietary interest in it.

When Mrs. Pollifax had enjoyed Mexico City for a week she bid her new friends adios and went by bus to Taxco, where for several days she wandered its crooked, cobblestoned alleys, looked over bargains in silver, and sunned herself in the market plaza. She then returned by way of Acapulco, stopping there overnight. Everywhere she went Mrs. Pollifax found people charming and friendly, and this spared her some of the loneliness of traveling alone. On the bus returning to Mexico City she was entertained by a widower from Chicago who showed her pictures of his six grandchildren, and in turn Mrs. Pollifax showed him pictures of Jane's two children and Roger's one. From the gentleman's conversation Mrs. Pollifax guessed that he was a professional gambler, but this in no way curtailed her interest—she had never before met a professional gambler.

As soon as she returned to Mexico City—it was August 15 on the day she came back—she found it convenient to walk down the Calle el Siglo and reassure herself about her store. It was still there, and Senor DeGamez looked just as elegant as ever. He really looked so pleasant that she thought, "Surely it wouldn't hurt just to step inside for a minute and buy something? Other tourists do, and I pass here so often, and I haven't a thing to read tonight." As she paused, considering, a party of tourists came out of the Parrot laughing and talking and carrying packages that could only be books tied up in white paper. On impulse Mrs. Pollifax crossed the street and went inside.

Four

After the briefest of glances around her—Senor DeGamez was busy at the counter—Mrs. Pollifax hurried to a corner table that bore the placard LATEST BOOKS FROM USA, and plucked one from the pile. The only sounds in the shop were the crackling of fresh paper, as Senor DeGamez wrapped books, and the sound of his voice as he spoke to his customer. Unfortunately, however, he was speaking the language of his country and so Mrs. Pollifax could not eavesdrop. She selected a volume of memoirs by a well-known American actress and groped in her purse for currency; she was mentally translating dollars into pesos when a strident voice broke the hushed, literary atmosphere. "Old books, new books, read a book," screeched the voice, and Mrs. Pollifax turned in astonishment to see a live parrot addressing her from a cage nearby.

"Well, for heaven's sake," she gasped.

"You like my parrot?" asked Senor DeGamez from the counter. His customer had departed and they were alone. "But he startled you, I think. My customers, they are used to him, but Olé surprises the new ones. Come see," he said, walking over to the cage. "You know parrots? Not many do —this one is exceptionally fine. Have you ever seen such color?"

"Beautiful," said Mrs. Pollifax in a hushed voice. "But seeing him was what startled me, rather than hearing him. He is so brilliantly colored, like a sunset—or are parrots she's rather than he's?"

Senor DeGamez smiled, and with courtly, old-fashioned humor said, "Well, some are he's and some are she's, no? And so it must always be."

Mrs. Pollifax smiled back at him. "Of course, I wasn't thinking, was I? I do say things without thinking, it's a very bad habit. And of course the name of your store is the Parrot. The bird adds just the right touch."

He lifted a hand. "No, no, my store is named after Olé, not the other way around. My Olé came first—she has been with me twelve years. What I do when she dies I don't know."

Mrs. Pollifax nodded sympathetically. "What *will* you do —exactly! Of course *they* would say find another parrot, but it's never the same, is it?"

He said gently, "That is so, never. You are very wise."

"No," said Mrs. Pollifax reflectively, "only experienced, which comes from living a good many years. Wisdom is something else, I think." Her eyes returned admiringly to the gaudy bird. "She is company for you?" When he looked blank she said, "Your parrot keeps you from being lonely?"

"Oh—*si*," he said, nodding in understanding. "Yes. My wife she is dead five years now, and my sons, they are grown and in business. When I wish to hear talk I uncover Olé's cage and we speak together. She says a few words in English, a few in Spanish, and when we are finished speaking I cover her cage again and she stops."

Mrs. Pollifax laughed. "The perfect companion!"

"Exactly. And you—you have children too perhaps?" Senor DeGamez was smiling.

Mrs. Pollifax gave her book and her money to him and they moved toward the counter. "Two," she told him, "a boy and girl, both grown up now. I've been a widow for eight years."

He at once looked compassionate. "I am so sorry. But you have surely not come to Mexico alone?"

Mrs. Pollifax nodded.

"Then you are courageous. That is good, very good."

"It's sometimes a little lonely," admitted Mrs. Pollifax.

"Yes, but like me with my Olé you can be alone when you choose. Some of these American women, they are like swarms of—you will forgive me—swarms of geese, always together, always making cackling noises." Here the senor stepped back and did a very humorous imitation of chattering women.

Mrs. Pollifax burst out laughing. "I'm afraid you're too good!"

"But think—when you are lonely you need only find some American geese and join them. And when you tire"—he snapped his fingers—"off you go. To read. You like to read? I understand that, or you would not be here. Solitaire? Do you play solitaire?"

Mrs. Pollifax shook her head.

"But senora," he cried, "you are missing a delight. I myself treasure the solitary cards." He tapped his forehead. "It clears the brain, it clears the thought, it is mentally sound, mentally healthy."

Mrs. Pollifax said doubtfully, "I remember trying a few games when I was a child—"

"*Si*, but you are a grown-up lady now," he told her, smiling. "Please—you are buying this book? Allow me then to add another as a small gift. No, no," he said, putting up a hand to cut off her protests, and he walked to a shelf, fingered a few titles and chose one with a bright blue jacket. "This one," he said, handing it to her with a flourish. *"77 Ways to Play Solitaire."*

"Well," murmured Mrs. Pollifax, charmed but not sure what to say.

"For the loneliness, *si?* Because you like my parrot and you are not a geese."

"Goose," said Mrs. Pollifax and began to laugh. "All right, I'll try it, I really will."

"Good, you accept my gift then. Better yet you read it and use it. Remember," he said as he finished tying up the book she had purchased, "remember you are not a child now, you will appreciate better the enjoyment." He nodded affably to a man and a woman who had entered the store. "This has been a pleasure to me, senora, may you have a beautiful visit."

Mrs. Pollifax felt deeply touched and warmed by his friendliness. "Thank you so much," she said, "and thank you for the book."

She had reached the door when he called across the store, "Oh, American senora . . ."

Mrs. Pollifax turned.

He was smiling. "How can you play seventy-seven games

of solitaire without cards?" He had picked up a deck from
below the counter and now he tossed the pack of playing
cards the length of the room to her.

Mrs. Pollifax said, "Oh but . . ." and reached up and
caught the cards in midair. Her son, Roger, would have been
proud of her.

"How do you Americans say it—'on the house!'" he
called out gaily.

How nice he was. Mrs. Pollifax gave in graciously—after
all, he had other customers waiting. She held up the playing
cards to show that she had caught them, dropped them into
her purse and with a wave of her hand walked out.

Mrs. Pollifax had gone less than a block when she stopped,
aghast, her mouth forming a stricken O. She had just realized that the charming gentleman with whom she had
been chatting for half an hour was no other than Mr. Carstairs' Senor DeGamez. She had not intended to speak to him
at all, she had meant only to walk in and very discreetly
make a purchase and leave. How could she have allowed
herself to be carried away like that? What on earth would
Mr. Carstairs think of her now? For that matter what would
Senor DeGamez think when on the nineteenth of August he
looked for Mr. Carstairs' courier and it turned out to be the
American tourist lady who was not a geese.

"How awful," she thought, hurrying along with burning
cheeks. "How terribly undignified of me. This is not the way
secret agents behave at all."

Thoroughly penitent, Mrs. Pollifax returned to her hotel,
and as punishment resolved not to go near the Calle el Siglo
again until the nineteenth. To further punish herself she made
a list of *Things To Do* during the next four days: souvenirs
to be found for Roger, Jane and the grandchildren, postcards
to be sent to friends at home, and she even went as far as to
carry her camera with her to Xochimilco and take a few
pictures. *Dear Miss Hartshorne,* she wrote without enthusiasm, *Mexico is lovely. I have visited . . ."* and she listed
some of the places she had seen. *I hope you are having a
pleasant August. Sincerely, your neighbor, Emily Pollifax.*
All of this seemed to her exceedingly dull because it deprived
her of the opportunity to observe the Parrot, toward which
she felt an almost maternal solicitude after this length of
time. It was this frustration that led her to open the book
that Senor DeGamez had given her, and to her surprise she
discovered that she really could enjoy solitaire. Instead of

going to bed with a book each night she invested in a tray upon which she could spread out her playing cards. The first ten games in the book were quite easy and she quickly mastered them; as the nineteenth of August drew nearer and she became increasingly restless she went on to more difficult games, sometimes playing them in the hotel lobby after breakfast or carrying the cards in her purse to spread out on a park bench or a cafe table. She found that solitaire not only relaxed her nerves but entertained her mind, and she wondered if she ought to mention this to Senor DeGamez when they met again.

"Better not," she decided regretfully; this time she really must play the part of secret agent to perfection. She would be cool, impersonal, businesslike.

On the eighteenth Mrs. Pollifax ventured out to complete her shopping for the family and when she retired that night there were serapes draped across desk, bureau and chairs. "Not the very best serapes," reflected Mrs. Pollifax as she turned out the lights, "but buying six is so expensive and of course I'm paying for these myself." She had kept a conscientious account of every dollar spent, recalling how grimly Jane's husband talked of waste in Washington. She had the distinct feeling that as a taxpayer Jane's husband would not enjoy contributing to her three-week holiday in Mexico. For the first time it occurred to Mrs. Pollifax to wonder why Mr. Carstairs had sent her here for three weeks. Why not one week, she wondered, or two at the most, and for a fleeting moment she toyed with the idea that her visit to the Parrot Bookstore might be more important than Mr. Carstairs had led her to believe.

Nonsense, she thought, he wanted to be sure everyone knew her as a tourist. Nothing was worth doing unless doing well, she added piously.

She fell asleep thinking of serapes and dreamed of serapes spread across chairs, desk and bureau with a talking parrot guarding them.

Five

When Mrs. Pollifax opened her eyes the next morning she knew it was *The Day* she had been waiting for, but she felt no flicker of excitement. She had waited too long, and during the last few days—she had to admit this—she had been quite bored. In fact nothing but her games of solitaire had kept her amused, and remembering this she tucked the playing cards into her purse to carry with her for the day. Glancing into the interior of the purse she noted that again it had become the repository of an astonishing assortment of odds and ends: a pocket knife for her grandson's birthday, two chocolate bars, a package of paper handkerchiefs, a tin of Band-Aids, stubs of travelers' checks, two new lipsticks and one old tube that was worn flat—she would have to clear this out soon. But not now. She zipped up the back of her best navy-blue dress, and because it was cool this morning she added the gorgeous hand-loomed Guatemalan wool jacket that she had given herself as a gift.

She ate a small breakfast in the hotel dining room and passed the hour that followed in playing solitaire in the lobby. At 9:45 she was walking up the Calle el Siglo and repeating to herself the words *A Tale of Two Cities* and Madame Defarge. The door of the Parrot Bookstore was open. Mrs. Pollifax walked in with what she believed to be exquisite casualness, blinked a little at the sudden change from sunlight to shadow and nervously cleared her throat.

"*Buenos dias,*" said the man behind the counter, looking up with a smile, and after a second glance he added, "Good morning."

Mrs. Pollifax glanced uncertainly around the room, but there was no one else there. "Good morning," she said. This was not her friend Senor DeGamez whom she had met on her earlier visit. This man was small and dapper, with black hair, spectacles and no moustache at all; when he smiled a gold tooth gleamed at one side of his lip. To cover her confusion she gave him a bright smile in return and moved to the table on which the books from America were displayed. She began picking up one volume after another.

"May I be of help?" suggested the man with a bow.

Mrs. Pollifax had gained a moment to reflect. She decided there was no alternative but to ask just when Senor DeGamez would be back. Perhaps he had been taken suddenly ill, or had run out for cigarettes. "When I was here before," she told the man confidingly, "the proprietor was so helpful, he chose just the right book for me. Will he be in soon?"

The man looked surprised. "But I am the proprietor, senora. I am Senor DeGamez."

Mrs. Pollifax, taken aback, said, "Oh."

Smiling, the man added, "That would have been my cousin, I think, who comes in to the store to help when I am away on business. It happens that way, you know? He is Senor DeGamez too. But he is not here."

"He was so extremely charming and kind," explained Mrs. Pollifax eagerly. "He gave me a book on solitaire—*77 Ways to Play,* and—" She gasped. "Oh dear, perhaps I shouldn't have mentioned that. After all, it's your shop—but I would be happy to pay you for it, indeed I insisted at the time—"

"Yes, that is José," said the man with a rueful smile. "Definitely that is José, but what is one to do with him?" He shrugged, his gold tooth gleaming. "José is always impulsive; if the store were his he would be bankrupt in one month. Still . . ." His second shrug was even more eloquent. "Still, it is José's charm that brought you back, no?"

"Yes indeed—and for *A Tale of Two Cities,*" she told him boldly.

"*A Tale of Two Cities,*" he mused. He returned to the counter to thumb through a pile of papers. Extracting one, he ran a finger down its list. "That book we do not have, I am so sorry."

"I believe there's a copy in your window," she told him breathlessly.

"*Si?*" He said it with just the proper note of surprise and she walked with him to the low curtain that divided the window from the store.

"Yes." They both looked, but Mrs. Pollifax could see no copy of *A Tale of Two Cities* and with a sinking sensation she realized that she ought to have looked for it before coming inside. Nothing seemed to be going well; it was as if fate was putting up little barriers everywhere to test her. She said with a frown, "It was here the other day, I ought to have stopped then. Or perhaps I have the wrong store. I think

Madame Defarge is simply gruesome, don't you?" She waited
now for him to say something, her eyes alert.

Senor DeGamez continued to lean over the curtain and
study the books in the window. When he stood erect he
looked at Mrs. Pollifax and his eyes behind the glasses had
grown thoughtful. She thought that he, too, appeared to be
assessing. "It is not there," he said, watching her.

"No, it is not there."

He said quietly, "But I think that we understand each
other nevertheless, you and I."

"I beg your pardon?"

"I mean that we have something in common, no? I have
been expecting you. Please—a cup of tea while I get for you
what you have come for. I was just brewing the tea in my
little back room."

Mrs. Pollifax said cautiously, "I'm sure that's very nice of
you." She wasn't sure that it was nice of him at all; the
absence of the book in the window was a jarring note and
made her feel like a fool. Yet the man said he had been expecting her. Perhaps the book had been accidentally sold or
mislaid—even spies must have their bad days. "Very kind
indeed," she added more firmly, and since he was holding the
curtain that separated the back room from the shop, she
walked past him into the rear. There seemed nothing else to
do.

"Please forgive the untidiness," he said with a sweeping
gesture.

It was indeed untidy, with cartons of books piled to the
ceiling and the floor littered with scraps of wrapping paper.
But Senor DeGamez had not lied, he really had been brewing
tea on a Sterno and was not luring her behind the curtain
to hit her over the head. The tea was here and visible, and
at sight of this domestic detail—there was something so cozy
about tea-making and all its accouterments—her confidence
returned.

"Milk, lemon, sugar?" he asked, leading her to the desk
and clearing a place for her.

"Milk and one sugar, please," she said, sitting down in the
swivel chair and looking around her with interest. "Although
really I mustn't stop more than a minute."

"No, of course not, that would be most unwise," he agreed,
bringing her a steaming cup. "I will not take long. Tea is my
breakfast. I often share it with early customers." He placed a

paper napkin before her. "Please relax, I will be back in a minute."

He disappeared behind the curtain and Mrs. Pollifax obediently relaxed by slipping off one shoe and sipping the tea. He was certainly a very polite man, she decided, but he lacked the warmth of his cousin. She wondered what he would bring her, another book or something in a package? Tiring of the calendars on the wall in front of her, she turned in the chair to regard the room behind her. Her glance roamed over the cartons, a smock hanging on a peg, a sink in the corner—a very dirty sink, she noted disapprovingly —and she thought what a hot and stuffy room this was. Very hot. She drained the cup of tea, wriggled into her shoe again and stood up. It was kind of him to have invited her back here, but it would have been kinder of him to open a window; she would wait for him in the shop. An odd but vaguely familiar shape caught her eye; it was domelike and mounted on a pedestal and covered with a cloth. She walked over to it and pulled the cloth aside. It was a large bird cage, empty now of all but one vivid blue feather.

"The parrot!" she thought in astonishment.

In her confusion she had forgotten the parrot, and remembering Olé she at once recalled the first Senor DeGamez with great clarity. "My store is named after Olé, not the other way around," he had said. "My Olé came first, she has been with me twelve years."

My store . . . *my* Olé . . . yes, he had definitely referred to both of them as his. It was not so much that she had forgotten this as that today's Senor DeGamez had not given her the time to think. Nor could she think clearly now for it was very close in this room and her head was beginning to ache. She stared at the cage and forced herself to think about it. The cage was here. The parrot was not here. "But if this is the Parrot Bookstore, and if the parrot belonged to the first Senor DeGamez . . ."

There was something else, too, and she struggled to think of it. If the parrot belonged to the first Senor DeGamez, and the shop belonged to the first Senor DeGamez—there was a conclusion that ought to be drawn but Mrs. Pollifax found that she could not draw it. Something was terribly wrong, and not only with this shop but with herself, for her mind felt dazed, groggy, unable to reason or to reach conclusions. And it *wasn't* the heat, she realized, it wasn't the heat at all. It was the tea. Mrs. Pollifax had been drinking tea for years and it had never before left such a very peculiar taste in her mouth.

"There was something in that tea," cried Mrs. Pollifax, taking a step toward the door, but her words made no sound, her cry was only a whisper, and she took no more than the one step before she sank, unconscious, to the floor.

Mrs. Pollifax opened one eye, dimly aware that someone was methodically slapping her face, first the left cheek and then the right. She closed her eye and the rhythmic slapping began again. When she next roused Mrs. Pollifax made an attempt to focus on the face that loomed only a few inches away. "Fu Manchu," she murmured wittily, and giggled a little.

"You will wake up now, pliss," said a disembodied voice.

Mrs. Pollifax sighed. "Very well—except I don't really want to, and certainly not when you keep slapping my face." This time she made a distinct effort to open her eyes and keep them open, but the dismal sight that confronted her was not rewarding. She and the cheek slapper appeared to be sharing a small tar-paper shack that listed slightly to one side. A kerosene lamp hung from a rafter and sent grotesque shadows over the earthen floor and rough walls. There was a smell of kerosene and mustiness and wet earth. She saw no windows in the shack and the only bright new piece of equipment in the room was the lock on its door. Her eyes arrived at the cheek slapper and as she pondered him, too, she saw why she had burbled in her sleep about Fu Manchu: the man was Chinese. The resemblance ended, however, because he was neatly dressed in Western clothes and looked like a serious and kindly young student.

Then Mrs. Pollifax realized that her hands were bound tightly behind her with wire and she decided that the young man was not so kind after all. "Where am I, anyway?" she asked indignantly.

"I wouldn't bother asking if I were you," said a voice behind her. The voice was male and very definitely American, and Mrs. Pollifax squirmed in her chair to look but discovered that she couldn't.

"We're tied together," explained the voice. "Back to back, wrist to wrist—very chummy. Farrell's my name, by the way. Nice to meet you."

"Nice?" said Mrs. Pollifax weakly.

"I was only being polite, actually. Who the devil are you, anyway?"

She said stiffly, "Mrs. Virgil Pollifax from New Brunswick, New Jersey. Look here, young man," she told their guard firmly, "I know enough about first aid to tell you that you will presently have to amputate my left hand if you don't allow it some circulation."

The man said calmly, "Soon you will eat and be given an opportunity to exercise the hands."

As he said this the door opened and a man walked in, and Mrs. Pollifax, glancing beyond him, saw that it was dark outside. Night already! "Then I've been unconscious all afternoon," she thought in astonishment. Her eyes fell to the tray the man carried and she realized how hungry she was. The cheek slapper brought a pair of pliers from his pocket, and while he leaned over to free her wrists Mrs. Pollifax kept her eyes on the food, which consisted of tired-looking tortillas, two slices of dry gray bread and two cups of either coffee or soup. It was just as well that she had this to divert her because her captor was none too gentle; tears rose in Mrs. Pollifax's eyes as he worked, and when her numbed hands were free she placed them in her lap and tried not to notice the blood trickling into her palms.

The young Chinese said, "Eat," and he and the other man walked to the door, glanced back at them once, and went out. Mrs. Pollifax could hear the grate of the key in the lock. She turned at once to look for the man behind her and found him staring at her incredulously. "Bless my soul," he said, his jaw dropping.

"What's the matter?" asked Mrs. Pollifax.

"I've never seen you before in my life. Damn it, where do you fit into this? No, don't touch the coffee," he added quickly, "it's probably drugged."

Mrs. Pollifax regarded him with suspicion, his reference to drugs reminding her that not so long ago she had drunk tea with Senor DeGamez. Now she was less inclined to trust strangers. Nor was this man a type that she could approve of even though he was American; he had a lean, hard-bitten face—very hard, she thought severely, with a Hollywood kind of handsomeness about it that had grown worn from careless living. It was such a *type* face—such a ladies' man's face, she amended disapprovingly—that it lent itself to caricature. You could draw a perfect, deeply tanned oval for the face, square it a little at the jaw, cap it with an almost horizontal line of straight black hair, add an exquisitely slender black moustache to the upper lip and there was Mr. Farrell —tough, hard and an inhabitant of a world that Mrs. Pollifax knew would shock her: perhaps he even dealt in the drugs that he was mentioning so lightly. "But why?" she demanded. "Where are we, and who are these dreadful people?" The circulation was returning to her raw, chafed wrists and the pain of it brought fresh tears to her eyes. She picked up a tortilla and resolutely chewed on it.

"These are Mao Tse-tung's boys," said Farrell. "Cuba is full of them now, you know." He put a finger warningly to his lips and tiptoed to a corner of the room where he pressed his face against the boards. He came back shaking his head. "Too dark. But I definitely heard a plane land outside while they were trying to bring you back to consciousness."

"A plane?" said Mrs. Pollifax falteringly. "Then we're at an airport? But what airport can this be?"

He shrugged and sat down to resume eating his tortilla. "If the stars had been out I could have done some figuring. I think they've brought us to some remote part of Mexico where the Reds have staked out a secret airfield. I've heard they have them."

Mrs. Pollifax said stiffly, "You certainly seem well informed. How do you know all this unless you're one of them?"

He grinned. "Don't trust me? Now that makes me suspicious of you for the very first time, Duchess. But I'm being abducted, too, in case you hadn't noticed. Whisked away from a theater date with the beautiful Miss Willow Lee— the bitch."

"I *beg* your pardon!" gasped Mrs. Pollifax.

"Sorry," he said after one swift amused glance at her face. "But she is, you know. Very high connections in Peking."

Mrs. Pollifax was astonished. "And you were going to take her to the theater?"

He grinned. "My dear lady, I knew all about her when I met her. What I didn't realize until now—at least it's beginning to dawn on me slowly here—is that she knew all about me too. Now just how did *you* land in this?"

The question startled Mrs. Pollifax. She thought to herself, "I'm here because I carried geraniums to the rooftop one day, and because there seemed no purpose in my life." And Mrs. Pollifax, who had been feeling a little frightened and very small, suddenly laughed. She thought, "I have no right to complain, I don't even have the right to be afraid. It's true that I haven't the slightest idea of what's ahead for me—and at my age this can be especially disconcerting—but I asked for a little adventure and it's precisely what I'm having." She felt at once calmed and unafraid. "I don't think it really matters how I got here," she pointed out to Farrell. "But I think I'm here because I walked into a little shop in Mexico City to buy a book."

Farrell was looking at her strangely. "Not El Papagayo," he said slowly. "Not the Parrot Bookstore!"

His face swam toward her and then receded. She heard him say in a thick voice, "Damn it, they must have put it in the tortillas."

Mrs. Pollifax nodded wisely. Just enough food to keep them alive, and then new drugs in the food to dope them again. Very clever, she thought, and this time took the precaution of carefully sitting down so that she would not fall to the floor. "I'm becoming quite experienced," she thought proudly, and even smiled a little as the familiar blackness descended, blotting out Farrell and all consciousness.

Six

Carstairs had spent most of the morning of August 20 conferring with a State Department official about a revolution that had erupted in one of the small South American countries. His was the only department with a comprehensive file on the very obscure young man who had emerged overnight as head of the junta. He was able to tell the official that this young man was not a Communist. He was not particularly democratic either, but he was definitely not a Communist.

Then Bishop brought him a carton of black coffee and a slip of paper from the teletype marked CARSTAIRS, URGENT. "Better have the coffee first," he said dryly, and Carstairs gave him a quick glance before he picked up the message.

It said simply:

BODY IDENTIFIED AS RAFAEL DEGAMEZ PROPRIETOR PARROT BOOKSTORE, CALLE EL SIGLO, MEXICO CITY, FOUND DEAD IN CANAL LAST NIGHT AUGUST 19 OF KNIFE WOUNDS AND/OR

DROWNING STOP POLICE ESTIMATE DEATH OCCURED TWO DAYS
EARLIER ON AUGUST 17 STOP INVESTIGATION UNDERWAY.

Carstairs stared at the impersonal black letters and felt a
hot rage grow in him. He knew that in time this rage in him
would pass and that it would be supplanted, as it always was,
by a cold and ruthless efficiency, but now he allowed himself this brief moment to mourn DeGamez, whom he had
known personally. It was no way for any man to die and it
was not always enough to remind himself that his people
knew the risks.

When he was under control again Carstairs lifted his head
and said coldly, "I want the complete file on this. And the
message—did it come from the Mexico City police or from
our friend in Monterey?"

"Monterey," said Bishop, and slipped the file on DeGamez
under Carstairs' hand.

"I want a direct wire to Mexico City immediately to get
this verified by the police. You know who to contact there."

"Yes, sir."

"Tell them we have a definite interest in the man and want
to be kept in touch. Oh God," he added suddenly and ex-
plosively.

"Yes, sir?"

"Mrs. Pollifax."

"I beg your pardon?"

"She was to visit DeGamez yesterday." He picked up the
telephone and barked an order for a connection to the Hotel
Reforma Intercontinental, and Bishop went out, marveling at
Carstairs' memory. The man must have nursed along half a
dozen intricate operations since first meeting Mrs. Pollifax
and yet he had remembered precisely the date on which she
was to pick up Tirpak's microfilm at the Parrot.

Five minutes later Bishop returned to verify the murder
of DeGamez. Carstairs was still on the line to Mexico City,
listening, giving orders in fluent Spanish and listening again.
"Mrs. Pollifax is being paged at the hotel," he told Bishop,
hanging up. "Now get me Johnny at the Galeria de Artes in
Mexico City."

Bishop presently came back with the report that he had
talked with the man who swept the floors at the Galeria de
Artes and Johnny had not come in to open the gallery that
morning. Carstairs picked up the connection and began
speaking. Had this happened before? When had the sweeper

last seen the owner of the Galeria? Carstairs began looking grim.

"Trouble," said Bishop. He did not bother to make a question of it.

"Trouble," repeated Carstairs flatly. He deliberated a moment, and then said, "Take this down. TEMPERATURE 102 IN MEXICO CITY WORRIED ABOUT HEALTH OF AUNT JOSEPHINE SUGGEST COMPLETE REST IN HOSPITAL." He wrote names on a sheet of paper. "Translate and send out at once, top priority, to these people."

"Right," said Bishop, and hurried out. No lunch today, he was thinking, and wondered how stale the peanut butter crackers were that he kept in his desk for such emergencies.

By two o'clock messages had begun filtering in from various points. Mrs. Pollifax had been paged but there was no answer. She was not in the hotel. She had not been seen in the hotel since the morning of the nineteenth when she had played solitaire in the lobby after breakfast.

"Damn," said Carstairs. "Bishop, get me the hotel again— I want her room checked by the hotel detective, everything in it gone over thoroughly. And try the Galeria de Artes again, I've got to reach Johnny." He could not face the thought yet that they might have snatched Johnny too. Damn it, if that had happened then the whole thing had blown higher than a kite.

The police in Mexico City called in to report that it was only by a freak accident that DeGamez' body had been discovered at all. It had been weighted with cement and tossed into an abandoned canal which the sanitation department had just last week earmarked for drainage under a newly launched insect-control drive. DeGamez' shop had been thoroughly checked. The peculiar thing there was that, although DeGamez had been murdered on the seventeenth, the Parrot Bookstore had been kept open until noon of August 19. They were looking into this and checking out descriptions of the man who had continued selling books there.

There was still nothing from the Galeria de Artes.

"Get me the police again," he told Bishop. "I want Johnny's apartment searched too. Tell them he lives behind the Galeria."

More reports came in. The hotel detective had done a competent job at the Hotel Reforma Intercontinental. The chambermaid reported that on August 19, at her usual hour of eleven, she had arrived to clean the room that Mrs. Pollifax occupied. There had been a number of serapes hung over chairs, and there had been two books on the bureau that the maid remembered picking up to dust. The hotel detective, checking it today, found the books and the serapes gone. Clothes belonging to Mrs. Pollifax still hung in the closet but linings had been slit open in two coats and the clothes ruined. Her suitcase, the mattress of her bed and the pillow on it had also been slit with a knife and hurriedly searched.

"Hell," said Carstairs, looking haggard.

At four o'clock the police reported again. They had searched Johnny's apartment behind the Galeria de Artes. Nothing had been touched except a small safe in the kitchen. This had been tidily blown open with nitroglycerine.

Carstairs swore savagely. "They've got Johnny then," he said. "Johnny and the code as well. More telegrams—take them down. REGRET TO INFORM YOU AUNT JOSEPHINE DIED . . ." He paused. "Bishop, Code Five is clear, isn't it? All right, REGRET TO INFORM YOU AUNT JOSEPHINE DIED 5 O'CLOCK KINDLY VERIFY ACKNOWLEDGMENT OF THIS AT ONCE.

He now had to face the fact that they might have caught Tirpak too. "Get Costa Rica," he told Bishop. "There must have been some kind of contact set up between Tirpak and our chap in San José. Someone's got to know where Tirpak is. We've got to break silence and locate him."

"Yes, sir."

The Mexico City police were back on the wires at five o'clock to report that they now had descriptions of the man who had been running DeGamez' shop for two days. He was short, of Spanish extraction, had receding black hair, was clean-shaven, well dressed, wore glasses and showed a gold tooth on the left side of his jaw when he smiled. No one in the neighborhood had ever seen him before.

The description made Carstairs thoughtful.

"Recognize him?" asked Bishop.

"God, I only hope I'm wrong. Get me File 6X." It arrived and Carstairs scowled at two pictures of the same man, one an enlargement showing him standing in a crowd next to Mao Tse-tung, and the other a candid snapshot taken secretly in Cuba. "We'll teletype these to Mexico City and have them shown for identification. Take away the glasses," he said, holding a picture up to Bishop, "and who do we have?"

Bishop whistled. "Good God!"

Carstairs nodded. "Our brilliant and ruthless old friend General Perdido. Mao's hand-picked man for his South American operations—the one person who's responsible for bringing Castro closer to Red China than to Red Russia." Now he knew they must have found Tirpak; he could feel it in his bones. "There's only one very feeble hope," he said at last. "General Perdido was in Cuba last week, wasn't he?"

Bishop was glancing through innumerable reports. "Seen there on August 15."

Carstairs said slowly, "He just might take one of them— Johnny or Tirpak or Mrs. Pollifax—back to Cuba with him. General Perdido has always enjoyed his little trophies. I'll shortwave descriptions to agents in Cuba." He glanced at Bishop and smiled faintly. "For heaven's sake, go and have lunch or dinner or breakfast or whatever it's time for, Bishop. You can bring me back some fresh coffee and a chocolate bar." The door closed behind Bishop and Carstairs lit a cigarette, relieved at being alone for a few moments. Tirpak . . . DeGamez . . . Johnny . . . he thought about them, his face like granite as he weighed all the angles. From the point of view of the department it meant failure, of course—a clean sweep for the other side, an utter rout, eight months of invaluable work gone up in smoke, no microfilms and three top agents missing and presumed dead. But it was in the broader sense that it cut more deeply. He thought of the years that DeGamez and Johnny had spent in carefully building up their respective reputations in Mexico City as cover for their real work. They had been good, very good. All of this was gone now, swept away overnight, the work of years wiped out.

But in this game these things happened and Carstairs could accept the failure. One started all over again every day— Tirpak, DeGamez and Johnny had been aware of this. They had all—he was already using the past tense, he realized— been seasoned agents. They were trained and knowledgeable; once in trouble they would weigh the odds against themselves and the odds in their favor; they knew the tricks of the enemy, they had their own tricks and if all else failed they knew how to kill themselves quickly and efficiently. It was Mrs. Pollifax who must be on his conscience. He had misjudged the job he had given her. She had been exactly right for it and he had taken ruthless advantage of that rightness. He had not been able to resist the unexpected twinkle, the preposterous hat, the little absurdities that gave her so much character. Who would suspect her as anything but a tourist? She had been given the simplest, most routine job that any agent could be given. Nothing had been asked of her but accuracy, yet the fact remained that even as a courier he had sent her off totally unprepared and untrained for emergencies. She had not even been given a cyanide pill. She was not a woman of the world, nor was she even aware of General Perdido's kind of world, and although he did not want to be ungallant she was an old woman, with neither the stamina nor the nerves to withstand these ruthless people. He had unwittingly sent a lamb into a wolves' den—a fluffy, innocent, trusting white lamb, and the wolves would make short work of devouring his lamb.

God help her, Carstairs thought devoutly.

Seven

"I'm wondering if they'll try to brainwash us," Mrs. Pollifax was saying cheerfully. "Do you know anything about brainwashing, Mr. Farrell?"

"Uh—no," Farrell said politely.

"It might prove rather interesting." She was remembering the lie detector test she had been given in Washington, and she wondered if there were similarities. Life was really very scientific these days. She looked at Farrell because there was nothing else to look at. She had been alert for an hour now, and it was still night, and they were still flying through the air, and once she had examined the seats and the floor of the plane she had exhausted the possibilities. There was at least one blessing in being airborne, however—her wrists were no longer bound. Instead there was a very medieval-looking shackle around each of her ankles with a chain that led to a ring set into the seat. It was not uncomfortable but it did give her a perverse longing to cross her legs now that she couldn't.

"Feeling better now?" she asked Farrell smypathetically. She had opened her eyes at least half an hour before he did.

"You didn't answer my question," he said suddenly. "About that bookstore you walked into."

"I don't believe I heard you," lied Mrs. Pollifax smoothly. "I asked if it was El Papagayo."

"I'm afraid I didn't notice its name. I seldom do, you know. Of course I know when I'm in Bam's or Macy's or Gimbels but this was a very little store. *Very* little."

There was a glimmer of amusement in Farrell's eyes. "I get the point—a very little store. And what happened there?"

"I went in," said Mrs. Pollifax, "and I asked for a book and this man seemed very friendly. He invited me into his back room for tea, he said it was his breakfast and he often offered it to early customers. And I drank it and began to feel rather peculiar. That's when I saw the—I mean, I suddenly realized the tea had left a very strange taste in my mouth. The next thing I knew I was tied up with you back in that dirty little shack." Mrs. Pollifax suddenly remembered that the best defense was an offense and she said, "How did *you* come to be here?"

He shrugged. "I, too, entered a bookshop."

"Are you a tourist then?"

He shook his head. "I've lived in Mexico since '45." He reached into his pocket, searched and swore. "I did have a card," he explained. "I run the Galeria de Artes in downtown Mexico City. John Sebastian Farrell's the name, Galeria de Artes."

Mrs. Pollifax, relieved, said, "Oh, I thought at first you might be a dope peddler, or—or . . ."

He grinned. "I've done some rum things in my life, and some of them outside the law, but I'll be damned if anybody's ever taken me for a dope peddler before."

Mrs. Pollifax at once apologized. "I've lived a very sheltered life," she explained, "and you do have a rather—well, I don't think I've known anyone—I mean, you look as if you'd done some rum things, you see."

"It's beginning to show? Well, at forty-one I daresay it's bound to—a pity." He said it with mock despair.

Mrs. Pollifax paid his mockery no attention. "What are some of the rum things you've done?"

"Good heavens, should you be interested? I hope you're not planning to write a book on your travels." He was still grinning at her.

She considered this seriously and shook her head. "No, it had never occurred to me, although I'll be very interested in seeing Cuba. You still believe it's where they're taking us?"

Farrell said irritably, "By all rights its where we ought to land, but it's taking us a hell of a long time to get there. Sorry —what were you asking?"

"You were going to tell me what a rum life consists of."

He grinned. "You don't think I'd dare give you an unlaundered version, do you? After all, I've bummed around Mexico since '45, ever since I was discharged from the Marines, and that's a long time. I used to run a charter boat out of Acapulco—at least until I lost the boat in a poker game. I've given painting lessons to debutantes—you may not believe it but I do occasionally move in the best circles."

"As well as the worst?" asked Mrs. Pollifax, hoping he wasn't going to disappoint her.

"As well as the worst. For a year I smuggled guns in to Castro before he won his revolution. Rather a good friend of mine although I've not seen him lately," he added with a roguish glint. "And I might add modestly that women constantly fall at my feet. I have that effect on them."

Mrs. Pollifax could not allow this weakness in her sex to go undefended. She said very blandly, "Like the Chinese woman you were going to take to the theater tonight?"

Farrell gazed at her for a moment and then said frankly, "Duchess—and I hope you don't mind my calling you that— you interest and surprise me. I've decided you're not a member of the D.A.R. after all."

"No, I've never joined that one," mused Mrs. Pollifax. "Do you think I should? But I *am* a member of the Garden Club, the Art Association, the Woman's Hospital Auxiliary, the—"

"Good God, spare me," he said, throwing up his hands. "If General Perdido knew these things he'd turn pale."

"General who?"

He turned his glance to the window. "Just someone I know." He leaned forward. "We're still flying very high but I thought I saw some lights down there." He added savagely, "You do understand what you've gotten yourself into, don't you? You do know what the odds are?"

Mrs. Pollifax blinked. She thought of expressing ignorance of what he meant, but to feign innocence indefinitely was tiresome. She said very quietly, "Yes."

"Yes what?" he demanded.

She did hope he wasn't going to shout at her. She added with dignity, "I am quite aware that I have been abducted by dangerous people, and that it's possible I may never see Mexico City again."

"*Or* your Garden Club *or* your Hospital Auxiliary *or* your

Art Association," he told her flatly. "It doesn't bother you?"

Mrs. Pollifax wanted to tell him that of course it bothered her. She had enjoyed herself very much in Mexico City and she had enjoyed being a secret agent and now she would like very much to be flying home to New Brunswick, New Jersey, to bandage her torn wrists and soak her bruises in a hot tub. There was, after all, a distinct difference between nearly deciding to step from the roof of an apartment house and in having such a decision wrested from her by men who appeared to be quite brutal. She did not want to die in a strange country and she did not labor under any illusions about Mr. Carstairs or her country coming to her rescue. If life was like a body of water, she had asked that she be allowed to walk again in its shallows; instead she had been abruptly seized by strong currents and pushed into deep water. It was a lonely situation, but Mrs. Pollifax was well acquainted with loneliness and it did not frighten her. What did frighten her was the thought of losing her dignity. The limits of her endurance had never been tested, and she had never met with cruelty before. If her life had to end soon she only hoped that it could end with dignity.

But she saw no point in saying these things to the man who shared her predicament and who must also be thinking of these matters. He had more to lose than she; his life was only half completed and he would be thinking of the women he would never make love to again, and the children he would never have. A pity about the children, she mused . . . but in any case she must be very careful not to display any unsteadiness; it was the very least that the old could do for the young. "There's no point in your being angry at *me*," she said calmly. Her gaze fell to the seat beside Farrell and she gasped. "Look —my purse! They haven't taken it away, it's squashed down between your seat and the next."

"Thoroughly searched, of course," he said, handing it to her. "What's in it?" He leaned forward to watch as she opened the clasp.

She, too, felt as if she were opening a Christmas grab bag. "It's a good deal emptier," she agreed, peering inside. "Yes, they've taken things. Oh dear, my aspirin's gone," she said mournfully.

"Extremely suspect."

"And they've taken Bobby's pocket knife—he's my eleven-year-old grandson," she exclaimed.

"No, they wouldn't approve of that at all."

"But the Band-Aids are here, and my wallet and coin purse and lipsticks—oh, and look," she cried happily, "they've left me my playing cards!" She greeted them as old friends, slipping them tenderly out of their box.

"Small comfort," growled Farrell.

"Oh, but you don't know how comforting they can be," she told him with the enthusiasm of a convert. "I already know twenty-two games. It's true there are fifty-five more to learn—I have a book on it, you see—but it's so relaxing and it will give me something to do." She was already laying out cards in a circle on the seat beside her for a game of Clock Solitaire. "They left the chocolate bars too," she said absently. "You can eat one if you'd like."

"You're not particularly hungry, either?" he asked.

She shook her head, her eyes on the cards.

He said in a funny voice, "We ought to be hungry, you know. We ought to be terribly hungry."

Mrs. Pollifax put down a card and looked at him. "Why, yes, that's true, we should be," she said wonderingly. She frowned. "I had breakfast, and then that man's tea, and nothing until night, and then I had only a slice of bread and a stale tortilla—I ought to be ravenous."

He hesitated and then said quietly, rolling up his sleeve, "I'm wondering if you have needle marks on your arm, too."

"Marks?" faltered Mrs. Pollifax, and stared in dismay at the arm he showed her. There were several angry red dots there, and a faint outline of gum where adhesive tape had been affixed and then removed. It was all the more unnerving to Mrs. Pollifax because she had been idly scratching at her arm since she awoke. She slipped out of her jacket and stared at her arm. "What are they?" she asked at last.

"I think we've been fed intravenously."

"Intravenously!" she gasped. "But *why?*"

"To keep us alive." He leaned forward and said in a low voice, "That's not all, there's something else. The plane I heard landing back there in Mexico was a propeller job. The plane we're traveling in now is a jet."

In astonishment Mrs. Pollifax took note of the sound of the engines. "Why so it is!" She stared at him with incredulous eyes. "Wh-what does it mean, do you think?"

He said quietly, "I think we've been unconscious for a longer time than we realized. I think we've been unconscious for a whole day instead of a few hours. I think this must be *another* night, and we met *yesterday* in that shack, not today.

I think they must have landed us somewhere during the day where they switched planes and took the precaution of feeding us intravenously so that we wouldn't die on their hands."

Mrs. Pollifax put down her cards with finality. It was not difficult to follow his reasoning to its obvious conclusion. "But jets travel very fast," she said, her eyes fastened on his face. "And if we have been traveling for such a long time—"

He nodded. "Exactly. I don't think that you are going to see Cuba after all."

"Not see Cuba," she echoed, and then, "but where . . . ?" On second thought Mrs. Pollifax stifled this question; it was much better left unsaid. Instead she said in a voice that trembled only a little, "I do hope Miss Hartshorne is remembering to water my geraniums."

Eight

It was still night when they began their descent through the clouds—through the very stars, seemingly—and Mrs. Pollifax felt a flutter of excited dread such as she had often felt as a child when the dentist beckoned her into his office, saying it was her turn now. She pressed her face to the glass, staring in amazement at the unearthly convolutions and formations below.

"Mountains," said Farrell, frowning. "High ones, some of them snow-covered." His gaze went from them to the stars, assessing, appraising, judging, his eyes narrowed.

Mrs. Pollifax watched him hopefully, but he did not say what he was thinking or on what continent such mountains might be. The flight continued, with Farrell's glance constantly moving from earth to sky. "We're going to land," he said suddenly.

Mrs. Pollifax leaned forward. A scattering of lights increased in density, the plane wheeled and began its approach to the runway. Mrs. Pollifax braced herself—there were no seat belts on this plane—and suddenly the earth was rushing past her with dizzying speed, they touched land and taxied to a very bumpy stop. Mrs. Pollifax gathered up her playing cards and put them in her purse. The door to the cockpit opened and two men they had not seen before walked in, one of them carrying a revolver. The other drew out keys and unshackled their ankles. Both were Chinese. The door was pulled away and by gestures it was indicated that Mrs. Pollifax and Farrell were to get out. This was accomplished only with difficulty because there was nothing more than a wooden ladder propped against the side of the plane, and for illumination a flashlight was shone on its rungs. Mrs. Pollifax descended into an oppressively warm night that gave the feeling of new heat lying in wait for sunrise. The two men waiting for them at the bottom of the ladder were not Orientals and she saw Farrell stare intently into their faces. To Mrs. Pollifax they looked—perhaps Greek, she decided, recalling an evening spent in Miss Hartshorne's apartment viewing slides on Greece; at least to Mrs. Pollifax their skin had that same similarity to the skin of an olive, moist and supple and smooth. She saw Farrell glance from them to the mountains behind the plane and then again at the stars in the sky. She said anxiously, "It's not Cuba, is it."

He shook his head.

"Do you know—have you any idea *where* we may be?"

His eyes narrowed. He said grimly, "If my guess is right, Duchess—I hope to God it's not—I should now turn to you and say, 'Welcome to Albania.' "

"Albania!" gasped Mrs. Pollifax, and peering incredulously into his face she repeated blankly, *"Albania?"*

"Albania."

"But I don't *want* to be in Albania," Mrs. Pollifax told him despairingly. "I don't know anything *about* Albania, I've scarcely even heard of the place, the idea's preposterous!"

"Nevertheless," said Farrell, "I think it's where we are."

A long car, once black but nearly white with dust now, drew into the periphery of the flashlights and they were ushered to its door and prodded into the rear. "A Rolls," Farrell said out of the corner of his mouth, and Mrs. Pollifax nodded politely. The two men with Grecian profiles climbed in and sat down on a drop seat facing them, guns in hand, and the car began to move at reckless speed over incredibly bumpy ground. Mrs. Pollifax clung to its sides and longed for an aspirin. The headlights of the car illuminated the road onto which they turned but the road held as many ruts as the airfield. They appeared to be entering a town, and presently they were threading narrow streets where garbage flowed sluggishly in gutters. They passed cobbled alleys and shuttered cafes and what appeared to be a bazaar. They met no other cars and saw no people. Even the homes that showed briefly in the glare of the headlights looked inhospitable, their rooftops barely seen over the tops of high walls that surrounded them. The walls were guarded by huge gateways with iron-studded doors—clearly not a trusting neighborhood, thought Mrs. Pollifax—and then they had left the town behind. Looking out of the window at her side Mrs. Pollifax saw the mountains again silhouetted against the night-blue sky; not comfortable-looking mountains at all, but harsh craggy ones with jutting peaks and cliffs and towering, rocky summits. The mountains, decided Mrs. Pollifax, looked even less hospitable then the homes. It was toward these mountains that they appeared to be heading.

Their guards stared at them impassively and without curiosity. Mrs. Pollifax turned to Farrell and said, "But why Albania? Surely you're wrong!"

"Well, this isn't Cuba."

"No," responded Mrs. Pollifax sadly, "it isn't Cuba."

"I thought at first these mountains might be the Himalayas, but this isn't China. The mountains aren't high enough, there aren't enough of them and the whole topography is wrong."

"I shouldn't care at all for China," Mrs. Pollifax agreed.

"One has to think of the few parts of the world where the Red Chinese are welcome. There aren't many, you know. That town we passed through was definitely not Chinese, it was Balkan in flavor. These mountains must belong to the Albanian Alps, and certainly these men are Europeans."

Mrs. Pollifax nodded. "I thought they looked Greek."

"If this is Albania then Greece is only a few hundred miles away," he pointed out. "You saw how primitive the airport was, and you see how primitive the country is. If we're in Europe there's no other country but Albania where the Red Chinese can come and go at will."

"I didn't know they could come and go *anywhere* in Europe," said Mrs. Pollifax indignantly.

"It happened about 1960," he mused, his brow furrowed. "Until then Russia was Albania's big brother and pretty much in control of the country. Then Stalin was denounced—that was a surprise to the world, you must remember that. It rocked Albania, too—they're Stalinists here, you see. I don't recall the details, it happened at one of their Big Party Congresses, but there was rather ugly name-calling, with China and Albania siding against Khrushchev. Russia pun-

ished Albania by withdrawing all its aid, all its technicians,
all its military, and China very happily moved in to help. The
chance of a lifetime, giving Red China a toehold in Europe."

"I didn't know," faltered Mrs. Pollifax. "The very idea—
and to think that I subscribe to *Time* magazine. I really *must*
stop skipping the Balkan news. But why bring us here? Why
go to such a great deal of trouble?"

Farrell gave her a quick glance and looked away. "Perhaps
they feel we're worth the trouble," he pointed out gently.

"Oh," said Mrs. Pollifax in a small voice and was silent.

The car had been climbing steeply for the past twenty
minutes on a road that appeared to be carved out of the side
of the mountain. On the left the car lights picked out weird
rock shapes, on the right side nothing, and Mrs. Pollifax had
a terrible suspicion that there really was nothing there, and
that any nervous turning of the wheel would send them
hurtling through space into the valley. Higher and higher
they climbed until at last the car came to a stop and their two
guards came to life and jumped out. They spoke rapidly to
the driver in a strange, oddly nasal language, and gestured
to Farrell and Mrs. Pollifax to leave the car. Once outside
they found themselves in a vast basin of desolate gray rock,
and noting this, Mrs. Pollifax realized the darkness was dis-
solving and that dawn must be near. Another day, she
thought wonderingly, and suddenly, quite absurdly, recalled
her son Roger telling her to wire him if she found herself in
a jam.

"This is extremely sticky jam I'm in," she reflected. "Treacly, oozy black raspberry, I think. And no Western Unions."

One of the guards had disappeared behind a rock. Now he
reappeared leading four donkeys, and to Mrs. Pollifax's
consternation the man signaled that she mount one of them.
"I can't," she said in a low voice to Farrell, and to the guard
she said in a louder voice, "I can't."

"I believe you're going to have to," Farrell pointed out in
amusement.

She eyed the animal with distaste and in turn it eyed her
with suspicion. Farrell moved forward to help; it was only
with his intercession that a truce was accomplished between
the two, and this was mainly because, once upon its back, the
donkey could no longer see Mrs. Pollifax. When Farrell and
the guards had also mounted donkeys they formed a procession and moved on.

The wilderness path along which they moved was desolate

beyond belief. This was a country where all life had been extinguished, to be supplanted by rocks of every color, shape and formation. The air was thin but only a little cooler than the valley. There was no shade of any kind. Slowly, as they traveled, the sunrise spread a golden light across the valley and Mrs. Pollifax could look down upon green slopes and occasional trees, but the rising of the sun brought warmth as well, followed by heat, and between this and the donkey Mrs. Pollifax was soon extremely uncomfortable. Horseback riding had never been her métier, and sitting sidesaddle on a donkey was taxing; it took a great deal of energy simply to keep from falling off, and the donkey moved with unexpected lurches. They had traveled for perhaps an hour when Farrell said suddenly, "Psst—look."

Mrs. Pollifax reluctantly lifted her eyes. They had left behind the bleak gray rocks and cliffs of the first leg of their journey and had come out upon a small plateau literally carpeted with stones. The ground was like a brook bed that had been emptied of silt and water—the stones were scattered everywhere in such profusion that not a blade of grass could grow. The sun beat down mercilessly on the landscape, turning everything into a tawny color of yellow dust. At the edge of the cliff overlooking the valley stood a square, fortresslike building made of stone piled upon stone, with only black slits for windows. It stood at the very edge of the precipice, and after a drop of a hundred or so feet the earth formed a rock-strewn terrace, and below this another, showing tentative signs of green, and then the earth flowed like a green river down to the floor of the valley. As her donkey picked its way over the stones Mrs. Pollifax saw a second, smaller building at some distance from the first, also built of rocks and precisely like the other except in size. If she were a tourist, thought Mrs. Pollifax wistfully, this would be a wild and romantic scene; one could imagine bandit chieftains holing up in these impregnable buildings, completely safe against attack. But unfortunately she was not a tourist, she was an American spy who had been abducted—no, captured, she thought uneasily —and no one on God's green earth knew where she was except the people who had brought her here. For just the briefest of moments she allowed herself to think of her children, of Jane having a safe and happy vacation in Canada, of Roger, who had told her to wire him if she got into a jam. "If it just didn't seem so *unreal*," thought Mrs. Pollifax unhappily. "I mean—what on earth am I doing *here?* I'm in

Albania—at least Farrell *thinks* it's Albania." And again she felt it was preposterous, her being in Albania. Why, she didn't even own a passport.

"Journey's end," commented Farrell dryly, with a nod at the smaller building toward which they were heading.

She said crossly, "I really don't think you need put it in just that manner." But as they approached the second of the two buildings she realized that unconsciously she had begun bracing herself for the worst. She drew herself up to her full height—it was a little difficult on a donkey—and said primly, "I have always found that in painful situations it is a sensible idea to take each hour as it comes and not to anticipate beyond. But oh how I wish I could have a bath!"

Someone must have noted their approach through the slits in the wall beause the iron door of the building opened as they drew near. A man stepped out into the blazing sun with a rifle under his arm but Mrs. Pollifax was too busy to pay him any attention; she was involved in separating herself from the animal to which she had become welded during the past hour. No sooner did she stand upright, all her bones protesting, when the guard grasped her arm and led her into the building.

"Journey's end," she thought bleakly, looking around her at more stone—really she was growing very tired of stones. In shape the building was a rectangle about thirty feet long. The door through which they entered was set at one end of the long rectangle, and as they entered they faced a room that occupied the precipice end of the structure. On their left was a dark hall that ran across the front, and looking down it Mrs. Pollifax saw two iron cell doors opening from it. She quickly turned her gaze back to the room, which contained a desk, a chair, a water cooler, a well-stocked gun rack, a small switchboard and a gray-haired man dressed in a uniform. He greeted them curtly in English.

"I am Major Vassovic." With this announcement he took a huge iron key from the wall and led them down the hall to the first door and opened it. "In, please," he said.

"I don't suppose you have an aspirin," Mrs. Pollifax told him hopefully. "I've had the most ridiculous headache for hours. I don't often get them, you know, and I don't mean to complain, but I've been doped twice and apparently fed intravenously, and it's been a rather exhausting plane ride——"

The major looked at her in astonishment, and then carefully wiped all expression from his face. "I have no orders to give you anything," he told her stiffly.

Farrell gently pulled her into the room, the door clanged shut behind them and Mrs. Pollifax said, "I don't see how one aspirin could . . ." Her voice died away at sight of their prison. It was quite decent in size, but so dark—lighted only by the two slits in the wall—that it was twilight inside. There was to be no privacy for her or Farrell, she noted; none at all except for the dimness. There was an iron cot at each end of the room, with a night chamber under each; there were two small tables and that was all. No chairs, no screens, no lavatory, no clothespegs, nothing else except the oppressive stone walls and floor.

"Well," said Farrell, and sat down on a cot.

"Well," said Mrs. Pollifax, and sat down on the other cot. They stared at each other through the gloom, a distance of perhaps twelve feet, and Mrs. Pollifax realized that the silence was becoming long and much too dismal. "Well," she said again, briskly, and getting up she carried one of the tables to the cot, reached into her purse and began spreading out her deck of playing cards.

"Not again," groaned Farrell. "Not *here.*"

"Whyever not?" said Mrs. Pollifax and was glad to see him diverted.

She had played three games when the door was unlocked and opened and a guard gestured that she come with him. Farrell also stood up but the guard shook his head. Farrell said lightly, "Well—I do feel snubbed. Good luck, Duchess."

Mrs. Pollifax did not look back. Her knees were trembling, and this unexpected separation from Farrell—on whom she had once looked askance—left her feeling very lonely. She was led out into the blazing sun to stumble over the stones to the other, larger building. The door was opened from inside and Mrs. Pollifax was led into a large cool room of white-washed stone. The room was furnished like Major Vassovic's office except that everything was larger. There were two men in the room, both in uniform, but Mrs. Pollifax's glance flew to the man seated at the desk.

"Why, Senor DeGamez," she gasped. "How did you get here?"

His gold tooth flashed in a brief smile. "In the same manner that you did, Mrs. Pollifax. Allow me to present General Hoong, who is in charge of the—uh—buildings here."

"How do you do," Mrs. Pollifax said politely to the Chinese. He bowed, his expression remote, and Mrs. Pollifax immediately forgot him. "Except that of course you're not the real Senor DeGamez, I know that now," she went on. "I realized it as soon as I saw the empty parrot cage. It had one feather in it."

"Actually I am General Raoul Perdido," he said, motioning her to take the chair beside his desk. "Do sit down, Mrs. Pollifax, we have a few things to discuss. Pleasantly or unpleasantly, depending upon your attitude."

Brainwashing, thought Mrs. Pollifax contemptuously, and suddenly realized that she was not afraid. She had endured other crises without losing her dignity—births, widowhood, illnesses—and she was experienced enough to know now that everything worthwhile took time and loneliness, perhaps even one's death as well. "I don't mean to be morbid," she told herself. "It's just that I refuse to be frightened by a man whose only weapon over me is the cessation of life. After all, I have nothing to hide. I only wish I did. I'm not even a spy. I almost was, but then this horrid man rushed in to spoil everything." She sat down and faced him with growing indignation. Aloud she said, "May I ask, General Perdido, just why you had to abduct me like this?"

He leaned back in his chair, lit a cigar and suddenly impaled her with a sharp glance. "I had hoped for a more intelligent question from you than this, Mrs. Pollifax. I abhor pretended innocence."

"And I have a great deal to complain about," she retorted, "and no consul to whom I can complain. I was having a very pleasant vacation in Mexico, and now I am informed that I am in Albania. Is this true?"

"I am in charge of the questioning," said General Perdido.

"Then you have been very extravagant," she told him coldly. "You have flown me thousands of miles across the world to ask questions that could have been very easily asked in Mexico. I don't know what country you work for, General Perdido, but your taxpayers would certainly have every right to be furious if they knew."

The general's face darkened. "I see that you are going to deny you are an American spy."

"Spy?" said Mrs. Pollifax scornfully. "Is that what you take me for? This is one more grievance I must hold against you, General."

"Fool," spat the general. "You are not in the United States now, and you are not in Mexico, Mrs. Pollifax, and—"

"Then I wish that you would tell me where I *am*," she reminded him.

"Never mind," he shouted. "Wherever it is, you are far from home and no one knows where you are. No one, do you understand? You are removed from all influence and all hope of rescue. I have methods for extracting the truth—very refined or very brutal but all of them painful. I am extremely accomplished in all of them."

"I'm sure you are at the very top of your profession," she said tartly, "but I do not find it a very admirable profession."

General Hoong turned from the window and spoke rapidly to General Perdido. There was silence and then General Perdido said reluctantly, "Let us try to be reasonable, Mrs. Pollifax."

"Yes, let's," she agreed.

"You visited the Parrot Bookstore a few days ago, did you not?"

"Yes, of course."

"For what purpose?"

"To buy a book. Naturally."

"At this time you confided in me that you had visited the Parrot Bookstore on a previous day, is this not correct?"

Mrs. Pollifax nodded.

"Also at this time you inquired of me where the other Senor DeGamez was. You told me you had talked with him at some length, is this not so, Mrs. Pollifax?"

"But of course," said Mrs. Pollifax warmly. "He was most enjoyable, a thoroughly charming man."

The general said patiently, "You said he made you the gift of a book?"

"Yes, he did, it was very kind of him." In this matter Mrs. Pollifax could be completely frank. "We began talking, you see—about his parrot, and then about grandchildren and traveling alone. That's when he gave me the book. He told me that solitaire was something I would enjoy very much. Have you tried it, General? He was quite right, I have found it enormously stimulating."

The general opened a desk drawer and brought out two books. "Then it is the book on solitaire that he gave you," he said triumphantly.

He held up the books and Mrs. Pollifax gasped. "Why— you have both of them! You *stole* them from my hotel room."

"But of course," replied the general with a flash of gold tooth. "We are very thorough."

Mrs. Pollifax said indignantly, "Of course it's your conscience and you'll have to live with it, but I would like to point out that those are *my* books."

He nodded. "Yes, but one of them was presented to you by an extremely dangerous man."

"Was he really?" said Mrs. Pollifax.

The general leaned back in his chair and studied her. "I think you are being a little ingenuous Mrs. Pollifax, I do not know. We have gone through these books with what you Americans call a fine-toothed comb and we have not found anything. For the moment it is sufficiently rewarding to learn that it is this particular book that he gave you. 77 *Ways to Play Solitaire,*" he read with distaste, and pushed it away from him. "We shall examine it many more times."

Mrs. Pollifax said stiffly, "Really, General, don't you think you can become too devious, too suspicious? That book was given to me out of kindness, I can assure you of that. If you insist that it is full of secret messages written in invisible ink—"

"Please," said the general, looking pained.

"Well, whatever you people use these days," she pointed out. "At any rate, his gift of a book to me a few weeks ago seems a very feeble reason for my abduction."

The general stared at her with dislike. "If you are innocent you chose a most inauspicious morning to visit the Parrot Bookstore, Mrs. Pollifax."

"On the contrary, I chose a most auspicious morning," she said coldly. "The sun was shining and I wanted a book to read."

"What is more you behaved very suspiciously when the book was not in the window."

"I did not behave suspiciously at all," replied Mrs. Pollifax. "I was in hopes that you might prove just as charming as the earlier Senor DeGamez. You didn't," she reminded him sternly.

"You did not so much as demur when I suggested I had something to give you."

"I was allowing you every opportunity to be as hospitable as the first Senor DeGamez," she snapped. "After all, he gave me a book."

"Why did you accept tea from me?" he demanded. "Just what were you expecting?"

"A chat," said Mrs. Pollifax firmly.

"A what?"

"A little chat," she said. "Is that so difficult for you to believe? My government expects each and every one of us to be traveling ambassadors when we go abroad. I was *trying*," she added piously, "to know you better."

General Perdido exploded in what sounded like an oath. He and General Hoong exchanged glances and General Perdido said bitterly, "You may go back to your cell."

Mrs. Pollifax nodded and arose. "There is one other matter," she said. "Please could I be given one aspirin?"

Nine

The guard inserted the huge, comic-opera key in the lock and opened the door for Mrs. Pollifax, slamming it shut behind her. At once Farrell sprang to his feet. "Are you all right?"

Mrs. Pollifax was deeply touched by his concern. "Yes, I really am," she told him. "I was asked questions by that man I met in a bookstore in Mexico City, except now he's here in Albania. Imagine." She sat down on her cot and picked up her playing cards and shuffled them. In a low voice she said, "Farrell, I must apologize to you for something quite dreadful."

"Good heavens, what can that be?"

Mrs. Pollifax tried to think of the word the professionals used. "Are we being bugged?" she asked.

Farrell walked over and sat down beside her on the cot. "If you mean are there microphones hidden in here I don't know, but there must be some kind of listening device. I'm sure it's why they put us together—but where on earth did you pick up that word bugging, Duchess?"

"At the hairdresser's. One learns a great deal there about life."

"And the apology?" Farrell whispered the question.

She turned and faced him. "It's really quite terrible," she whispered back. "It seems the reason they brought us here is that they believe I'm a dangerous American spy."

"You?" The corners of his mouth twitched a little at this revelation. "You're not, are you?"

Mrs. Pollifax hesitated. "In one sense, no," she admitted. "In another, yes. But certainly not *dangerous*."

Farrell said flatly, "I don't like the way you say that, Duchess, you'd better be much more specific. Do you trust me?"

Mrs. Pollifax nodded.

"Good. Then for heaven's sake, are you or aren't you?"

Still whispering, Mrs. Pollifax plunged into her confession, beginning with her visit to CIA headquarters, describing the simple courier work that she was to do and how this man with the gold tooth had totally ruined her assignment. "And he's the same man who questioned me here, but now he calls himself General Raoul Perdido."

"Oh God," said Farrell.

"You mentioned his name once—quite lightly—on the plane. Do you know him too?"

He said grimly, "Nobody mentions Perdido lightly, and if I did I ought to have my head examined. Yes, I've heard of him, and he's a cruel, vicious bas—sorry," he added, and glancing at her face a smile lit up his eyes, "You of all people, Duchess!" The smile abruptly left his eyes and he became thoughtful. "You've certainly outflanked the general for the moment at least." He frowned. "You've bought yourself more time, which is the most important concession, but I only wish —I'm very much afraid—"

"It's all right," she told him gently. "I know what you're thinking. Even if they believe everything I've told them they can't afford to let me go home again."

He smiled wryly. "You continue to surprise me, Duchess, but let's not be gloomy, they may save you for an international incident and trade you for one of their own." Glancing up he said, "Oh-oh, we have company again."

The door swung wide and a man walked in carrying a tray of food, followed by a guard who insisted upon dramatically covering them with his rifle. Mrs. Pollifax thought it extremely ill-bred of him and turned her back on him, ignoring him just as she would have ignored a rude waiter. "Can you explain this odd-looking food?" she asked Farrell conversationally, hoping he knew what lay on her dish like a piece of melted rubber. "And is it drugged, do you think?"

Farrell said evenly, "Not likely. They'll be questioning me soon and I'd be no good to them drugged. It's some sort of cheese dish," he added, pushing a spoon into it. "Go ahead and try it. Not bad."

"It just looks such a mess," said Mrs. Pollifax with a sigh.

"Rather like Welsh rarebit," he told her, nodding approvingly. "Cheese and milk cooked together."

They ate quietly. There was coffee, very strong, and cakes drenched in honey. When they had finished Farrell brought out a crumpled pack of cigarettes, extracted one and lighted it, saying dryly, "The condemned man ate a hearty meal. And now, Duchess, there is something I believe I should tell *you*."

Mrs. Pollifax was feeling much more cheerful now, and her headache was virtually gone. "Fire ahead," she said gaily.

"You've been frank with me. I think it only politic to tell you what General Perdido already knows about me—namely that I, too, work for Carstairs."

Mrs. Pollifax drew in her breath sharply.

"I've been an agent since '47 when the CIA was formed," he went on. "You might say that I'm their man in Mexico City. Or one of them," he added absently. "A long time ago I did a job with DeGamez, so I knew what his real work was, and therein lies the rub, as old Billy Shakespeare would say. I hadn't seen DeGamez for years, not that we had to avoid each other, we just didn't move in the same circles. But on the nineteenth, just after I'd finished lunch, I received a crazy, garbled message from him and I went off at once to his bookstore. You see, the message had a code word inserted into it, a word meaning SOS. All the words in the message should have been in code—I knew that when I set out—but when a friend sounds in trouble how can a guy hang back? I should have been more cautious; I was impulsive instead. I went to see what the hell DeGamez meant and walked right into their trap. I realize now that Perdido must have pried just that one word out of DeGamez or some poor soul who knew it, but there's no use crying over spilt milk. By going to the bookstore—by reacting to that code word—I proved I was just who they thought I was, an agent they'd been looking for since '47." He was silent, smiling a twisted smile as he looked into his thoughts. "It takes only one goof and the others follow like one-two-three. The first thing they took from me was the cyanide pill I'm never without. The second thing they took from me was my identity, and then my freedom. So here I am, as full of information for them as Santa's knapsack. A real Christmas present in August for General Perdido."

Mrs. Pollifax stared at him in astonishment, understanding for the first time the hardness in him. "I thought him a reckless adventurer," she remembered. "I thought him a philanderer and a professional charmer and a man of no scruples, and he is perhaps all of these things, but I completely missed the truth in him: namely that he is all of these things and yet none of them."

To Farrell she said simply, "You are very brave."

He lifted an eyebrow mockingly. "Not at the moment, Duchess, not at the moment. You see, I can't allow General Perdido to question me. You understand what I've got to do, don't you?"

"What do you mean?" faltered Mrs. Pollifax.

"I mean that no one can hold out indefinitely against their methods of torture, and the general is considered an expert in the field. I mustn't be taken alive into that building."

As the meaning of his words penetrated Mrs. Pollifax became very still.

Farrell got to his feet and began pacing the floor. "For me it's part of the job," he said, "but I hate leaving you in the lurch. It's not very gallant of me, but under the circumstances—"

Mrs. Pollifax said breathlessly, "You mustn't concern yourself with me at all. *Please*. But what do you intend to do?"

He shrugged. "Whatever presents itself. Try to break away between here and the other building and hope they'll shoot me. Throw a rock at somebody." He shrugged again. *"Che sera, sera,* as they say—except I must not enter that building and meet General Perdido."

"You can't think of any other way?" she asked anxiously. "You don't think the general . . . ?"

He smiled cryptically. "Not on your life, Duchess, not on your life."

She averted her eyes so that she need not embarrass him with her compassion. She thought of her son Roger and daughter Jane, of Miss Hartshorne in apartment 4-C, and of the simple life she herself had lived, and then she thought of men like Farrell who for years must have been dying in queer parts of the world without her ever knowing of their existence. Life was certainly very strange, she reflected, but in spite of its uncertainty she was extremely grateful to have known Farrell.

"I don't know how to advise you," he continued, pacing and frowning. "There's no possibility of your getting away or being rescued. I hate deserting you. If I just didn't know so much—but Carstairs would never approve of my staying alive, there's too much at stake." Hearing the guard at the door he stamped his cigarette out on the floor. "Take what's left of them," he said, handing her the flattened pack. "You never know who's bribable in this world."

"Thank you," said Mrs. Pollifax, standing up, and as the door opened she and Farrell gravely shook hands.

This time the two guards were heavily armed. Major Vassovic had come as well to superintend Farrell's removal. "It's been so nice meeting you, Major," said Farrell as he went out.

"God go with you," whispered Mrs. Pollifax, staring after him.

Major Vassovic pointedly coughed. "The—uh—order has been received now. One aspirin for you, to be taken in my presence. Come."

Mrs. Pollifax realized that her headache had returned doublefold. She humbly followed the man into the guardroom and stood patiently while he brought her a cup of water and the pill. As she placed the tablet on her tongue her gaze came to rest on the collection of weapons on the wall, a number of guns and knives beautifully decorated with carved-silver ornamentation. They were works of art belonging in a museum and she told the major so.

"The long guns are called *pushkas*," he said gruffly. "The sabres we call *yataghans* in this country."

There were also an assortment of undecorated and very lethal-looking pistols and revolvers but she ignored these, her glance falling to the three drawers set into the base of the gun rack. One of them held a key in its lock; a small brass key, really quite distinctive. She kept her glance riveted to this, every nerve in her body waiting. "I am admiring a brass key," she told herself. "I am in Albania and presently Farrell will be killed and I mustn't think about it." She did not have long to wait. Her concentration was interrupted by harsh shouts from outside the building, and then by the sound of guns being fired. Mrs. Pollifax very carefully placed the cup of water on the major's desk and was pleased to see that her hand was not trembling. "I mustn't look," she told herself. "I don't want to look. There was nothing else for him to do."

At the sound of firing Major Vassovic uttered an explosive oath. After one glance from the window he said, "Back—back," and roughly pushed Mrs. Pollifax down the hall to her cell and slammed the door upon her. The firing had not continued beyond that one frenzied burst. There was only silence now in the building. Mrs. Pollifax sat down on Farrell's cot and said in a quiet voice, "I didn't look." For some reason this was very important to her. "I didn't look," she repeated in a louder voice, and fumbling in her purse she brought out a handkerchief and angrily blew her nose. Then she resolutely shuffled her deck of cards and laid them out for a game of Spider.

Mrs. Pollifax had played for several minutes, the silence like a shroud in the stone cell—like Farrell's shroud, she thought bitterly—when slowly her thoughts became diverted by a small sound emanating from the wall behind her. She turned her head to hear it better. It was not a metallic noise, it was more like a clenched fist rhythmically striking the stone wall. Recalling the second iron door set into the hall outside Mrs. Pollifax frowned. Kneeling on Farrell's cot she tapped with both hands. Immediately the sound stopped, as if in astonishment, and just when Mrs. Pollifax decided it must be someone repairing a drain, the fist beat an excited staccato reply. This fist had a personality all its own, thought Mrs. Pollifax in surprise; at first it had seemed to be hitting the wall in a monotonous rhythm of despair, then finding itself answered the Fist had panicked and stopped, afraid. But perhaps the Fist had remembered that another cell stood between it and Major Vassovic, for after its hesitation it had replied with joy.

"Yes with joy," repeated Mrs. Pollifax firmly, and reflected that if this were anything but real life they would now exchange urgent messages in Morse code. Unfortunately Mrs. Pollifax knew no Morse. She tapped again once more and received a reply, but it was a little like communicating with a newly born infant or someone who spoke only Swahili; once the initial greeting had been made there was really not much more to manage. Besides, her mind was on Farrell and she returned sadly to her game of solitaire.

It seemed a long time later when the building filled with noise again. A number of booted feet tramped down the hall and Mrs. Pollifax heard Major Vassovic issuing orders in an irritable voice. He sounded like a frustrated and angry man. Mrs. Pollifax placed a black ace on a red two and waited for the inevitable grating of the key in the lock—it was a sound she was beginning to dread. The door swung open. Mrs. Pollifax looked up and the cards slipped from her hand to the floor.

"Farrell!" she gasped.

He was propped between two guards, one leg dangling uselessly, his clothes smeared with blood. At her cry he lifted his head and opened one eye. "Goofed again, Duchess," he said, and as the men lowered him none too gently to the cot he added peevishly, "Damn cliff. If *you* jumped from a hundred-foot cliff wouldn't *you* bloody well expect to be killed?" Having delivered himself of this diatribe he fell back unconscious on the bed.

Ten

The two slits in the wall of the cell gradually darkened as night fell. Mrs. Pollifax sat beside Farrell and listened to his ravings as he slipped in and out of feverish dreams. She knew his leg was broken in two places and she had neither water nor bandages for him. There was a great deal of blood all over him, but as far as she could see only one bullet had entered his body and this was embedded in his right arm above the elbow. She had staunched the bleeding by removing the coarse blanket from her cot and using it as a tourniquet. When General Perdido arrived she had worked herself into a cold fury over the cruelty of the situation and her own helplessness. "Good evening," she said icily.

The guard accompanying Perdido carried a candle which he inserted into a metal ring set into the wall for this purpose. The general walked over to Farrell and looked down at him contemptuously. Clearly he, too, was furious.

Mrs. Pollifax said coldly, "I have asked for water and bandages and no one brings them. If I may be so presumptuous as to make a suggestion, General, why don't you shoot Mr. Farrell? It would be much more efficient because he is making a great deal of bothersome noise and what's worse he is bleeding all over your furniture."

General Perdido turned on her angrily. "I find you insolent, Mrs. Pollifax."

"I *feel* insolent," retorted Mrs. Pollifax. "Perhaps you would like to shoot me as well."

For a moment she thought that General Perdido was going to strike her. She almost hoped that he would for her rage was nearly uncontainable and she would have welcomed violence, even if directed at herself. But his hand fell. He glared again at the moaning Farrell and turned on his heel. At the door he said to Major Vassovic, "Give the woman the water and bandages she asks for. Perhaps she can revive the prisoner for questioning." He turned and gave Mrs. Pollifax a tight, sadistic smile. "For questioning and other things." With this he marched out.

Major Vassovic looked doubtfully at Mrs. Pollifax. "Water? Bandages? You are a nurse?"

"No, a human being," she snapped, and sat down again beside Farrell's cot.

The major returned with strips of cloth and a pitcher of water. He stood and watched while Mrs. Pollifax moistened Farrell's lips and untied the tourniquet. "You have been loosening it?" he asked.

She nodded. The bleeding had stopped; Mrs. Pollifax placed the blanket to one side and walked over to her cot and rolled back the mattress. The cot was made of wood, with rough slats to support the thin hard mattress. She removed two of the slats and carried them back to Farrell's bed.

"What do you do now?" asked Major Vassovic curiously.

"I intend to set his leg."

Major Vassovic looked astonished. "*Zott!* You know how?"

"No," replied Mrs. Pollifax, "but someone has to. I'm hoping you will help me."

He said stiffly, "I have no orders."

"But you are here, and you are a man and he is a man, and do you think any leg should look like that?"

"I have no orders," he repeated, and went out.

Mrs. Pollifax felt suddenly very tired. She looked at Farrell and she looked at his leg and she knew that she would bungle the job alone. Gritting her teeth she leaned over him and began ripping away his trouser leg. "I will not faint," she told herself, "I will not, I will not. Surely I can push one of those bones back myself. It certainly ought to be done now, while he's unconscious." She stood back and looked at the leg, already swollen and red and turning black and blue, and she thought forlornly, "I wish I had another aspirin."

The door behind her opened so quietly that Mrs. Pollifax started when a low voice said, "Lulash."

She turned. One of the guards stood there, his finger to his lips, nodding and smiling nervously. "My name is Lulash."

"I see," said Mrs. Pollifax blankly. "Lulash. Well, how do you do, Mr. Lulash."

He tiptoed back to the door, listened a moment and gently closed it. "The major has gone for the night. He sleeps."

He walked to the cot and stared down at Farrell. "I have worked in hospital," he said suddenly. "I can set this man's leg. *Zott,* but it looks bad."

Mrs. Pollifax's eyes weakly filled with tears at this offer of help. "He jumped from the cliff," she explained in a strangled voice. "He was trying to kill himself."

Lulash only nodded. "I wish him better good fortune the next time." He leaned over to examine Farrell's leg more closely. "*Zott,* but this is not good."

"But you can do something?"

"Something, yes. Better a doctor, but they will not bring a doctor. I do my best." His eyes fell to the slats that Mrs. Pollifax still held in her arms. He took them from her and leaned them against the wall. "Later," he said. "Now you must sit on the man's chest and hold him down. I bid you do it." Numbly Mrs. Pollifax obeyed.

Ten minutes later Farrell's leg was set and Mrs. Pollifax, feeling shaken and a little ill, sat on her cot and watched Lulash bind the slats against Farrell's straightened leg. After one enraged scream Farrell had lost consciousness again, and he was still unconscious. Lulash placed a hand on Farrell's heart and then on his pulse, counting the beat. With a nod he came to sit down beside Mrs. Pollifax and mop his brow with a soiled handkerchief.

"Would you like an American cigarette?" asked Mrs. Pollifax humbly. She brought from her purse the crumpled pack that Farrell had given her.

"Thank you."

"We are both Americans," said Mrs. Pollifax, with a nod toward Farrell. "Do you think—that is, is it all right for me to ask if this is Albania?"

The guard shrugged. "We call it Shkyperi, which in your language would mean Land of the Mountain Eagle. But yes, it is called Albania."

"Where did you learn to speak such fine English? Do all the Albanians speak it? Major Vassovic does, and you."

"I was brought here two days ago because I speak the English. Before then I was in Sarande. It was the same with Major Vassovic, who came from Tirana. They went searching for those of us in the Sigurimi who speak your language."

"The Sigur—what?" asked Mrs. Pollifax.

"That is the name of the secret police in this country."

Mrs. Pollifax gasped. "That means that you—I mean—"

He shrugged. "The time is very difficult here. Those of us

who can read and write have two choices, to join the Sigurimi or not to join. Those who do not join can usually be seen on the roads any day. They smash rock. They carry rock. They have no hope."

"I'm sorry," said Mrs. Pollifax. "It sounds quite sad." She looked at him with curiosity, studying him carefully because of his extraordinary kindness to Farrell, but unable to find anything in his face to explain him. It was a dark, secretive face with pointed features: black brows, a long, thin nose, a sharp thin jaw, a thin sharp mouth. She would not have taken him for a kind man or an unselfish one, and yet he had flouted orders to help a sick man.

"It was not always this way," he said. "Albanians are a proud, fiercely independent people. But without luck," he added. "First the Turks ruled us, then the Russians, now the Chinese. Whatever the master the country stays the same. Poor, primitive, frightened too."

"You speak English so well," she pointed out.

His face brightened. "My cousin and I learned the English as children from a man who had come here to write a book about the country. He was a travel man, you know. He wrote the book the year I was born but each year he came back to visit my father. It pleased him to teach us. He was friend to all the tribes, a very good man."

"Tribes?" said Mrs. Pollifax.

He nodded. "You know nothing of our country?"

"Nothing at all, I'm afraid," she admitted.

"The most beautiful country in the world," he said firmly. "Here the rocks and the high mountains, below the flatlands, the valley, the rivers. And oh, the sea," he added with nostalgia. "Patrolled now, of course. But the Adriatic is the most beautiful sea in the world."

"Yes, I've heard that," said Mrs. Pollifax quietly.

"This man, this Mr. Allistair, gave us the book he wrote of my country. He loved it too." He pinched out the cigarette and placed the butt carefully in the pocket of his shirt. "Your friend is stirring, I will find for him one aspirin."

He got up and opened the door to the hall and stood there, waiting. Mrs. Pollifax realized that he was waiting for her to accompany him, Surprised, she followed him out, quite touched by his trust. Once in the guardroom he began opening and closing drawers of the desk while Mrs. Pollifax stood beside him. She heard his murmur of satisfaction as he brought up a flask containing what looked to be brandy. While he attacked a new drawer Mrs. Pollifax's glance wandered and came to rest, mesmerized, upon the gun rack behind the desk.

The little brass key to the drawer in the gun rack was still there in its lock.

What, she wondered, would people keep in the drawer of a gun rack?

"If they put ammunition there they certainly wouldn't be so careless as to leave the key in the lock," she reflected. "It's probably filled with paper clips or something idiotic. Except, why paper clips in a gun rack?"

It was an interesting thought. If it *was* a drawer for ammunition a person could steal the key and hide it and later hope to come back and remove whatever was there. Then perhaps some use could be made of it, or a gun taken from the rack—

She looked at Lulash, at his narrow back bent over the bottom drawer. Still watching him she took several steps backward, until she felt the gun rack between her shoulder blades. Fumblingly she tugged at the drawer and felt it slide open. Lulash was still leaning over the desk and she quickly turned and glanced down. She had been right about its holding ammunition: the drawer was filled with neat stacks of bullets, cartridges and clips, all of them unwrapped and accessible. She slid the drawer closed and placed her fingers around the key. Then she hesitated.

"I can't" she thought bleakly. "I just can't.

"Lulash would be blamed," she realized. "It wouldn't be fair. He would be blamed for its loss and punished and he has just set Farrell's leg and now he is going to give him brandy and an aspirin.

"I am an utter failure as an agent," she decided with anger. "It should have occurred to me before that I would have to be ruthless and unscrupulous. These people are planning to kill me and still I can't steal this key or so much as a bullet because this man has helped me and would be blamed for it."

Lulash stood erect, brandishing a bottle of white pills and smiling at her. Automatically she smiled back, her mind totally occupied with her defeat. Lulash found a paper cup and drew water from the cooler and she accompanied him back to her cell.

"What goes?" asked Farrell shakily.

"This gentleman set your leg," she told him, patting his arm. "We've brought you some brandy for your nerves, and aspirin for your fever. Could you manage to sit up just a little if I help?"

Farrell struggled to one elbow. "I hope I haven't given away any state secrets. I have the feeling I've been talking like an idiot."

She smiled faintly. "Exactly like an idiot, but not like any friend of Mr. Carstairs."

"Thank God for that." He swallowed some brandy, winced, and saluted Lulash with a wave of a hand. "Does he speak English?"

"Yes."

"The brandy isn't bad. More?"

"Aspirin next," she said firmly, and placed one tablet on his tongue. "If you prefer washing it down with brandy we can dispense with the water."

"Loathe water," he said, and gulped down two aspirin with huge draughts of brandy. "What are the prospects?" he gasped, lying back.

"Dim," replied Mrs. Pollifax dryly. "General Perdido has been in to look you over. You have considerably frustrated him by injuring yourself so badly, and he left in disgust." She added in a low voice that Lulash could not hear, "It might be wise of you, when anyone comes in again, to continue talking as wildly as possible, and to see things crawling up and down the walls."

He whispered back, "That's delirium tremens, not fever. You'll make a bloody alcoholic out of me."

In a louder voice, and tartly, she said, "In your weakened condition, and with all the brandy you've just consumed, you will soon be in precisely that state."

Lulash slipped the aspirin bottle into his pocket and showed signs of leaving. Mrs. Pollifax arose and reached for his hand. "Thank you," she said warmly, shaking it. "We both thank you very much."

"Is all right," he said, nodding and smiling.

When he had gone Mrs. Pollifax sat down abruptly on her cot, realizing how terribly tired she was. Farrell, watching her, said, "You look exhausted, Duchess, for God's sake get some sleep. I'll try to limit my ravings for a while."

Mrs. Pollifax looked at him in the flickering eerie light of the candle and realized how very fond of him she was becoming. "It *is* comforting not to be alone," she thought. She stood up and rolled back the mattress to arrange the slats around the two that were missing. "It has been rather a long day," she admitted aloud, and lying down she fell at once into an exhausted sleep.

Eleven

On the twenty-third of August Carstairs sat down in his office to review the Mexico City fiasco with a man named Thaddeus Peattie. Peattie came from another department; he was extremely interested in all matters concerning Mao Tse-tung and he was one of the few Americans to have personally known Rauol Perdido—they had met frequently in China during the war when Perdido was a member of Mao's guerrillas and Peattie was a liaison officer between Chiang Kai-shek and the guerrillas.

"There hasn't been a sign of Farrell or Mrs. Pollifax being smuggled into Cuba," Carstairs said, offering Peattie and Bishop cigarettes. "This doesn't for a moment exclude their being there. They could have landed at night in some secluded area and been whisked into solitary confinement or killed at once. But General Perdido hasn't been sighted in Cuba, either. I think we can say without any doubt at all that Perdido is not in Cuba at the moment."

"South America?" suggested Peattie. "Mexico? Perdido is a Mexican by birth, after all. Need he have left Mexico at all?"

"He's not particularly welcome there," pointed out Carstairs. "If he's still there he would certainly be in hiding. What we want to know is where he would go if he left the country. Where's that report from Belmonte?" he asked of Bishop.

Bishop riffled through the pile of papers on his lap and efficiently extracted the needed sheet. Carstairs handed it over to Peattie. "It's common knowledge that the Russians have used Mexico as a takeoff point for spies and defectors in this hemisphere. We know of two secret landing strips used by the Reds for smuggling people out. These strips," he added pointedly, "are not entirely unobserved, as you will see by this report from—an observer, shall we say?"

Peattie picked up the report.

"As you will note," continued Carstairs, "there has been

some activity observed in this lower California landing strip. A plane—a four-engine prop—was reported landing there on the night of August 19. It was on this day that General Perdido closed the doors of the Parrot Bookstore and vanished from sight. It is also on this day that Farrell and Mrs. Pollifax visited the Parrot Bookstore and vanished."

"Mmm," murmured Peattie, frowning. "This report says that two people were carried aboard this plane."

"Yes, carried. On stretchers."

"Definitely a Russian-made plane," read Peattie aloud. "Markings thought to be Cuban." He returned the sheet to Carstairs. "You say that our beautiful Miss Willow Lee has also left Mexico City?"

Carstairs nodded. "Yes, but she left on a registered flight, destination Peking, and has already arrived in Hong Kong."

"Then it's not likely that she and General Perdido were the passengers taken aboard that plane," mused Peattie.

"Not on stretchers," remarked Carstairs dryly.

"No, not on stretchers," agreed Peattie with a quick smile. "Perdido is of course the key to this. If he's involved—and from what you've implied this whole affair is big enough to interest him—then he's the man to trace, of course. The two others, dead or alive, could be anywhere but are doubtless with him. Or were." He stood up and walked to the map on the wall and stood before it, his hands locked behind his back. "I hate to say this," he remarked. "At least I assume you're grimly hoping to regain or trace these two agents of yours. But if General Perdido is not in Cuba—and surely by now he would have been seen there by someone—then I fear the general would have headed for Red China."

"This department does not grimly hope," said Carstairs in a hard voice. "No, my dear Peattie, the names of Farrell and Pollifax have been crossed off all earthly lists as far as we are concerned."

"Then I don't think I understand," said Peattie, returning to his chair and sitting down.

Carstairs hesitated. "You might call our investigation fifty per cent precaution and fifty per cent conscience. We don't want any international incidents growing out of it, for instance."

"You mean like the U-2 affair," cut in Peattie dryly.

"Right. We want to"—his voice softened apologetically—"we *have* to be sure these two people are dead. We have to have *proof*."

Peattie nodded. "I'll send out feelers at once, of course. I think that within four days—a week at the most—I can tell you whether General Perdido is or has been in China." He gave Carstairs a curious glance and said, "And the fifty per cent conscience—or isn't that any of my business?"

Carstairs sighed. "I'm thinking of Mrs. Pollifax. The late Mrs. Pollifax, I fear. You didn't know her, of course. Perhaps I can give you a capsule picture of her if I tell you that she strolled in here one day and asked if we needed any spies."

Peattie looked at Carstairs in open-mouthed astonishment.

Carstairs nodded. "A comfortable little woman in her sixties, with a charmingly direct way of going about things. Asked Mason if there was something she could do for us. Rather like volunteering for work at a charity fete. Hellishly innocent and naïve, but so patently right for the tourist I needed that I gobbled her up, so to speak."

Peattie gave him a sympathetic glance. "I see," he said quietly. "She knew the risks?"

"Oh yes, she knew the risks. But she left without indoctrination, without training, without a cyanide pill."

"Fortunes of war," pointed out Peattie softly. "Necessity is a ruthless mistress."

Carstairs sighed. "No one knows that better than I, but I haven't been sleeping too well these past three nights. From a practical viewpoint it's she who could become the international incident—she is so clearly usable, because of her innocence. But what is far more likely—"

He stopped and Peattie said wryly, "Don't torture yourself, my friend—don't."

"I try not to," Carstairs said with a bitter smile. "Let us say very simply that I must now think of plausible telegrams to send to the woman's relatives explaining why she is not en route home from Mexico at this moment, and that eventually—once her death is substantiated—I must arrange some plausible death for her in Mexico."

"Stevens is working on that now," put in Bishop. "A boating accident has been suggested, with no body recovered. Either a chartered boat off Acapulco or a freak drowning at Xochimilco. Mexico is being very helpful."

"How nice," said Carstairs sourly. "Then her son and daughter will hold a memorial service for her and have her name cut on a stone in the family plot and say 'What a way for Mother to go' and they will never guess how their mother did die, or for what purpose, or know that half a dozen people in Washington, D.C., and Mexico City worked over the details, making their mother's death palatable and acceptable to them."

"I get the point, you needn't labor it," said Peattie gently. "But you must know by now that inevitably there's one person for whom one feels unusually responsible."

Carstairs nodded, a faint smile on his lips. "I ought to know that by now, Peattie. Rum job, what?"

"Rum job," agreed Peattie, and stood up. "I've got the picture now. I can promise you information, positive or negative, within the week. I wish it could be sooner but China still moves pretty much by oxcart in spite of Mao's boasts to the contrary."

"Thanks—we'll take anything we can get."

When he had gone Carstairs lit a cigarette, leaned back in his chair and gave Bishop a weary smile. "I don't know whether you saw the message that came in late last evening or not. Tirpak is dead. A knife in the back in Guatemala about a week ago, the identification just made."

Bishop sighed. "What you'd call a clean sweep then. No, I haven't had time to catch up on last night's communiques."

"They make lively reading—there's even more," added Carstairs wryly. "Our photographic-supply friend in Costa Rica processed all the information that Tirpak brought him, and duly burned the papers. It took three days to get all of Tirpak's documents on film. There were six microfilms, but here's the sad news: Tirpak gave no indication of how these films were going to be conveyed to Mexico City, or in what form. Whatever he did next with them was done secretly. According to our friend in Costa Rica Tirpak picked up each microfilm with a pair of tweezers, dropped them one by one into a plain white envelope, and left."

"Ouch," said Bishop.

Carstairs nodded. "Three days later he was murdered, but he must have started moving them toward Mexico City before then. What he did with them is anybody's guess but I would assume he planned to insert them into something printed— say a letter or a book."

"You do think the microfilms reached Mexico City then."

Carstairs nodded. "Tirpak would have seen to that even at the cost of his life. He was that kind of man. What he couldn't have realized was just how closely he was being followed and watched—and just how closely those mircofilms were being watched. Yes, I believe they reached Mexico City. They reached the Parrot Bookstore and DeGamez was killed because of them."

"So General Perdido has the microfilms then."

Carstairs frowned. "They're lost to us in any case, Bishop, but I'm not so sure that General Perdido has them, either. Take a close look at this timetable of events I've written out—see if it suggests anything to you."

Bishop took the memo and read:

August 17: probable date of DeGamez' murder
August 17: General Perdido poses as DeGamez and in-
            stalls himself at the Parrot Bookstore
August 19: Mrs. Pollifax visits the Parrot Bookstore to
            pick up microfilms and vanishes
August 19: Farrell visits the Parrot Bookstore for un-
            known reasons, and also vanishes
August 19   Mrs. Pollifax's room at the Hotel Reforma
  or 20:   Intercontinental entered and searched.

Bishop was thoughtful. "I see what you mean. Why go to the bother of keeping the bookstore open after DeGamez' demise, and why search Mrs. Pollifax's room, if they'd gotten what they wanted."

Carstairs nodded. "Exactly. It implies a certain lack of success. If General Perdido had gotten the microfilms from DeGamez before DeGamez was killed, then I don't really see what purpose was served by his turning into a bookstore clerk to set a trap for Mrs. Pollifax and Farrell. And that's another thing: their including Farrell bothers me very much. Farrell's only link with the Chinese Reds was the friendship with Miss Willow Lee that he was busy cultivating at our orders. He had no knowledge of either Tirpak or Mrs. Pollifax, and as to the microfilms, he didn't even know of their existence."

Bishop nodded. "Snatching him *does* imply desperation on the part of General Perdido."

"Yes. And that's why I'm reasonably sure that he chose to keep Farrell and Mrs. Pollifax alive—at least for a day or two. And that, my dear Bishop, is why I am not sleeping well these nights, because General Perdido's methods of extracting information are neither polite nor pretty."

"But Mrs. Pollifax had no information to extract," pointed out Bishop.

Carstairs gave him a hard look. "Let's not be naïve, Bishop. Do you think Perdido would believe that?"

There was a long silence during which Bishop tried to think of something tactful to say. Finally, with a forced brightness, he concluded, "Well if Perdido doesn't have the microfilms, that's something, isn't it?"

Carstairs gave a short laugh. "Oh yes—yes, indeed. It means they're lost to everyone, floating in space, so to speak, and of no use to anyone. If they were appended to a book sold in DeGamez' shop then someone at this very moment may be reading that book, never realizing that it's the repository of secrets costing eight months work and the lives of innumerable people who would otherwise be alive today. And that is what I call waste. Where is the telegram sent to Mrs. Pollifax's next of kin?"

Bishop drew copies from his file. "Here they are, sir. They went off late yesterday from Mexico City; this one to Mr. Roger Pollifax in Chicago, this one to Mrs. Conrad Kempf in Arizona."

Carstairs read them with irony:

HAVING WONDERFUL TIME STOP POSTPONING RETURN A WEEK OR MORE STOP MEXICO CHARMING STOP LOVE TO ALL MOTHER

Twelve

General Perdido returned to the cell the next afternoon, but Mrs. Pollifax had been forewarned by the sound of his voice in the hall. The general, entering, found Mrs. Pollifax playing a quiet game of solitaire and Farrell tossing feverishly on his cot.

"Good afternoon," said Mrs. Pollifax coldly.

"Where?" shouted Farrell, thrashing feebly. "Take the green ones away, for God's sake!"

Both the general and Mrs. Pollifax turned to look at Farrell, one with exasperation, the other with admiration. To the general Mrs. Pollifax said bitingly, "I have set his leg but he still has a bullet in his arm and I am *not* Dr. Schweitzer. The wound is infected."

General Perdido crossed the cell to Farrell and looked down at him. "Senor Farrell," he said harshly.

Farrell opened his eyes and stared into the face above him. "Carmelita?" he said tenderly, and then, hopefully, "My darling?"

General Perdido drew back his arm and sent his fist crashing against Farrell's cheekbone. There was a sickening sound of bone meeting bone. Mrs. Pollifax turned away and thought, "I really can't bear this."

There was, for the next few minutes, a great deal more to bear. The general was a thorough man, a determined and an intelligent man, and he intended to leave no stone unturned in his search to learn whether Farrell was shamming or if his mind could still be reached. Mrs. Pollifax moved to the attenuated window and forced herself to look beyond it to the narrow rectangle of stones glittering in the sun, and the thin slice of bleached white sky. "I won't listen," she thought. "I will detach myself forever from this room and this moment." It was an exercise in deception that she had practiced before but never so desperately as now. But when at last the general desisted she was more calm than he—the general's face was distorted with fury. Pausing with his hand on the cell door he said stiffly, "I will be going away until I am informed that Mr. Farrell is well enough to be questioned. You may tell him so. You may also tell him that I will look forward to his speedy recovery." He opened the door and turned back dramatically. "As for you, Mrs. Pollifax, you have inconvenienced me so greatly that I resent your very existence." The door slammed behind him and she heard the bolt drawn outside. Only then did she dare look at Farrell. "I think General Perdido has been seeing too many B movies," she said lightly, and wanted to cry at the sight of Farrell's battered face.

Farrell said evenly, his words slurred by two very puffy lips, "Let's give him to Hollywood then with our compliments." He sat up. "Did he break my nose, damn him?"

Mrs. Pollifax sat down beside him and for the next few minutes they took inventory. The list was encouraging: it consisted of bruises, two loosened teeth—both molars—and a split upper lip; but there appeared to be no bones broken and Mrs. Pollifax felt it was reasonable to hope there was no concussion of the cheekbone. She said gently, "You managed very well. Have you had to endure this sort of thing before?"

He glanced away. "Once, during the war. That was when I knew Carstairs." He looked at her thoughtfully. "There are limitations, you know, especially after the first time. The second time the mind knows what to expect. It anticipates. Actually the mind can become a worse enemy than the person inflicting the pain. But this was brief—mercifully."

Mrs. Pollifax considered his words and nodded. "Yes, I see how that can be." She felt his forehead and sighed. "You still have a fever, you know. About a hundred and one, I'd guess."

"But not the raving kind," he said, and winced as he tried to smile.

"No, not the raving kind—you put on a very good act." She brought from her purse the package of cigarettes he had given her and held out the last one to him. "Could you manage this with your torn lip?"

"Pure nectar," he said longingly. He took it and began stabbing his mouth with it to find a comfortable corner for it. She lighted it for him and he inhaled deeply. "Duchess," he said gratefully, "I've known an incredible number of young, beautiful and nubile women—more than any one man deserves—but I would have to nominate you as the Woman I Would Most Like to Be Captured with in Albania. You are a true blessing to me in my old age—and I feel I'm aging pretty damn fast in this place."

"Ah, you are feeling better, I'm delighted," said Mrs. Pollifax with a twinkle. She returned to her own cot, carrying her small table with her, and laid out her playing cards for a game of Clock Solitaire. "How did you fall into this preposterous sort of life?" she asked, thinking he might like to talk now. "This preposterous life with beautiful nubile women and General Perdidos in it. You're American, aren't you?"

"As American as San Francisco," he said, sending streams of blue smoke toward the ceiling from his horizontal position. "My mother was Spanish—I learned to speak Spanish before I knew English. And I got the wandering bug from them. They were both vaudeville people—dancers."

"How very nice," said Mrs. Pollifax, charmed by the thought. "I always did enjoy the flamenco. Did you live out of a suitcase?"

"Mmm, just about."

"Do you dance?"

"Only a waltz," he said cheerfully. "In me the talent came out in art. I was in the war very early, and when I got out I headed for Mexico to paint. It may surprise you to hear that I really do paint—off and on. By the time Carstairs found me I had already acquired just the reputation he wanted: half playboy, half adventurer, half artist."

"You have too many halves there," pointed out Mrs. Pollifax primly.

"You don't feel that exaggeration adds flavor?" he inquired.

Mrs. Pollifax struggled and lost. "Actually, I have been guilty of a small amount of exaggeration myself at times."

He chuckled. "I'll bet you have, Duchess, I'll bet you have. But lived a very quiet and respectable life in spite of it?"

"Oh yes," she said. "Very quiet and very respectable. My husband was a lawyer, a very fine one. My son is a lawyer, too," she added, and thinking back added with nostalgia, "Yes, it was a very pleasant and peaceful life."

Farrell turned his head to look at her through the gloom. He said tactfully, "Think I'll have a little nap now, Duchess." Carefully adjusting his position to his wounded arm he left Mrs. Pollifax to her thoughts and pretended to fall asleep.

It was at mealtime that the new prisoner arrived. He was pushed in ahead of the trays and kicked ungenerously by Major Vassovic and apparently sworn at in the language of the country. A third cot was then brought in and placed along the third wall. Mrs. Pollifax was too busy feeding Farrell with a spoon to pay much attention, but while she ate her own meal—reluctantly putting away her playing cards to make room for it—she eyed the man curiously. He lay on his side, with his face resting on his two hands, but all that she could really see of him was a bristling, white, walrus moustache jutting up, and the top of a bald pink head fringed with white about the ears. It was a very elegant, splendidly Victorian moustache—she hadn't seen one like it since she was a child. She realized that Farrell, propped against the opposite wall, was also studying the man. He said suddenly, "My name's Farrell, what is yours, sir?"

The man's head shifted, aware of Farrell's voice, but his face remained blank and he said nothing.

"Speak English?" asked Farrell.

"Inglese?" repeated the man, and with a shake of his head added a jumble of words in a language that neither of them understood.

"He doesn't speak English—that's good," said Mrs. Pollifax. "What did we eat tonight, by the way?"

Farrell said broodingly, "Heaven only knows." He was still

watching the stranger. He said suddenly, in a particularly meaningful voice, "Look at the candle!"

Mrs. Pollifax's glance went at once to the candle over the newcomer's head, and she frowned because there was nothing wrong with it, nothing to see but the one sputtering flame that gave little more than an illusion of lighting the shadows. Then she realized that the new man, who had been lying on his side, had thrown back his head so that he, too, was looking at the candle. How very curious, she thought, he had understood perfectly what Farrell said. It occurred to her that he was arriving in their cell just as General Perdido had announced that he was leaving for a few days, and she pondered the connection. Yes, it was quite possible; it would be very inefficient of the general to leave without making some arrangements to learn more about her and Farrell. The general would not care to waste time, and what better way to make time work for him than to place a spy in their cell to eavesdrop on them while he was gone? Apparently the general had unearthed another English-speaking member of the Sigurimi. She smiled at Farrell to show him that she understood his warning.

Tonight it was Lulash who came to remove their trays and he went first to Mrs. Pollifax after directing a quick glance at the new prisoner. "We are late tonight in collecting your tray. General Perdido had to be driven to his airplane."

Mrs. Pollifax saw that he had deposited two aspirins on her table and she gave him a grateful glance.

"Also for you, to read in the English about my country." He spoke in a very low voice, and with his back still to the new prisoner he leaned over and slipped a book under her pillow. "It is *the* book, the one I told you about," he added reverently. "I carry it everywhere with me, it is even inscribed to me."

Mrs. Pollifax had to content herself with another grateful glance, for she dared not speak. Lulash moved away to Farrell's table and after removing his tray went out. With her table again empty Mrs. Pollifax arranged her cards for a new game of solitaire and played doggedly for an hour. Farrell was the first to fall into a restless sleep. Soon the stranger turned his back to the room and filled the air with rhythmic snores, and Mrs. Pollifax, growing drowsy herself, put away the cards and lay down.

The book that Lulash had placed beneath her pillow proved uncomfortable to lie upon—she had forgotten its existence as soon as Lulash went away. Since no one was awake to see her she brought out the book and opened it. It was an old volume; the first thing she noted was its copyright date—1919—and at sight of this Mrs. Pollifax was touched that it was still such a treasure to Lulash, and then she was disappointed because a book written forty-five years ago could not possibly be informative; too many wars had been fought since then, too many political parties gone from the scene, making the book a virtual antique. She thumbed through it, however, with a feeling of nostalgia, recalling books in her childhood with the same gray, sunless photographs, the same pictures of people in national costume, with the author himself posed artfully beside monuments and graves and on horseback. The book was entitled *Albania: Land of Primitive Beauty,* and it was written in the florid verbiage of the day. The plainest sentence in the book stated simply that in size the country was equal to the state of Maryland. Its last chapter ended with the words, "And so I bade farewell to the head of the clan of Trijepsi, leaving him by the leaping flames of his campfire, a real friend whom I must always cherish. Rough, yes; but a pearl among men, truly a chief among men." Mrs. Pollifax winced at the style and turned a few more pages to come face to face with a very clearly rendered black and white map. A map . . . she idly turned another page and then came quickly back to the map. It was a very good, clear map. There was Albania fitted neatly between Greece to the south and what would now be Yugoslavia on the north, and there was the Adriatic Sea. . . . Water, thought Mrs. Pollifax, feeling her way toward a thought not yet expressible. Thoughtfully she turned the map closer to the light and began looking for mountains, wondering just where they might be at this moment. In the south there was a thin line of mountain range facing the sea, but according to the description these were hardly fifteen hundred feet in height—the ones they had traveled through were higher and so she ignored these for the time being. The central part of the country was flat and open with the exception of one mountain rising out of the plains, but she and Farrell had been brought to a very long, high range of mountains and she dismissed this solitary peak. Her glance fastened on the north, narrowing as she spied the words *North Albanian Alps.* Farrell had said something about Alps, and the mountains to which they had been brought resembled Switzerland in their naked ruggedness. These mountains ran from east to west across the top of the country like a necklace—a necklace extremely close to Yugoslavia, she noticed—and, if the country was no larger than Maryland, they were not excessively far from the Adriatic Sea, either.

"We have to be somewhere in these mountains," she mused. She would have to begin reading the book tomorrow because in forty-five years the topography would remain the same. But still she lingered over the map. They had landed by plane in a town that was plainly old and well established, and after driving toward the mountains they had traveled for one or two hours by donkey. Would it be possible to figure out in what direction they had traveled?

"The sun," gasped Mrs. Pollifax. From the heaving, slippery back of her donkey she had watched the sun rise and spread across the valley in a flood of gold. Sleep left her as she concentrated on remembering. Yes, the sun had definitely risen in front of her and slightly to the right. Therefore they had been traveling eastward. If she reversed this, moving her finger westward, there was only one city, named Scutari, printed in bold print, that would be large enough to sustain a crude airfield. The other towns were all in small print—villages, no doubt, none of them large enough to drive through for a period of ten minutes. If it was Scutari where they had landed then they must be about *here,* she decided, scratching an X with her fingernail. It was a point astonishingly close to Yugoslavia, and surprisingly near the Adriatic, and across the Adriatic lay Italy. . . .

She placed the book carefully under the mattress at her feet and lay down, almost frightened by the thought that the map engendered. "But how very difficult it is to dismiss an idea once it has presented itself to the mind," she mused. She would have to look at the map again more carefully tomorrow and read about the North Albanian Alps. Perhaps Farrell would have noticed landmarks she had missed. She tried to tame her thoughts, but it was a long time before she fell asleep.

Thirteen

"You may come out," said Lulash the next afternoon, standing in the doorway and speaking to Mrs. Pollifax. "General Hoong has said you may have a little walk for the exercise."

"How very kind," gasped Mrs. Pollifax.

Lulash said cheerfully, "General Hoong has wired for instructions about you. Everyone has wired for instructions about you. Now with General Perdido gone we only wait."

Mrs. Pollifax nodded and went to look at Farrell. During the night his temperature had flared dangerously and she was very worried about him. If he was to survive at all the bullet would have to be removed from his arm; for what purpose he must survive she did not know, but it went against all of her instincts to let a man die without making every effort to save him. He was flushed and drowsy and his appetite had vanished; his temperature must be 104 or 105, she judged, and he was not always lucid. Mrs. Pollifax leaned over him and said gently, "I will be back in a few minutes."

Farrell opened one eye and grinned weakly. "Have fun."

Before leaving Mrs. Pollifax went to her cot and picked up the Guatemalan jacket which an eternity ago she had worn when she left her Mexico City hotel room. She had lived in the same dress for six days and nights, and had passed the point of fastidiousness; but the jacket she guarded with feminine illogic. During the day it was spread carefully atop her pillow; at night it was folded across the table on which she played her card games—it had become almost a fetish with her. As she plucked it now from the pillow her left hand groped underneath for the book on Albania. She slipped it under the jacket and without even a glance at the Gremlin—this nickname had been bestowed upon their stool pigeon by Farrell—she walked out.

"Did you like my book, will you read it?" asked Lulash once they gained the hall.

She nodded with vivacity. She had already done much reading and she was in the process of assimilating some extremely interesting information. She had been wrong to think that a book written in 1919 could yield nothing pertinent;

she had entirely overlooked the fact that political parties and wars could sweep like clouds across a country but leave its terrain untouched. Mrs. Pollifax was becoming very interested in Albania's topography and she eagerly welcomed a few minutes outside her prison to view it.

In the guardroom, as she passed through it, the key to the ammunition drawer had again been left in the lock.

Lulash led her outside. The sun, dazzling even to a normal eye, had an almost searing effect upon Mrs. Pollifax's eyeballs after the darkness of the cell, and she covered both eyes with her hands, gasping at the pain.

"Here," said Lulash, and gravely handed her his pair of dark glasses.

"Really you are so kind," said Mrs. Pollifax, and found that a few seconds after putting them on she was able to look around her without discomfort. They were not a great distance from the precipice from which Farrell had jumped. From here to its edge there were nothing but yellow rocks— boulders, stones, pebbles of every possible shape and size and texture, some worn smooth, others sharp and jagged. On their left the larger stone building cast a sharp black shadow across the stones, its edges as precise as if they were lines drawn with a ruler. On Mrs. Pollifax's right, not too far away, stood a hill of rock lightly screened by fir trees—it was from this direction that they had come. But Mrs. Pollifax was more interested in what lay in front of her. "I am to walk?" she asked of Lulash.

He nodded, and lowering himself to the bench beside the door he explained, "Better today if you walk within my eye, you understand? From there to there." With his hands he indicated boundaries.

Mrs. Pollifax nodded, and limping over the uneven stones made her way to the edge of the cliff. There she began what she hoped looked like an aimless stroll back and forth but was in reality a reconnaissance. The valley especially interested her, and from this height she could look far across it. Some distance away she traced with her eyes the winding skein of a riverbed that ran from east to west across the plain. Between herself and the river she could see four small towns, clusters of buildings baking in the brutal heat. The floor of the valley was almost a checkerboard of symmetrical lines dividing field after field—or possibly rice paddies, decided Mrs. Pollifax, having already dipped into four chapters of the book. Off to her right—or to the west, if her reasoning was correct—a road ran toward her into the mountains, and on its surface she could see men at work, so tiny they resembled little black insects. Mrs. Pollifax turned to look at what lay behind her, beyond Lulash and the stone house, and her head had to go up and far back before her eyes found the sky—the mountain towered above her. She concluded that this stony cut upon which she stood, and into which the two fortresslike buildings had been inserted, was an accident of nature, the path of some long-ago landslide or avalanche that had killed the soil for every growing thing. But of one fact she was certain: there could be no efficient escape over the peak above them into Yugoslavia, the only possibilities lay to the west, along the route they had come, or below, through the valley.

Escape . . . for the first time she acknowledged the direction of her thoughts, and having at last formed the word in her mind she took it out and examined it. Escape . . . the idea was quite mad—she admitted this cheerfully—but surely some effort had to be made? It struck her as extremely characterless for any human being to sit around waiting for execution. It wasn't that she had so much character, thought Mrs. Pollifax, but rather that always in her life she had found it difficult to *submit*. The list of her small rebellions was endless. Surely there was room for one more?

She smiled and waved at Lulash and sat down on a rock near the cliff's edge, her back to him as she carefully removed the book from under her arm. She had already marked the map's page and now she opened to it at once. A valley, an alp and a river . . . yes, there *was* a river in exactly the right place. On the assumption that her directions were correct she quickly compared its location on the valley's floor with its location on the map.

"The River Drin," she exclaimed in a pleased voice, memorizing the name, "Drin . . ." About fifteen miles away, according to the scale of the map, and if her sense of direction was accurate then it flowed westward into the Adriatic Sea.

Walking back to Lulash she said pleasantly, "The city with the airport, is that Scutari, your capital?"

His face lit up. "Ah, you really did read my book. No, it is not the capital any longer, nor is it called Scutari now," he said. "Its name is Shkoder. But yes, that is where the airport is, in the north."

"You are a mine of information about your interesting

country," Mrs. Pollifax told him with complete honesty. "I shall hope to learn much more from your book. Forgive me, but I think I will go inside now, this sun—this heat . . ." She placed a hand daintily on her brow, impatient to get inside and begin new calculations on her map.

Lulash jumped to open the door for her before he sat down again on his bench.

Considerably refreshed by her small excursion Mrs. Pollifax walked back into the ice-house coolness of the stone building, and closed the door behind her. "Oh—I do beg your pardon!" she said, discovering Major Vassovic kneeling in a corner on the floor. For one fleeting moment Mrs. Pollifax wondered if she had interrupted the major in prayer, but then she remembered where she was and put this thought aside. Curiosity drew her closer. "Is that some form of Yogi you're practicing?" she asked.

"*Zott,* no," he said heavily.

Mrs. Pollifax knew by now that *Zott* was a derivative of Zeus and a favored exclamation of the country; this much had not changed since 1919; and she nodded.

"The electric wire, there is only the one—ah! I have it!" The major climbed laboriously to his feet, and finding her still watching him he added, "For my heat brick. The electric is difficult here."

"Yes, it would be," she agreed. "How on earth do you get electricity? Surely not from the valley."

"*Zott,* no," he said, untangling the wire that ran from the floor to his desk. "We have, what do you call it, a big machine in the other building. But here, only the one wire."

Mrs. Pollifax brightened. "Oh yes, a generator. That's clever. And this is your heat brick?" She reached out and touched it. "Why, this is what we call a heating pad at home."

"Yes, for the back," he said, nodding. "These stones are hard to live with."

"Back?" repeated Mrs. Pollifax, puzzled.

"My back. Very cold, very sore."

Mrs. Pollifax understood at last. "You mean a cold has settled in your back!"

He nodded morosely. "To get up, to get down, it hurts."

"You poor man," said Mrs. Pollifax, genuinely concerned. "I know exactly what that's like. How long has it been bothering you?"

"Since they moved me here."

Mrs. Pollifax frowned. "Have you tried any deep heat, have you tried massage?"

He only stared at her, uncomprehending, and Mrs. Pollifax made an exasperated sound. "Take off your shirt," she said firmly. "Yes, take it off, I won't hurt you, it's the only thing that really helps. Have you rubbing alcohol?"

"Alcohol?" He reached into a drawer of the desk and dubiously held up a flask of brandy.

"Yes, why not?" she said cheerfully. "Now the shirt, please, and if you would be so kind as to lie across your desk—"

He retreated in alarm.

"No, no, you don't understand, I will rub your back. Massage it. This has . . ." She was making no headway with him. She went to the door and opened it. "Mr. Lulash," she called, "could you please come and translate for me? I want to rub the major's back."

"You want to what?" said Lulash, entering.

"His heating pad will do very little for him, he needs a sound back rub. Please ask him to remove his shirt and lie across his desk."

With a grin Lulash translated the words. Major Vassovic said, "Ah!" and then, "Oh?"

"He did not understand you," said Lulash. "He thought you were insisting he lie down and drink the alcohol and his instructions are to never drink while on duty."

"I see." The major was removing his shirt.

"He says," translated Lulash, "that he did not bring long winter underwear here because it is summer. He did not expect a stone house."

"Nor did any of us," murmured Mrs. Pollifax, her eyes running expertly over his back. Once the major had lowered himself to the desk she rolled up her sleeves, poured brandy into the palm of one hand, and approached him. She was a knowledgeable back-rubber; at one period in her life she had visited a Swedish masseur and had seen no reason why she should not apply the same principles to the backs of her family. Experience added a special fillip to her technique, and now she pummeled, pushed, kneaded and slapped the major's back with enthusiasm. His small shrieks of protest presently became sighs of joy.

"He will need a blanket now," Mrs. Pollifax told Lulash. "He must lie still for several minutes before getting up." Lulash nodded and returned with a blanket. Mrs. Pollifax threw it over the major and collapsed into the desk chair. "Now that was good exercise," she said happily. "I haven't done it in years."

"Was good, good," grunted the major from the desk.

"You must be extremely careful in getting up," she told him sternly. "When the muscles are inflamed and swollen they push little bones out of place. This is what hurts you."

Lulash went to the water cooler and brought back two paper cups. "Allow me," he said, and with a bow poured brandy into each cup.

Mrs. Pollifax said doubtfully, "I suppose I could call it a late afternoon cocktail?" She accepted the drink with her right hand. Very casually she dangled her left hand in the vicinity of the ammunition drawer and felt for the protruding brass key.

"Half-past three," said Lulash, and seated himself in the chair on the other side of the desk. He and Mrs. Pollifax exchanged friendly smiles across the lumpy, prostrate form of Major Vassovic. "*Skoal!*" called Lulash, lifting his cup.

"*Skoal,*" returned Mrs. Pollifax gaily, pulling open the drawer behind her. In the comfortable silence that followed she filled her hand with gun cartridges and pushed the drawer closed again.

The lumpy figure stirred and sat up. "But that was delicious," gasped the major. "You do that for my back again sometime?"

Mrs. Pollifax beamed at him. She now had four gun clips in her lap and was feeling congenial indeed. "Of course, Major. At least until they decide how to dispose of me."

Lulash said in surprise, "Dispose? Dispose?"

She said cheerfully, "Oh yes, I'm sure they'll eventually have to kill me. What else can they do with me?"

"But you cannot be dangerous," protested Lulash.

Mrs. Pollifax shrugged. "Does anyone care? This isn't a democracy, you know."

"They do not shoot people in a democracy?"

"Oh dear, no. Not unless they've committed a murder, and even then—no, really, people do not get shot as punishment in a democracy." She sipped her brandy appreciatively. "And then it's in the hands of a jury, you know. It takes twelve people to decide on a person's guilt."

Major Vassovic stared at her. "Twelve officers, you mean."

"Oh no," said Mrs. Pollifax. "Twelve people. Citizens. Ordinary people. Working people."

The two men stared at her incredulously. Major Vassovic said, "But then no one would ever be found guilty. Who instructs them?"

Mrs. Pollifax smiled forgivingly. "They are free to make up their own minds from the evidence that's presented."

Major Vassovic looked thoroughly alarmed; Lulash looked interested. "Explain to me how it works," he said.

Mrs. Pollifax hesitated, not from any lack of articulateness but because she was holding four gun cartridges in her lap. She said, "First I must put on my jacket, I'm cold." She left her chair and walked over to the stool upon which she had arranged her jacket so that it would conceal *Albania: Land of Primitive Beauty*. Slipping the gun clips into the pocket she shrugged on her jacket and managed to squeeze the book tightly under one arm. Her activity reminded Major Vassovic of his own condition and he started buttoning on his tunic.

"It works like this," Mrs. Pollifax said, and returning to the desk drew pencil and paper toward her and began diagraming a courtroom. "The judge sits here," she announced, drawing a circle, "and we will call this the jury box and put twelve circles here. You will be one of them, and I will be another, and the major will be a third."

"Please no," said the major in alarm.

"It's only on paper," she told him soothingly. "And we will pretend that you, Mr. Lulash, are a farmer, and I am a housewife, and Major Vassovic sells ties in a store."

"What are our political affiliations?" asked Lulash quickly.

"Oh, but that doesn't matter at all."

"But it must."

She shook her head. "No, because this is a court of law and justice. We would be concerned only with truth."

Lulash said, "But surely the jury would have been appointed by party officials?"

"No," said Mrs. Pollifax firmly. "Not appointed at all. No commitments, no ties, no obligations. Absolute freedom to decide."

"*Zott*," cried Major Vassovic despairingly.

"Then surely the judge is appointed?"

"Yes," said Mrs. Pollifax.

"Ah!" cried Lulash triumphantly.

"But the judge has nothing to do with the verdict," emphasized Mrs. Pollifax. "He cannot decide whether a man is guilty or innocent. That responsibility rests with the twelve jurors."

Lulash looked bewildered. "He cannot tell the twelve jurors they're wrong? He cannot punish them if they bring in the wrong verdict?"

"Absolutely not," replied Mrs. Pollifax.

From the doorway General Hoong said coldly, "Good afternoon, Mrs. Pollifax."

Mrs. Pollifax turned. She had not realized before how very much the general's face resembled a fresh brown egg. The skin fitted his bones so snugly that she could not find a single line of laughter or of sadness, and she wondered if he could have had his face lifted. There was something very sinister about a man of forty or fifty who looked so remote and untouched by life. "Good afternoon," she said.

His nostrils quivered fastidiously. "There is a smell of alcohol in this room. Private Lulash, Major Vassovic, have you been drinking?"

"It's entirely my fault," intervened Mrs. Pollifax. "I was allowed a small walk and I had a touch of sunstroke. They offered me the brandy for medicinal purposes."

Seeing the general's gaze drift from Lulash to Major Vassovic she continued in a firmer voice. "I'm glad you are here, General Hoong. I would like permission to extract the bullet from Mr. Farrell's arm. You have seen Mr. Farrell today?"

The general's glance rested upon her and his left eyebrow lifted. Mrs. Pollifax was relieved to see that this caused two lines above the brow without cracking the surface of his face.

"It is obvious to me," she said in her most imperious Woman's Club voice, "that he will die if the bullet is not removed. This will make General Perdido quite angry, don't you think? I don't believe he will appreciate his dying at all. Not at all."

The general's gaze lingered on her face. He might have been pondering a piece of rare jade, a beautiful sunset or the fish he was to eat for dinner.

"I will need a knife," she went on recklessly. "A knife and some boiling water to sterilize it, and a bandage. This is possible?"

The general's right eyebrow was lifted this time. His lips moved. "It is possible, yes."

"Good."

Gradually something resembling an expression stirred the shell-like surface of his face. "There is nothing else?" His voice was brushed with the most delicate sarcasm.

"I don't believe so," Mrs. Pollifax told him, ignoring the

sarcasm. "Your food is quite good and I'm growing accustomed to the mattress. It's not exactly posturpedic, but it's firm. No, I think this is all."

He bowed slightly. "I am so glad."

"And now I believe I'd like to go back to my cell and lie down," she finished. "If you will excuse me?"

Major Vassovic at once produced the key and led her down the hall. As he swung the cell door open for her he whispered, "Tomorrow, same time?"

Feeling like a paramour making an assignation Mrs. Pollifax told him gravely, "Tomorrow, yes." She entered the cell to discover that the Gremlin had disappeared and Farrell was asleep. As soon as the door closed behind her she hurried to her cot and hid the book on Albania under the mattress. Only then did she bring from the pocket of her Guatemalan jacket the items she had stolen from the ammunition drawer. It was a little like opening up a mystery prize, she reflected, as she held them up to the light to see what she had won. Carrying them to the nearest window slit for a closer scrutiny she found that two belonged to a Beretta pistol, and two to something called a Nambu. Very good, she thought, nodding. Next she wondered where to hide them and she decided at last upon diversification; she placed one in her purse, another inside her underclothes in a time-honored place of concealment, a third she trusted to a hole in her mattress and the fourth she hid in Farrell's mattress. Since Farrell was still asleep she took out Lulash's book and turned again to the map.

"What, no solitaire?" asked Farrell suddenly from across the room, turning his head toward her.

"For the moment I have something better to do," she told him absently. "Lulash has loaned me a book on Albania, much prized by him in spite of its being published in 1919. What is particularly interesting is that it has a very good map of the country. He really should have remembered it was there and removed it."

Farrell's mouth dropped open. "Good God," he gasped, "you can't possibly be thinking of escape!"

She thought it tactless to mention the alternative. Instead she said calmly, "But why not? You don't think I want to spend my sunset years in Albania, do you? The winters are extremely cold, the book says so, as cold as the summers are hot. If I only apply myself there must be a way to get us out, preferably before General Perdido returns."

"Us?" echoed Farrell in astonishment. "You said 'us'?"

Mrs. Pollifax looked up from her map in surprise. "You can't possibly think I'd leave you behind!"

Farrell shook his head. "My dear Duchess, it must have escaped your notice that for most of today I've been off my rocker with fever. I also have a broken right leg and a bullet in my right arm."

Mrs. Pollifax nodded indifferently. "Yes, I'd noticed. But I've asked for permission to cut the bullet out of your arm, and if you can bear another operation—I know it won't be pleasant—then your temperature ought to go down, and that will leave only the healing leg."

"That's right—only a broken leg," rasped Farrell.

Mrs. Pollifax returned impatiently to her book. "It isn't clear to me yet, but I'm hoping it will come. The simplest way would be lowering you over the cliff, but we would need at least a hundred feet of rope for that. We ought to have a gun, too, and some sort of clothes for disguise, and food, and I suppose to be really efficient we ought to have a compass, although if the stars are out—"

She found that Farrell was regarding her as if she had gone mad. He said with sarcasm, "A rope, a gun, a disguise, food and a compass—anything else? How about ordering a limousine?"

"I don't think you're being at all receptive," she told him stiffly.

It was their first quarrel. He said scornfully, "I think you've gone off your rocker, too, Duchess, but if it gives you something to keep your mind occupied—well, have lots and lots of fun. And now if you'll forgive me I'll go back to sleep, which is the best escape *I* can think of. You know—'sleep that knits the raveled sleeve of care' and all that?"

"Coward," said Mrs. Pollifax with a sniff, and then was sorry for the word as soon as it left her lips. But it was too late; Farrell's eyes were closed and a kind of gentle snore was issuing from his half-open mouth. Mrs. Pollifax, watching him, wondered if he knew how becoming a beard would be to the shape of his face. A few more days, she mused, and he would have a very striking one, and then with a start she went back to *Albania: Land of Primitive Beauty*.

The boiling water, a penknife and a towel arrived at dusk, brought in by Major Vassovic, who looked disapproving and then somewhat distraught as he added that he had been

ordered to remain behind to help with the operation. In a
gruff, nervous voice he addressed the walrus-moustached
man who now shared their cell. "His name is Adhem Nexdhet," he told Mrs. Pollifax. "I have asked him to hold the
candle for you, Lulash is not on duty tonight."

"For me," thought Mrs. Pollifax, "he means hold the candle for me," and her knees suddenly felt very wobbly. She
put down the pack of playing cards and stood up, trying to
recall the dozens of splinters and the broken glass she had
extracted from small knees and fingers in her lifetime, but
finding little comfort in the thought. She remembered only
one bit of advice given her by a doctor: never bleed for the
patient, let him do the bleeding, you just get the job done.

Mrs. Pollifax took the knife from Major Vassovic, saw to
its sterilization, glanced just once at Farrell, whose eyes were
open, and proceeded to go about getting the job done. She
mentally granted to Farrell his own right to dignity, assuming
he could manage his own hell just as she must somehow
manage hers. Quickly and ruthlessly, knowing that speed was
kinder than gentleness, she probed the rotting flesh for the
bullet. When the knife met its hard resistance she thanked
heaven that it was not embedded in a muscle and with one
swift, cruel turning of the knife she lifted the pellet to the
surface and heard it drop to the stone floor. Not knowing
how else to complete the job she poured the hot water over
the infected skin, and this at last brought from Farrell a yelp
of pain.

"I wondered when we'd hear from you," she told him.

"They'd never hire you at Mount Sinai, Duchess." His face
glistened with perspiration.

"Really? And I was planning to apply next week—what a
pity."

He grinned weakly. "Just can't keep you from volunteering for things, can we. Have you finished your butchery?"

"Quite."

Farrell nodded and turned his face to the wall, and Mrs.
Pollifax realized what he had already endured and must still
face, and the resolve to escape hardened in her. She would
not, *must* not, save Farrell only for General Perdido. Even if
an escape attempt brought only death it was certainly a
cleaner way to die than by whatever means the general was
planning. In that moment she realized they were going to
have to try it, and with this all her doubts ended; it was no
longer a matter of *whether* but *when* and *how*.

Major Vassovic had disappeared, leaving her the basin of water and several towels. Mrs. Pollifax dipped a towel into the water and began swabbing blood from Farrell's mattress.

"You did that well," said Adhem Nexdhet suddenly. "Without emotion."

Mrs. Pollifax stepped back in surprise. "You really do speak English," she said accusingly.

He smiled wryly. "But you already knew this, did you not? I am not unaware of the little trick Mr. Farrell played on me. Allow me," he said, taking the towel from her. "You are not young, you must be tired."

Mrs. Pollifax backed to her cot and sat down. "I suppose you're also in the secret police then!"

"Yes, I am Colonel Nexdhet of the Sigurimi."

Mrs. Pollifax winced. "I see. That makes you the major's superior then." She sighed. "It also makes it especially kind of you to help. Thank you."

He shrugged. "A good officer knows when to break rules here and there. Major Vassovic is not a good officer, except for his rigid obedience, which is the mark of a follower, not a leader. He is afraid of life." The colonel wrung out one towel and picked up another, saying over his shoulder, "There is one thing that General Perdido does not know about you, Mrs. Pollifax."

Startled, she said, "Oh? What is that?"

He turned to look at her. "He does not know how well you perform under pressure."

There was a long silence. Nexdhet's words were ambiguous, but the man's stare made Mrs. Pollifax feel distinctly uneasy. Until now the comic moustache had obscured the fact that his eyes were both penetrating and intelligent. As pleasantly as possible Mrs. Pollifax said, "I'm glad to hear that."

"You are more than you appear to be," he said, smiling.

"Really?" He was clearly testing her, she decided. "I have no idea how I appear."

"It is very interesting to me," continued Nexdhet. "I underestimated you at first glance. To General Perdido you are an embarrassing mistake. Now I wonder if he may not have underestimated you as well."

"What you have underestimated," retorted Mrs. Pollifax firmly, "is my experience in first aid. However, if it pleases you to think otherwise—"

The cell door opened. The guard who did not speak English came in to collect the dinner trays and the conversation was mercifully ended. Mrs. Pollifax spread out her playing cards for a last game of solitaire, but whenever she glanced up she was aware of Colonel Nexdhet watching her with a mixture of speculation and amusement.

Fourteen

The next morning Mrs. Pollifax began to plan in earnest. When Colonel Nexdhet was removed from their cell, presumably for his exercise, she brought from her purse everything that could be used as a bribe or trade, and spread the items across the little table. There were three lipsticks, two of them brand-new and in smart bejeweled gold cases; a tin of Band-Aids, her wallet containing five dollars and thirteen cents; travelers' checks amounting to fifty dollars (the rest were in her suitcase in Mexico City) and a small memo pad with gold pencil. To these she reluctantly added her Guatemalan jacket, and distributed the small items between the two pockets of the jacket, keeping only the memo pad. On one of its pages she had jotted down the few Albanian words with which the author of *Land of Primitive Beauty* had salted his book. The words were as follows:

> *dunti—hope chest*
> *shkep—rock*
> *zee—voice*
> *rhea—cloud*
> *gjumë—sleep*
> *bjer—bring*
> *pesë—five*
> *zgarm—fire*
> *natë—night*

It was meager fare for her purposes, but after an hour spent in arranging and rearranging the words she had selected four of them for the message she wished to write in Albanian. It was a crude affair but it was the best that she could manage, and now she carefully copied out the four words on a fresh sheet of memo paper. *Night—Sleep—Bring Voice.* To this she added hopefully in English, since everyone else here seemed to speak it, "We are two Americans here, who are you?"

"What's up?" asked Farrell from his cot, watching her.

"Nothing, nothing at all," said Mrs. Pollifax hastily, and slipped the memo into her pocket. "How are you feeling?"

"Weak but human at last."

She nodded. "Your temperature is almost normal, I felt your forehead while you were asleep." She stood up as the cell door groaned open and a guard appeared. "I believe it's time for my walk now," she told Farrell.

From his cot he said dryly, "You look like a cat planning to swallow the canary, Duchess. Whatever you're up to it won't work, you know. This is Albania."

"Yes, Albania, land of primitive beauty," she told him, and swept from the cell.

She had no more than closed the door behind her, however, when a familiar voice said, "There you are, Mrs. Pollifax, I have been waiting for you."

It was Colonel Nexdhet, the very man she would have preferred to avoid. He wore a pair of binoculars around his neck and carried a book under his arm. "We can walk together," he said.

"You are to guard me?" she inquired coldly, and then as they entered the guardroom she said warmly, "Good morning, Major Vassovic, and how is your back today?"

"Ah, Zoje Pollifax," said the major, beaming. "It is still sore, yes, but last night I sleep like the baby."

"Mrs. Pollifax," cried Lulash, coming in from outside and holding the door open for her. "You have good walk before the sun climbs high?"

"Thank you, I hope to," replied Mrs. Pollifax.

"Take my sunglasses, please," insisted Lulash, peeling them from his eyes. He winked. "Remember we are jurors, you and I."

"What did that mean?" asked Colonel Nexdhet as they emerged into the brilliant sun.

"Nothing important," Mrs. Pollifax assured him airily. She stopped a moment, adjusting to the bright tawny landscape, and then moved on. "There are so many of you here to guard so few of us, it seems such waste."

"We will go in this direction," said Colonel Nexdhet, gesturing to the east. "No, it is not waste. There are other prisoners in the larger building."

"I didn't know that. How long have you been here, Colonel?"

"Oh, for several months. I was brought here to be second in command to General Hoong."

"You must find it bleak?"

"At times. I take many walks, I fancy myself as a bird watcher." He gestured toward the binoculars around his neck. "I enjoy walks."

"So I gather," she said dryly.

He helped her across a deep cut in the earth, and they began to climb a little, toward the forest.

"And do you enjoy being a colonel in the Sigurimi?" she asked.

He shrugged. "It is my job." He looked at her and smiled. "You question everything, and this is good. But you doubt nobody, and this is bad. We are neither of us young, you and I, we are each nearing the end of long lives and so can speak frankly. I observe in you the desire to trust, even here. This is weakness in a human being, a foolish thing, the desire to lean."

Mrs. Pollifax followed him among the trees, her face thoughtful. She had already forgotten that he made her uneasy. "No," she said honestly, "no, I don't think I agree with you. I don't lean on people, as you put it. It only comforts me to know that people are there. You don't find this to be so?"

He looked at her and again she was aware of the tired wisdom in his eyes. "Then it is because you are a woman."

"Perhaps. You mean you trust no one at all?"

"No one but myself."

"Why?" asked Mrs. Pollifax.

He shrugged, and helped her over a fallen log. "That is only common sense. Perhaps I have seen too much of life, I don't know. I am sixty-three, I have perhaps watched too many knives in the back, too many sudden changes of the face. Nothing endures except the *idea*, the *mind*. I served Albania under the Turks, I served her under King Zog. We were friends with Mussolini and then Mussolini turned on us and conquered us and I fought in the resistance then, for communism. After the war it was Hoxher who came to power and ruled, with Russia our friend. Now we have quarreled with Russia and it is the Red Chinese who help us." He shrugged again. "It is the way life is. Nothing endures except the idea. This alone is clear, pure, not soiled by change."

Mrs. Pollifax nodded. "Yes, you have seen too much of life—the bitter side, at least."

"In the Balkans, in Albania, life *is* bitter," he said.

Mrs. Pollifax considered. "Of course by the idea you mean the political idea—communism—but aren't you wrong to say it never changes? There is this matter of Stalinism—"

"One adapts," he said. With a wry smile twisting his preposterous moustache he asked, "Politically you are what?"

"Republican," acknowledged Mrs. Pollifax. "Although twice I voted for Adlai Stevenson—*such* a charming man."

He smiled. "Then you, too, adapt." He touched her arm and directed her to the right. "We have gone far enough," he said. "We will follow the cliff back. There is a good view here, you will see the valley from a new angle."

There was indeed an excellent view, and she was grateful to stop walking for a minute. "Beautiful, is it not?" said Colonel Nexdhet, standing beside her. "And those men below, how small, like ants."

"Yes, I just noticed them," said Mrs. Pollifax. "What on earth are they building down there?"

"A missile site," he said without interest. "Seeing Man like this reminds me always of Man's fragileness, don't you agree?"

A missile site, he had said. *A missile site?* A shock of excitement moved down Mrs. Pollifax's spine disc by disc. The Chinese were building a missile site in Albania? She forgot her failure in Mexico; if she could bring news of a missile site to Mr. Carstairs then she would not have failed as a spy at all. It was obvious that Colonel Nexdhet would not have mentioned such a thing if he was not absolutely sure that both his secret and Mrs. Pollifax would remain in Albania, but this was only a new goad. Aloud she said disapprovingly, "They would do better to build roads, why do you need a missile site?"

Colonel Nexdhet gave her his arm. "Shall we start back? The Chinese are very patient, Mrs. Pollifax, they build for the future. They are not taken seriously yet as a major power, but see what they have already accomplished! They have fought and won a small slice of India. They have their finger in a dozen pies in southeast Asia. They are proving extremely successful in infiltrating Latin America—every Communist party there has its Mao-ist wing. They now have trade relations with most of western Europe and with Canada, Australia and Japan. They have exploded a primitive atom bomb. But most of all they are here to help and to protect my country, which you must not forget is a European country. The Chinese have arrived in Europe."

"Good heavens," said Mrs. Pollifax as she absorbed the meaning of all that he said. "It's really quite shocking."

"If you are an American, yes," he said with a shrug. "As for the Chinese—they look ahead."

"Very enterprising of them," she said weakly, and wondered how to change the subject before she gave away her profound interest. "But I have not seen any of your birds, Colonel Nexdhet."

He said gravely, "That is what makes bird-watching so fascinating, Mrs. Pollifax. There are so few of them up here along the cliffs."

Presently they came out into the hot sun again, and the stone buildings lay ahead.

Mrs. Pollifax had left her cell at half-past nine in the morning. It was quarter-past five when she returned, flushed from the sun and a string of small, happy accomplishments. She found Farrell livid.

"Don't you ever do this to me again," he sputtered, sitting up on his cot and glaring at her. "Don't you dare."

"Do what?" she said in astonishment.

"Go off for a whole day like this. I've been nearly out of my mind picturing you in front of a firing squad or being stretched on a rack somewhere being tortured. And now you have the audacity, the unmitigated gall to walk in here looking happy."

She walked over and kissed him fondly on the top of his head. "Bless you for worrying. I'm sorry."

"Then try to look sorry," he snapped. "I'm a very sick man. Where have you been?"

"Oh, here and there," she said airily. "Walking with Colonel Nexdhet, picnicking on the cliff with Lulash, rubbing Major Vassovic's back. We have even been discussing holding a small party in the guardroom tomorrow night."

"Party!" exploded Farrell.

"Yes, you see Lulash knows some old Albanian mountain songs and he wants to sing them to me, and Colonel Nexdhet will bring a musical instrument and Major Vassovic went so far as to volunteer something alcoholic for the occasion, and one thing led to another, and now it's to be a party."

Farrell stared at her open-mouthed. After a minute he

closed his mouth with a snap. "All right," he said crossly, "what exactly *have* you been up to, Duchess?"

She sat down beside him and drew from the pocket of her jacket a sheet of onionskin paper and placed it in his lap. "For tracing the map in Lulash's book," she whispered. Drawing out a flat, round, metal case she added it to the sheet of paper. "And I won't have to tell you what this is."

He pried open its lid and whistled. "A compass! But how on earth—and who—"

"I traded with the major after I rubbed his back. I said I was getting rid of my effects early. It cost two new lipsticks, one Petal Pink and one Hug Me."

"Yes, but didn't he wonder at a *compass?*"

She smiled reminiscently. "He gave me several things to choose from in return, it was quite fun. He offered an old watch, a pen and this surveyor's compass that has been in the guardroom for years, he said. Does it work?"

"It moves," Farrell said, frowning over it.

"East," she told him, "would be in the direction of the guardroom, and west behind the wall you're leaning against."

He looked up. "And just how do you know that?"

"Because we traveled into the rising sun when we came here," she said. "We arrived from the west, from the city of Shkoder, where our plane landed. And according to the map the River Drin, which I can see from the precipice, flows from east to west, into the Adriatic, which places Yugoslavia just behind us."

She had captured his attention at last. He closed the lid of the compass with a snap and said quietly, "Perhaps you'd better tell me exactly what you're thinking of, Duchess, if it's not too late to ask. You really *have* been busy."

"Of course I'll tell you," she said warmly. "I'm only an amateur, you know—although a very determined one, I warn you—and I desperately need your professional advice. Have you been trained in escape procedures?"

"Afraid not," he said in amusement.

"Oh, what a pity. Well, I guess that can't be helped."

"Good of you to see it that way."

"What I do think I ought to tell you, though—and I would have sooner if you hadn't been in such a state—is about the person in the cell next to us." She described in a whisper the rappings on the wall that had taken place on the day that Farrell jumped from the cliff. "I've heard nothing since, you understand, but this afternoon, walking around the building, I dropped a note through the window slit of the cell next to us."

"A note?" echoed Farrell. "But this is Albania, and an Albanian jail. I really doubt that whoever it is would speak English, you know."

"Well, it wasn't the most articulate message, but I made it up out of scraps of Albanian from Lulash's book," explained Mrs. Pollifax. "It said *night—sleep—bring voice*, if I remember correctly, but I did rather hope our neighbor would get the point that we'd like to hear from him again somehow." Footsteps echoed in the hall and Mrs. Pollifax seized compass and paper, stuffed them into her purse and moved back to her cot. She was seated on it fingering her deck of cards when the door opened and Adhem Nexdhet—no, Colonel Nexdhet, she remembered—walked in. "Have a good walk?" she inquired pleasantly, and was suddenly all too conscious of the contraband book under her mattress, the gun cartridges distributed around the cell, the food and compass in her purse.

"What is this game you always play?" he asked, stopping beside her table.

"Different kinds," she told him. "All sorts of solitaire. Very healthy for the mind and the nerves, I enjoy it. Has General Perdido returned yet?" she added casually.

"He comes late Thursday, in the evening," Adhem Nexdhet said absently, his eyes on the cards she was arranging.

Mrs. Pollifax managed a rueful laugh. "And I don't even know what day it is today!"

"Tuesday." Nexdhet abruptly sat down beside her. "Show me," he said. "The cards in a circle, what is the key to this?"

"It's called Clock Solitaire," replied Mrs. Pollifax, and began to explain the rules. But her heart was thudding at the realization that General Perdido would return on Thursday, and already this was Tuesday. . . . At once the general's face came very clearly to her mind: impassive and observant with only the eyes, sans spectacles, betraying shrewdness and cruelty. Over the cards she glanced at Farrell and saw him chewing reflectively on the moustache that would in time resemble Adhem Nexdhet's walrus-type adornment—if ever given the time. Haste makes waste, she thought a little wildly; escape in haste, repent in leisure; she wondered if Farrell remembered any of General Perdido's parting promises; he had been feverish and in pain and she hoped he did not recall them. It was far kinder for him not to know what lay ahead of him.

But only two more days, and they had made almost no arrangements . . . !

Then something else occurred to her and she said in shocked astonishment, "But why is he coming back so soon? Is it you who told him Farrell is well enough to be questioned by then?"

Colonel Nexdhet met her glance with a faint smile. "I believe I warned you that you must trust no one," he pointed out gently.

On Wednesday morning during her walk along the cliff Mrs. Pollifax selected two round, fist-sized rocks from the ground and took them back to the cell and hid them. She then borrowed Lulash's sunglasses and walked a little farther, toward the clusters of fir through which she and Farrell had ridden on donkeys. What they needed most of all, she knew, was a crutch for Farrell; a very stout crutch or walking stick. Without this they might as well abandon all hope of reaching the valley.

"Lulash," she called across the rocks. He was sunning himself on the bench outside while he cleaned his gun. "Lulash, I've had the nicest idea." She walked up to him, smiling. "But first I'll need your permission and your help."

"What is that?" asked Lulash.

"It's Mr. Farrell," she explained. "He cannot take walks, as I do—"

"He would not be allowed," Lulash said bluntly.

"I know that, and it's very difficult for him, shut up all day in that cell. Lulash, I should so like to hang some branches in the cell. Fresh green branches."

"Branches?" repeated Lulash, scowling.

"Yes, branches. Surely it would be all right? Surely no one would mind?"

Lulash's brow cleared and he smiled indulgently. "Every woman, she likes to make things pretty, eh?"

"Uh, yes," said Mrs. Pollifax. "You do understand, I'm so glad. Should I ask the major's permission, too?"

"That I can do for you," Lulash said gallantly.

Major Vassovic not only gave permission but announced that he would come too, and they set out for the line of scattered firs together, with Mrs. Pollifax pointing out the beauties of the sky—a horrid bleached blue—the uniqueness of the rocks, and the wild scenery above them. She talked mercilessly until they reached the trees, whereupon she became reverently silent, and for such a long time that the men became restive.

"This one—or this one?" she asked at last, touching first one branch and then another. She stood still, struck with apparently spontaneous inspiration. "Or do you suppose we could take back a very small tree?"

"Tree?" echoed Major Vassovic in astonishment.

"Tree?" repeated Lulash.

"This little one, for instance. It looks just like a Christmas tree."

"But this is summer," pointed out Major Vassovic.

"Yes," Mrs. Pollifax said, nodding, and then, ruthlessly, she delivered the *coup de grace*. "But I will not—I will not be here—I will not see another Christmas."

That did it. Lulash angrily tightened his lips. "She will have the little tree," he told Major Vassovic.

"Of course," nodded the major, and at once twisted the tree to test the depth of its roots. Lulash gave a small assist and the young tree was uprooted.

"Lovely," murmured Mrs. Pollifax with feeling, and with the tree between them like a fourth member of the party they marched back to the stone building.

"What on earth!" exclaimed Farrell as Lulash leaned the tree against the wall of the cell.

"Isn't it beautiful? Christmas in August," said Mrs. Pollifax, and added a warning frown because Colonel Nexdhet was seated on his cot reading a newspaper on which the banner head proclaimed the words ZERI I POPULIT. But he had already begun folding up his paper, and presently, with a nod, he went out wearing his binoculars.

When he had gone Mrs. Pollifax sat down on her cot and said tartly, "I loathe myself. I have just given the most nauseating performance of my life—I, Emily Pollifax! I was girlish, I was kittenish, I very nearly fluttered my eyelashes at those two men, and at my age! Sickening."

"You didn't," exclaimed Farrell, grinning.

She nodded. "I pulled out all the stops. I nearly had them weeping for me."

"Not over this—this ragged specimen of evergreen, I hope."

Mrs. Pollifax said crossly, "That ragged-looking specimen

of evergreen, my dear Farrell, is shortly going to be transformed into the crutch that is going to help you walk across Albania to the Adriatic Sea."

Farrell whistled. "I've done it again, Duchess—my apologies." His glance ran appraisingly over the trunk and he nodded. "Yes, the shape is there all right."

"No crosspiece," she explained, "but we can use pieces of mattress and blanket to wad the top and protect the arm. Did you finish tracing the map?"

"Yes, in spite of Nexdhet. That man wanders in and out— if he has to keep up the pretense of being a fellow prisoner I wish he'd put his heart into it and suffer along with me. He obviously has bathroom privileges, a discrimination I deeply resent, and he never speaks to me, he only grunts."

"But you finished the tracing!"

"Oh yes. And something else happened, fortunately while Nexdhet wasn't here. About half an hour ago *this* fluttered through the window." He brought from his pocket a slip of paper.

"Our neighbor!" gasped Mrs. Pollifax. "He did reply after all!"

"In a fashion," said Farrell, and watched with ironic eyes as she held the slip of paper up to the light.

On it had been printed in beautiful script the following message:

天吾林為人好不好

Fifteen

That evening Colonel Nexdhet followed their dinner trays out of the cell, and as soon as he had gone Mrs. Pollifax crossed the room to Farrell and sat down on the cot beside him. She had spent the afternoon in playing solitaire and doing some private assessing which had definitely not aided her digestive juices. She was also beginning to scratch and she feared that she had lice, but this did not concern her nearly so much as the knowledge that within twenty-four hours General Perdido would be appearing. The general, she reflected, was the more compelling irritant.

"He's gone?" whispered Farrell, sitting up. They did little talking at all while Adhem Nexdhet was with them.

"He may not be gone long," Mrs. Pollifax reminded him. She thought that Farrell was no less haggard, but he looked brighter-eyed and more interested than she had seen him in a long time.

"All right, let's go over the list."

Mrs. Pollifax nodded. "We have one tree." She gave it a reproachful glance. "But no earthly way of cutting it down to a crutch."

On her memo pad he wrote *knife or facsimile*. "Go on."

She continued gloomily. "We have four magazine clips, apparently for Beretta or Nambu pistols but unfortunately we have no Beretta or Nambu pistols."

Farrell winced as he made a note of this.

"We have enough cheese and stale bread for two people—two pygmies, really—for two days. But no water."

"Mmm."

"We have one compass that works—we think. And one tracing of a 1919 map of Albania. And two rocks."

"Ah—rocks!" Farrell brightened. "But let's take the items one by one. The tree first of all: they'd never allow us a saw or a knife. I don't suppose you've seen one lying around that you could, uh, pinch? Make off with?"

"There are at least half a dozen knives in the gun rack in the guardroom," Mrs. Pollifax told him. "But they're under glass and locked up. There's always someone with me, and I doubt if they'd trade a knife."

"No, not likely. I could always ask to shave—"

"I'm sure they'd want the razor blade back."

He nodded, but without appearing in the least discouraged, which pleased Mrs. Pollifax because she was beginning to feel very discouraged indeed. He said, "The branches we can tear off at the last minute with our hands, but we do need a cutting edge to shape the top."

"How do we manage all this with Colonel Nexdhet here in the cell with us?" asked Mrs. Pollifax. "I thought—I mean I picked up one of those rocks thinking we could hit him over the head at the proper time but . . ." She shivered. "I couldn't, you know, could you?"

"Yes."

"But you can't even walk yet."

Farrell smiled faintly. "No, but I haven't been completely idle, Duchess. At night while you and our spy friend are asleep I've been trying to get my strength back. I stand. I do crazy exercises. Look." He got laboriously to his feet and stood, his weight on the good leg. "I don't get dizzy any more. I nearly fell over the first time, I was so lightheaded. I've been exercising my hands and arms, too. Yes, I could hit our friend over the head, at least I can if he gets close enough to me. Let's see those rocks, by the way, and whatever's left of your trading goods."

"Trading goods," repeated Mrs. Pollifax, smiling. "You mean for friendly natives?" She brought out the diminished contents of her pocket. "One lipstick, one handkerchief . . ."

He was examining both as if he had never seen either. "Always use men's handkerchiefs?" he asked with amusement.

"For a number of years, yes. They were my husband's, and so much more substantial."

"Excellent gag," he pointed out.

Mrs. Pollifax brightened. "I didn't think of that."

"One must," he murmured. He had taken apart her lipstick case and was studying it. He ran a finger over the rim of the metal tube and said quickly, "Let's see those rocks, are any of them rough?"

Mrs. Pollifax leaned eagerly over his shoulder. "You mean we may have found a cutting edge?"

"Only a peeling edge, I fear. I'll see if I can chisel a sharper point with the rock. Try to bring back a few more rocks if you're allowed a walk tomorrow. Except that without a gun . . ."

Mrs. Pollifax said reasonably, "But if we escape as far as the guardroom we can steal as many guns as we want."

"Yes, and a knife, too, except we can't leave the crutch until the last minute. It would take too long to make. We're going to have to manage it somehow during the last hour we're here, preferably after our spy has been rendered unconscious."

"And he's so pleasant, I like him," mourned Mrs. Pollifax. "You *will* hit him gently, won't you?"

"Gently, yes, but very thoroughly."

"When should we—that is, what hour tomorrow should we plan on?" asked Mrs. Pollifax timidly. "It will have to be a time when someone unlocks the cell and comes in, Lulash with a tray or whoever's on duty. We hit him over the head, too, I suppose?"

"Everybody. Major Vassovic, too—somehow."

"I could scream or do something like that to bring him in," suggested Mrs. Pollifax, getting into the spirit of the thing. "About six o'clock, do you think?"

Farrell shook his head. "Dinnertime's too early. Too light outside. We don't know how many people are left in the other building, the big one. They might see us stumbling around on the rocks."

Mrs. Pollifax said anxiously, "But if we wait until later, when they bring in the candle, that might be too late. General Perdido may have returned, and I'm sure he'll want to see us right away."

Farrell said firmly, "I'll think of something. I'm better now, trust me. Just don't worry."

"Not worry," echoed Mrs. Pollifax, and at once felt a trembling begin deep down inside her and run along her nerves until she began to shiver uncontrollably. Really this was madness, she realized—absolute madness, none of it could be real, neither Albania nor Farrell nor General Perdido nor this ridiculous cell in which she had been placed as a prisoner—and tomorrow evening they were going to try to escape with two rocks and a Christmas tree turned into a crutch. It was the final touch of madness.

The spasm passed, and Mrs. Pollifax regained her poise and was relieved to see that Farrell had not noticed her moment of weakness. He was staring at their pathetic heap of treasures and saying, "Not bad, really, not bad at all. Their letting you out for walks, and these rocks you picked up, are the two real miracles allowed us. Nobody can ask for more than two miracles, the rest is up to us."

"*I* could ask for another," said Mrs. Pollifax tartly.

He grinned. "Then go ahead, maybe you have more influence than I. But don't turn gloomy on me suddenly. Thanks to that map you spotted in Lulash's book we know fairly well where we are—"

"We think," added Mrs. Pollifax warningly.

"And thanks to your ingeniousness we have weapons, a bit primitive but no less effective."

"Yes, but if only we had a *knife!*"

Farrell said flippantly, "Maybe someone will start throwing knives at that party of yours and you can deftly catch one between your teeth and hide it in your pocket."

Unfortunately there was not a knife to be seen at the party. There were forks—Mrs. Pollifax at once secreted two of them—and various-sized spoons, but no knives, not even dull ones. Mrs. Pollifax might have become despondent again if it were not for the *raki* that Lulash had filched from the wine cellar in the larger building. He and Major Vassovic had obviously begun sampling it already. "Join us," said Lulash with shining eyes.

"I believe I will," said Mrs. Pollifax, and startled them by emptying her glass. "It is extremely sweet of you to have a party for me," she told him with feeling.

"Have an olive," said Lulash, embarrassed. "Have more *raki*."

"But you have no knives," pointed out Mrs. Pollifax.

"Why do you need a knife?"

"I always eat olives with a knife," Mrs. Pollifax told him hopefully. "A sharp knife."

"Americans do this?"

"Always."

Major Vassovic shook his head. "We have no knives. Try a fork."

Mrs. Pollifax philosophically accepted a second glass of *raki* instead, and was sipping it when Colonel Nexdhet arrived bearing a dish of cheese and what looked like a zither. Mrs. Pollifax's reaction to his arrival was ambivalent: she felt extremely wary of him and yet as a human being she liked him.

"General Hoong will be coming too," said the colonel. "It seems that he enjoys parties."

"Then I will sing before he comes," said Lulash, and promptly sat down on the floor and crossed his legs. "Please," he told Mrs. Pollifax, gesturing her toward the desk chair. The colonel plucked a few strings of his peculiar-looking instrument and Lulash began to sing a song filled with weird half notes and pauses.

How beautiful is the month of May
When we go with the flocks to the mountains!
On the mountains we heard the voice of the wind.
Do you remember how happy we were?

In the month of May, through the blossoming trees,
The sound of song is abroad on the mountains.
The song of the nightingale, ge re ge re ge re.
Do you remember how happy we were?

I would I had died in that month of May
When you leaned on my breast and kissed me, saying,

"I do not wish to live without you."
Do you remember how happy we were?

I wish again the month of May
That again we might be on the mountains,
That again we might hear the mountain voices.
Have you forgotten those days of beauty?

There was a long silence when he had finished. With his head still bowed Lulash said sadly, "There was a Russian engineer in Tirana, she once said to me those same words. Where is she now?"

Why was it, wondered Mrs. Pollifax crossly, that love songs everywhere had to be so terribly sad? Major Vassovic was noisily blowing his nose and Mrs. Pollifax realized that something was needed to cut the treacly sentiment that was submerging them. She herself did not feel sad; on the contrary the *raki* had left her lightheaded and a little belligerent. She turned to Colonel Nexdhet and said with unsteady dignity, "Colonel Nexdhet, I have been thinking about your country and I have decided it was immoral of you to give it to China."

Lulash looked appalled. *"He* gave us to China?"

The colonel said firmly, "Not personally, Private Lulash."

"Then who did? That's what I'd like to know, who did give us to China?"

The colonel shrugged. "Russia moved out, China moved in."

Major Vassovic looked up and said piously, "We needed and wanted China to help us. We gave ourselves to her gratefully, willingly."

Lulash looked insulted. "I didn't have anything to say about it, Major—did you? What this country needs is a George, a George . . ." He turned to Mrs. Pollifax. "Whoever he was you told me about."

"Washington."

"Tha's right, George Washington. And let me tell you something else, Colonel, if anybody was to ask me who to give this country to, I'd say, give it to Mrs. Pollifax."

"Why, thank you, Lulash," she said warmly.

Colonel Nexdhet said mildly, "Lulash, you have had too much *raki*."

"I? Too much? It is a lie. I will sing to you another song."

"Yes, please do," said Mrs. Pollifax.

"An old song," announced Lulash defiantly. "Full of old heroes who belong to Albanians and nobody else. I will dedicate it to—"

The door opened and General Hoong entered in full dress uniform, medals pinned to his chest, a pistol strapped to his belt.

"To democracy!" shouted Lulash, standing and emptying his glass of *raki*.

General Hoong looked around him and focused at last upon Lulash. He said distastefully, "Private Lulash, you are drunk." To Mrs. Pollifax he bowed and said, "I have come to your party. I have brought for it a bottle of vodka."

Mrs. Pollifax said eagerly, "Did you bring a knife with you to open the bottle?"

"A knife? No, a corkscrew," said the general reprovingly. "Vassovic, open the vodka."

"At once, General," cried Major Vassovic.

General Hoong removed the pistol from his side, held it at arm's length and fired six shots into the ceiling. "The party may begin now," he announced. Seating himself next to Mrs. Pollifax he said, "I like noise with a party."

"Yes, it is so convivial," she admitted, her eyes on the pistol which rested upon his knee. "What an interesting-looking gun, General," she said.

"Since it is empty you may look at it," he said condescendingly. "It is a Japanese pistol, called a Nambu."

"How very odd," murmured Mrs. Pollifax, and held it to the light admiringly. When she had finished admiring it she placed it carefully on the top of the desk between them.

"Some vodka?" suggested General Hoong.

"Oh, a very little," she said, and as he leaned forward she neatly slid the Nambu into her pocket.

"I sing my next song," cried Lulash, and reaching over to pluck the strings of the instrument on Nexdhet's lap he began chanting loudly,

Ahmet Bey, the Beautiful! O! O! Ahmet Bey!
Ahmet, the son of the Mountain Eagle . . .

From the stricken look on Major Vassovic's face Mrs. Pollifax at once deduced that this was a subversive song. She moved closer to General Hoong and said, "It really is so very kind of you to join us. Very considerate."

His empty eyes turned to look at her. "A general is always alone," he said.

"But soon General Perdido will be back and you can be alone together."

He said fastidiously, "Perdido is a barbarian."

Mrs. Pollifax thought about this and nodded, "Yes, he is." General Hoong sighed. "I am not the happiest of men."

"I'm sorry," Mrs. Pollifax told him with sincerity. "I can quite understand why, of course. You live a very isolated life up here. Have you hobbies?"

"I have a mistress."

Mrs. Pollifax considered this frank statement and gamely nodded. "Yes, that would help to pass the time."

"And I write poetry."

"Do you really! I wish that I might hear some."

"My most recent one I have committed to memory. I will recite it for you."

"Please do," said Mrs. Pollifax, and wished that Lulash would end his interminable song about Ahmet Bey.

Closing his eyes General Hoong recited in a sonorous voice:

Pale moon torn by white clouds:
Spool of purest light.
Enchanted. Timeless.
Without heart, lacking grief.
I gaze, and wish my soul
Lacked heart and bore no grief.

"But that is charming," said Mrs. Pollifax.

"Yes," he said simply.

"I had no idea you were so sensitive, General Hoong. I had no idea you suffered so. You seem so—so impervious to the demands of your job."

"I suffer," he announced firmly.

"Then you really must find another job," she urged him sympathetically. "You certainly must be qualified for some work where you don't have to shoot people, or beat them, or torture them to death."

"Job?" he said, frowning. "Job?" He sighed and drained his glass of vodka. "There is nothing wrong with my job. It is my mistress who causes me torment." He stopped talking and began staring broodingly into space.

Lulash had reached the end of his song. He said to Mrs.

Pollifax, "Now you must take a turn and sing to us a song of your country."

"I?" said Mrs. Pollifax.

"Yes, yes, for it must be a beautiful country, a country of justice," cried Lulash exuberantly. "Maybe one day Albania too will be like that, let us all drink a toast to that hope."

Major Vassovic gently belched. "Shplendid idea." He lifted his glass.

Colonel Nexdhet was smiling mockingly. "Well, Mrs. Polli-fax?"

Mrs. Pollifax accepted the challenge, arose and bowed to General Hoong. "We have your permission to drink Lulash's toast, General Hoong?"

General Hoong roused a little from his reverie. "What? Oh yes, I like noise with a party."

"To the United States of America," said Mrs. Pollifax in a ringing voice. Remaining on her feet, however unsteadily, she sang one chorus of "God Bless America." It was on this note, carrying with her the general's Nambu pistol but still lacking a knife, that Mrs. Pollifax withdrew from the party, pleading weariness.

"I tried," said Mrs. Pollifax, sitting on the edge of her cot and staring sadly at Farrell. "I tried to steal a knife, but all I could bring back was the pistol."

Farrell was still admiring it. "At this moment, Duchess, the odds against our escaping have just shrunken by about five hundred."

"But it isn't a knife," she pointed out. "It's true that you could blow the top of the tree off with a pistol but you can't make a crutch with a pistol."

"Nevertheless, you can't imagine how much more secure I feel," said Farrell. "Get me the cartridges and I'll load it." She gave him the two Nambu clips and he grinned. "You're turning into quite a scavenger, you know. How was the party?"

"Quite dismal, really. Except for Lulash." Mrs. Pollifax smiled reminiscently. "Lulash would like a George Washington for Albania."

"You haven't been planting seeds of insurrection, have you, Duchess?"

"Well, it's a change from planting geraniums," she retorted.

He finished loading the pistol, patted it lovingly and slipped it beneath his mattress. "I strongly advise getting some sleep now, considering what's ahead of us."

The effects of the *raki* were wearing off, leaving Mrs. Pollifax depressed. "Sleep?" she said resentfully. "Why?"

"Because if we're going to be shot tomorrow trying to escape I'd much prefer dying with someone who can say something jaunty, like 'I regret that I have only one life to give for my country,' or—"

"Jaunty!" exclaimed Mrs. Pollifax, but she was smiling. "That's all very well but I didn't bring *Bartlett's Quotations* with me, you know."

"A pity. Do come up with something magnificent, though, will you? Surprise me," he suggested with mischief in his eyes.

At that moment Colonel Nexdhet walked in, but Mrs. Pollifax's sense of humor had returned—Farrell had seen to this—and she realized that she could face the next day, if not with equanimity, at least with a philosophic stoicism. Then she realized that Farrell was pointedly staring at her and she raised her eyebrows questioningly. Slowly and deliberately his glance moved to Nexdhet, who was removing his jacket in preparation for a night's sleep. Mrs. Pollifax's eyes followed and abruptly widened. Colonel Nexdhet was wearing a knife strapped to a sheath on his belt.

"Our third miracle," said Farrell quietly.

Mrs. Pollifax could scarcely believe it, but being of a practical mind she at once said, "You or me?"

Farrell gestured ruefully toward his leg. "You, I'm afraid."

Mrs. Pollifax nodded. She put away her table, yawned elaborately, scratched her leg—lice, obviously—and lay down. "Good night, Colonel Nexdhet," she said sweetly. "It was a lovely party, wasn't it?"

"Oh?" He looked surprised. "Oh yes, good night." He nodded curtly to Farrell and stretched himself full length on his cot. It really was a pity, thought Mrs. Pollifax, that he had to continue sleeping in the cell with them; at his age he must long for clean pajamas, a comfortable mattress and a private room. Then she remembered that at least he had bathroom privileges, and this cut short her pity and she lay on her side with her eyes fixed upon the knife and tried, through the gloom, to figure just how it was affixed to his belt.

Farrell began to snore gently—she did not believe for a moment that he was sleeping—and Nexdhet began to snore loudly. There were no sounds from the hall or the guardroom. Mrs. Pollifax slowly sat up, the mattress producing even more ominous rustlings than usual, which only substantiated her suspicion that it was filled with corn husks. Once in a sitting position she remained so for a few minutes to make certain the snores continued. She stood up and waited again before moving slowly toward Nexdhet's cot. She was nearly there when she was attacked by an almost irrepressible urge to giggle; she had just remembered that when she was a child she had been given a part in a school play where she had to glide like a wraith. After it had been explained to her just what a wraith was the result had been this same gliding, tight-hipped movement. Firmly she controlled herself and leaned over Nexdhet. Neither his breathing nor his snores changed. Her hands moved to his belt and she fumbled with the strap on the sheath, gently drawing it up and out. When this had been accomplished she sank to one knee, and with one hand steadying the bottom of the sheath she placed the other on the handle of the knife and pulled. The knife came out easily. Still Nexdhet had not stirred, and after a moment's hesitation Mrs. Pollifax glided, still wraithlike, to Farrell's cot.

He was still snoring softly but his left hand reached out, open-palmed, to accept the knife that she placed in it; then he turned on his side, his back to her, and Mrs. Pollifax knew he was hiding it under his mattress. She returned to her own cot and sank upon it with relief, corn husks and all. Two minutes later she was asleep.

Sixteen

In the morning when Mrs. Pollifax awoke she realized at once that a fateful day was beginning. She lay and thought about this dispassionately, almost wonderingly, because to every life there eventually came a moment when one had to accept the fact that the shape, the pattern, the direction of the future was entirely out of one's hands, to be decided unalterably by chance, by fate or by God. There was nothing to do but accept, and from this to proceed, doing the very best that could be done. Without knowing the end, reflected

Mrs. Pollifax; like being wheeled into an operating room and wondering if one would ever see this or any other ceiling again. Twenty-four hours from now would she and Farrell be staring at these same stone walls, or would they be free, or would they even have survived to see that next day?

Farrell was sleeping soundly. She momentarily begrudged him such discipline until she remembered that he did his exercising at night. Colonel Nexdhet was sleeping too, and suddenly she remembered the knife she had taken from him and was afraid. He would wake up soon and find it gone and know at once that she or Farrell had taken it—who else could have stolen it from him while he was asleep in a locked cell? She wondered why on earth they hadn't thought of this last night. They had so badly wanted a knife and Nexdhet had walked in wearing a knife and it had seemed like their third miracle.

"When actually it may prove our undoing," she thought.

As if he had felt her thoughts Nexdhet sat up and yawned and rubbed his eyes. Meeting her gaze he nodded, and one hand went to his sweeping white moustache to smooth it. Mrs. Pollifax fought to keep her eyes from dropping to the empty knife sheath; she prayed that Colonel Nexdhet's talents did not include mind reading. Nexdhet's second move was to stand up and stretch, and then his hand went out to his jacket at the foot of the bed. While Mrs. Pollifax watched with alarm he lifted the jacket, patted one pocket and shrugged his arms into the sleeves. At least he had not *seen* the empty sheath, she thought wildly, and waited next for him to feel for the knife's presence. But he didn't. He leaned over and began tying his shoes.

Farrell sat upright. He, too, glanced quickly at Colonel Nexdhet and then anxiously at Mrs. Pollifax, who shook her head. At the same moment steps echoed in the hall, keys rattled, the door opened and the guard named Stefan walked in carrying breakfast trays. Nexdhet spoke curtly to him in Albanian, and then walked out.

"Bathroom privileges," muttered Farrell darkly.

"You don't suppose there's a bathtub on the premises?" asked Mrs. Pollifax breathlessly.

"A shower maybe."

Mrs. Pollifax closed her eyes and thought yearningly of hot water coursing down her body and taking with it the accumulation of dirt and dust, and then, most voluptuous of all, the feeling of being clean again and not itching. Life was incredibly simple when stripped to its essentials, she reflected, and for a moment her thoughts lingered on luxuries taken for granted during a long life. Except it was not really a long life, she amended, certainly not if it was to end today, and she began to feel quite angry with these people for wanting to kill her. "After all, it's my life, not theirs," she thought peevishly, "and all I did was . . ."

All she had done, she added more reasonably, and with a faint wry smile, was to walk into CIA headquarters and offer her services as a spy. This made her at once feel better, since it was obviously a spy they would wish to kill rather than Emily Pollifax of New Brunswick, New Jersey. Somehow this knowledge made it less personal; women were always so sensitive to snubs.

Stefan backed out, leaving the trays. Farrell whispered, "He doesn't know it's missing?"

"No, not yet. And now that he's out of here he can't blame it on *us*."

"Hooray for our side." Farrell stood up, wobbled dangerously but waved her away. "Let me show you what I did last night while you were sleeping." He half crawled, half limped to the tree that leaned so idiotically against the wall. Grasping it at the top he neatly removed the last twelve inches like a magician pulling a rabbit from a hat.

"Why, for heaven's sake," Mrs. Pollifax said in pleased surprise.

"I hollowed one end and sharpened the other so the two pieces fit into each other. It's a beginning, anyway, and just the right height now to fit under my arm. Later we'll rip and cut the branches off. Think you can collect some padding?"

Mrs. Pollifax nodded. "There's a very nice hole in my mattress. Not nice for sleeping but nice for taking out what's inside. Did you know we've been sleeping on horsehair? It may be why I itch." She was already extracting it from the mattress and making a bundle to fit the top of his crutch-stick.

"What will you wrap it in?"

"My petticoat—and therein lies a tale."

"I beg your pardon?"

"Pins," said Mrs. Pollifax. "I never was good at sewing and both straps are pinned together."

"I bless your sloppiness," said Farrell reverently.

"If you're going to call me sloppy I refuse to lend them to you," she told him indignantly.

"All right then, your charming lack of housewifery."

"Much better. Now if you'll turn your head I'll remove my petticoat."

"My head is turned. Better give me the stuff to work with, though, you may be summoned for your walk at any time."

"You can turn around now," said Mrs. Pollifax, and she presented him with slip, pins and horsehair, whereupon they both sat down to eat their breakfast, the bread and cheese disappearing automatically into Mrs. Pollifax's handbag, leaving them only a thin porridge with which to begin their day. What was most nourishing, however—to Mrs. Pollifax at least—was the realization that this was the day they were going to do something about their fate. They were going to act. Her fears had evaporated now. She had faced them, made her obeisance to them and now she could dismiss them. Anything was preferable to submission, and now she began to feel almost reckless at the thought of their attempt at freedom. She cleared her throat. "You still feel we should wait for dark?"

"From what I remember of the terrain it struck me that anything else would be suicidal."

Mrs. Pollifax put down her spoon and nodded. "Quite true. But in which direction should we head? Right away, I mean. They'll expect us to leave the way we came, won't they?"

"Yes, but can you think of anything better?" asked Farrell, and there was irony in his voice.

Mrs. Pollifax concentrated firmly on prospects she had entertained only lightly before, and she began to understand his irony. It would be very clever of them to head east, away from the sea, and throw General Perdido off the scent for a while, but eventually they would have to double back, either this way or through the valley, and in the end they would only have added extra miles to their journey. Farrell could never endure this. In fact it was doubtful whether he had the stamina to go anywhere at all, but the thought of leaving him behind was untenable; they had to try together or not at all. Then there was the mountain behind them, and the forest in which they could hide, but here, too, Farrell's condition prevented them from going far and General Perdido would be very aware of this.

She said sadly, "No, I can't think of anything better."

"So all we need is darkness and a great deal of luck." He smiled at her. "It's not too late to change your mind, you know—about including me in this wild venture, I mean. I would feel a great deal of relief if you left me behind."

"Absolutely not," said Mrs. Pollifax flatly. "If I made it
alone, which I doubt, I would only be extremely unhappy
when I got there, which would defeat the whole purpose."
She rose to her feet as the door swung open and Lulash
walked in. "Good morning, Lulash, I may go outside now?"

"Yes, Zoje Pollifax. It was a good party last night, was it
not?"

"Every minute of it," she told him with more cheerfulness
than she possessed. "And you're looking very well in spite of
so much *raki*."

"You make all of us feel like human beings again, Mrs.
Pollifax."

From his cot Farrell said, "Beware, Lulash, that is a very
bad way to feel in a place like this."

There was no one to guard her this morning, and it occurred to Mrs. Pollifax that she might try to find the missile
site again and observe more closely how it fitted into the
cliff. In some ways it made her uneasy to be given such freedom; it was pleasant to be considered harmless, but it also
proved how secure her captors felt. She wondered whether
she or her captors were the more naïve, but unfortunately
this would not be discovered until the escape had been committed. Life had never looked better than when death was
imminent, and Mrs. Pollifax found herself looking long and
ardently at earth, sky and clouds.

She cut across the seam in the rocks and climbed doggedly
toward the slanting pines in the wood. Once she had reached
the trees she stopped to recapture both her breath and her
sense of direction; she and the colonel had entered the woods
at this point, and gradually made their way downhill to meet
the cliff again a half mile beyond; she would therefore follow
the course that Colonel Nexdhet had set. Patting her moist
temples with her handkerchief Mrs. Pollifax resumed her
walk. She had moved only a few hundred yards deeper into
the trees when she began hearing a very peculiar noise ahead.
It was a familiar sound, but not customarily heard in a forest,
so that she could not for the life of her identify its source.
The feverish crackling sound came from between two large
boulders that leaned toward each other up ahead.

Deeply curious, Mrs. Pollifax hesitated and then tiptoed
across the fallen pine needles to the rocks. At once a voice

broke the stillness of the woods but the crackling sounds continued without interruption.

"Static!" thought Mrs. Pollifax, brightening. Of course, it was static and someone had carried a radio here into the woods.

The canned voice stopped speaking, and to Mrs. Pollifax's amazement a live voice began talking from behind the rock. Mrs. Pollifax poked her head between the two rocks and stared through the gloom at the man seated on the ground facing her in the small cavity there. "Why, Colonel Nexdhet!" she faltered. He was speaking into a telephone—no, a walkie-talkie, she recalled—and at the sound of her voice he dropped the mechanism as if it were a live coal.

"Mrs. Pollifax!" There was no doubt but that she was interrupting something clandestine; his eyes were blazing. He picked up the fallen walkie-talkie, spoke a stream of foreign words into it, and then placed the instrument in a hole of the rock.

"What are you doing here? Why are you allowed in the woods this morning?" he barked, crawling from the hole and standing beside her.

She said scornfully, "So this is how you report to General Perdido! And if you come out here to do it secretly then you must inform not only on Mr. Farrell and myself but on General Hoong as well. You're nothing but a paid informer, Colonel Nexdhet! Shame."

He glanced back once among the rocks and then firmly grasped Mrs. Pollifax by the arm. "I will take you back to your cell," he said firmly.

"I trust you told General Perdido that Mr. Farrell is in glowing health, and can scarcely wait to see the general again? And that a party took place last night, with subversive songs being sung under the influence of *raki?* You quite disillusion me, Colonel Nexdhet!"

He remained silent, his mouth in a grim line. They reached the edge of the wood and emerged into the blinding sunshine. He helped her over the stones toward the two buildings, his hand tight on her arm. Both Lulash and Major Vassovic were in the guardroom but he did not so much as look at them. He marched Mrs. Pollifax straight to her cell, closed the door behind her and turned the key in the lock. She heard him issuing curt orders in the guardroom.

"He sounds peeved about something," said Farrell pleasantly.

Mrs. Pollifax said indignantly, "Colonel Nexdhet is nothing more than a paid informer. A spy on his own men. An informer on everyone."

Farrell said mildly, "What on earth makes you say that?"

"Never mind, just beware of him. He's not to be trusted." She added in a kinder voice, "I'll tell you about it when we get out of here—if ever we do. Just remember he's not to be trusted."

"But I never did trust him," pointed out Farrell logically. "He's a colonel in their secret police, isn't he?"

"Yes," said Mrs. Pollifax forlornly. She sat down on her cot and stared into the long, desolate and nerve-racking day that lay ahead of them and she wanted to cry. Instead she brought out her deck of playing cards and shuffled them.

At noon it was not Lulash who brought lunch to them but the guard who did not speak English, and when he left he carefully locked the door behind him. Nor did anyone else come. The afternoon wore on, hour by hour. Mrs. Pollifax played every game of solitaire that she had learned, and then played each one again, and then chose her favorites and played them until she was tired to death of cards. She reflected that Senor DeGamez could certainly not have foreseen the conditions under which she would play his cherished game, and remembering his kindness she thought of him for a moment. He had been a spy too; perhaps he had played his games of solitaire under precisely such conditions. She did hope he was in good health because obviously Mr. Carstairs' friends proved very poor insurance risks.

The dinner trays arrived, and with them Colonel Nexdhet. "Good evening," he said in a pleasant voice, as if nothing unusual had happened. "We are getting ready for General Perdido's return, he arrives by plane about half-past eight and should be with us by nine or half past."

"That's interesting," said Mrs. Pollifax politely. It would be quite dark by then—good! "What time is it now, Colonel Nexdhet?"

"Half-past six."

She looked at him in surprise. "I always thought we ate at five although I never really knew. Is it really so late?"

He said primly, "Usually the trays are brought to you by five, yes. We are late tonight because we are understaffed. General Hoong and Lulash have gone to meet General Perdido, leaving only myself, Major Vassovic and Stefan here, and two guards in the other building."

Mrs. Pollifax met Farrell's glance; the colonel was a veritable mine of information.

Nexdhet added casually, "And when you have completed the crutch you are making—and I advise you to finish it at once—I would appreciate your returning my knife to me. I am very fond of it and would prefer that you not take it with you."

They stared at him incredulously—it was a full minute before his words were absorbed. Mrs. Pollifax gasped, "I beg your pardon?"

"You know?" said Farrell in a stunned voice.

"Of course."

"But how?"

Colonel Nexdhet shrugged. "It is my business to know."

Mrs. Pollifax was staring at him in astonishment. "You know and yet you're not going to give us away?"

"Give you away?" He frowned. "Like a bride?"

Farrell was studying the man intently. "She means you're not going to inform on us, you're not going to prevent us from this absolutely wild escape idea?"

"But how can I?" he inquired blandly. "I know nothing of such plans. And if I did I am quite weaponless, as you see, whereas you have my knife as well as a loaded Nambu pistol."

"You know that, too?" gasped Farrell.

Mrs. Pollifax's eyes narrowed. She took a deep breath. "Colonel Nexdhet," she said, "just what *were* you doing in the woods this morning?"

"I am extremely sorry you saw that, Mrs. Pollifax, it would have been much safer for all of us if you had not."

Farrell said, "What *did* you see in the woods this morning, Duchess?"

"I don't know," she faltered, watching the colonel. "That is, I must have leaped to the wrong conclusion. I thought —he was in the woods listening to a voice on the radio, and then he talked back into the radio. He was very upset when I saw him, he escorted me back here and locked the cell."

"He was in the woods—secretly?"

She nodded. "Hidden under two rocks."

Farrell drew in his breath sharply. "Over these mountains lies Yugoslavia, and to the east is Bulgaria; they're both within reach of radio." Farrell stared at Nexdhet and suddenly began laughing. "My God," he gasped, "you're a Russian agent!"

"He's a what?" echoed Mrs. Pollifax in a shocked voice.

"Of course! They left him behind to report on the Red Chinese!"

Colonel Nexdhet walked to the door, placed his ear against it and listened. "No one is there," he said, coming back, "but would you do me the kindness to speak in a lower voice?"

"My apologies," said Farrell, his eyes still brimming with laughter. "Don't you see, Duchess? He's the only one here who goes for walks. Bird-watching, you said. He has radio contact with someone across the mountains." To Nexdhet he said, "But why help *us*?"

Nexdhet sighed. "I strongly dislike the word help. I am *not* helping you."

"All right, you're not helping us."

Mrs. Pollifax suddenly blurted out, "But you *have* been helping, Colonel Nexdhet! That knife—you deliberately wore that knife in here last night, you've never worn one before. And you showed up wearing it just after we'd been talking about how badly we needed one!"

The colonel winced. "Please, Mrs. Pollifax . . ."

"And it was you who told us General Perdido was coming on Thursday night, we'd never have known, otherwise."

"Duchess," said Farrell firmly, "don't look a gift horse in the mouth. He has told us he is *not* helping us."

"And a Russian agent shouldn't be helping us," she added indignantly. "Why?"

"Yes, why?" asked Farrell. "Considering all we know about you already—"

The colonel sighed. "Far too much, I agree. Very well, I will say this much." He hesitated, choosing his words carefully. "You were brought to Albania because you are suspected of knowing the whereabouts of a missing report—well-documented—of Communist activities in Latin America."

"Oh?" said Mrs. Pollifax with interest.

"Red China is extremely interested in seizing that report. Red China will do anything to prevent the United States from learning how heavily involved it has become in Latin America. Red China has still another interest in that report: she would like to learn what Russia is up to in Latin America."

"Ah," said Farrell.

"Russia in turn would enjoy knowing what Red China is secretly doing in Latin America."

"Mmmm," murmured Farrell.

"But if there is a choice between Red China reading that report, or the United States reading that report, Russia would infinitely prefer the United States to have it."

Startled, Mrs. Pollifax said, "But you are both Communist countries!"

Colonel Nexdhet's voice was dry. "You bring up a subject that is—uh—very tender, Mrs. Pollifax, and one that I could wish we not explore. Let us simply say that between Red China and Russia there are certain conflicts. On the part of Russia, a certain amount of alarm, certain suspicions—"

"Russia is more afraid of Red China than of America!" gasped Mrs. Pollifax.

"In some areas, yes. There is something called the balance of power that must be preserved at all costs."

Farrell nodded. "This I understand, yes. But what guarantee have we that Russians aren't waiting somewhere to recapture us and throw us into a Russian prison?"

Nexdhet shrugged. "There are no guarantees at all, Mr. Farrell."

Farrell considered for a long moment. "I'm afraid we'll have to trust him," he told Mrs. Pollifax.

She smiled. "Should we trust you, Colonel? You have repeatedly advised me to trust no one here."

His answering smile was grave. "Nor should you even now, Mrs. Pollifax, for you must remember that I will be in the party that hunts you down after your escape."

Mrs. Pollifax thought about this and nodded. "Then could you do one more thing for us—shoot to kill?"

He said simply, "If you are caught I could not afford to let you survive."

"Thank you, that is all we can hope for."

Nexdhet stood up. "I help you no further. In return I ask only that when you hit me with your rock you do not hit me here." He pointed to the back of his skull. "I have already a small steel plate here from an old wound."

"Better than that we will only gag you," promised Farrell, taking out the knife and beginning to slash branches from the tree.

"With the male handkerchief?"

Farrell grinned. "No secrets at all. You have your own microphone in here?"

"Hidden in my cot, yes. You need not worry, however, I destroyed the tapes this afternoon."

But Mrs. Pollifax's mind was still fixed upon Colonel Nexdhet and she suddenly burst out again. "There's the missile site, too!" She turned to Farrell. "I didn't tell you about that because you still had a fever and might have babbled in your sleep, but the colonel took me for a walk a few days ago, a walk that just happened to include a missile site." To the colonel she said, "You *wanted* me to see it!"

"See *what?*" exploded Farrell.

She nodded. "The Red Chinese are building a missile site only a mile away from here."

"Good God," gasped Farrell.

Nexdhet looked apologetic. "A small detail, but a vital one lest your country underestimate Red China." He smiled wryly. "Russia no longer underestimates Red China."

"You've known our plans that long then?" asked Farrell.

Nexdhet smiled. "I had no interest in your possibilities at all when I first met you. A badly wounded man, a woman no longer young—I thought your escape plans hopelessly naïve, as they still are. It was after observing Mrs. Pollifax remove the bullet from your arm that I decided to do what I could for you. You were worth the risk." Turning to Mrs. Pollifax he said with a smile. "Wherever there is violence there is absurdity, also. And now is there anything else you would like to mention as reminder to me of how dangerous you both are becoming? Certainly it will be to my benefit to see that neither of you is ever questioned by Perdido."

Mrs. Pollifax shook her head. "I can't think of anything else, except . . ." She frowned. "I am wondering if it is quite ethical to let you help us. It feels terribly unpatriotic."

Farrell grinned. "World politics make strange bedfellows, Duchess. Do try to manage a small sense of expediency, will you?"

"If you think it's proper," she said doubtfully. Her eyes fell on the window slit and she jumped to her feet. "It's already twilight," she told Farrell in a shocked voice, and was suddenly struck by the meagerness of their preparations. "Is the crutch finished?"

"I'm just padding it," he told her, and stood up and tested it. "Not bad."

Mrs. Pollifax opened her purse and brought out the rocks and the gag. She collected the Beretta gun cartridges, the map and the compass from their various hiding places and added the cheese from tonight's dinner. She was contemplating them with a frown when Farrell said quietly, "Psst, they're coming for the empty trays, I think."

The trays. . . . She wondered what time it was, and at what hour the candle would be brought. To conceal the rocks she sat down on top of them just as Major Vassovic walked in rattling his keys. "Evening," he said.

Nexdhet grunted; he had brought out a newspaper in which to bury his head. Farrell nodded; he had hidden his crutch under the bed but the tree's absence was conspicuous, and Mrs. Pollifax decided she must divert the major's attention. "How is your back?" she asked, and then saw the candle he was carrying and her eyes widened. "But you're not—not going to light our cell so early?" she faltered.

"Busy tonight," said Major Vassovic, and struck the candle in its round metal ring. "No time for it later."

Farrell looked up, appalled, while Nexdhet put down his paper and regarded Mrs. Pollifax with a sardonic, challenging amusement. Mrs. Pollifax realized with a sinking heart that she was sitting on the rocks that were to knock their guard unconscious; the moment had come and neither of them was prepared. A fretful anger rose in her over changed plans, broken routines, unpredictable guards. It wasn't dark yet. The candle had never before been brought in so early. It could not be more that eight o'clock but the cell door would not be opened again unless to admit General Perdido, and she was sitting here like a brood hen on the rocks that Farrell ought to have if he was to hit Major Vassovic over the head.

"Farrell has to do it," she reminded herself. "He's the only one who knows how." But Farrell was across the room and without the rocks.

"I can't," she told herself fiercely—what on earth would the Garden Club think of her, or the pastor of her church?

Major Vassovic was bringing a match from his shirt pocket, his back turned to the room. In a moment he would strike that match against the wall, light the candle and then turn around. "I can't," she repeated to herself stubbornly.

He struck the match against the wall and Mrs. Pollifax watched it flame into life. "I've never hit anybody in my life," she remembered. "Never," she repeated. "Never never *never*."

Quietly, rock in hand, Mrs. Pollifax rose from her cot, walked up to Major Vassovic and hit him on the head. To her utter astonishment he collapsed at once, falling to the ground to lie there like a suit of old clothes. "For heaven's sake," she said, staring down at him in fascinated horror.

"Good girl," said Farrell, and reaching under the cot for his crutch he hobbled over to look at the major. "Out like a light."

"I do hope I didn't hurt his back again," said Mrs. Pollifax anxiously. "It was coming along so well."

Nexdhet said politely, "Not at all, I'm sure. What next?"

Farrell plucked Vassovic's huge, comic-opera keys from the floor and dropped them into Mrs. Pollifax's purse. "What next?" he repeated. "We call the other one in—Stefan—and to spare the Duchess I'll try *my* skill with the rock."

"Oh?" said Mrs. Pollifax wistfully. "Actually it was rather interesting."

"Then you'll jolly well have to sublimate, I'll be damned if I'm going to encourage you to hit men over the head. Here, help me arrange Major Vassovic in a more sprawling position. We'll say he's fainted. I do beg your pardon, Nexdhet," he added with a smile. "Damn funny doing all this in front of you."

"But he's isn't helping, he's just overlooking," Mrs. Pollifax reminded them both. "Now?" Farrell had taken a position behind the cell door, a rock in his good hand. When he nodded, Mrs. Pollifax gave a squeal, held her breath and followed this with a penetrating scream. "Guard! Guard!" She ran to the door and pounded on it.

Footsteps hurried down the hall and the unlocked cell door was pushed open. Stefan walked in and Farrell stepped forward and hit him. Stefan also sank into a heap. "You're quite right, it *is* fun," Farrell said.

"I'll go out and look for rope to tie them with," said Mrs. Pollifax, and hurried up the hall to the guardroom. It was not until she arrived there that she realized it might not have been empty; she made a mental note to develop more cunning, and at once locked the outside door so that no new guards could surprise them. Rummaging through the desk drawers she found a few lengths of rope and carried them back to Farrell.

Nexdhet said, "I really think you had better tie me up now, too, before I am tempted to change my mind or before General Perdido walks in. It surprises me, how alarmed I am beginning to feel."

"Frankly, I'm a little alarmed myself," said Farrell with a

grin. "It's the Duchess who gives this such an amateur quality. Delightful but alarming. Lie down, chum."

Nexdhet gratefully lay down and Farrell began linking him by rope to Major Vassovic and Stefan. "I'll gag you but not hit you. You'll have to play dead," explained Farrell. "Are you a good actor?"

"No, but I'm known as a very good Sigurimi man."

Farrell gave a bleat of a laugh. "Let's hope it protects you then. And Nexdhet—thanks."

The colonel smiled faintly. "Just spare me the trouble of shooting you, that's all."

The gag went into his mouth and Farrell knotted it securely. Over his shoulder he asked of Mrs. Pollifax, "Where are you off to now?"

"To look for a Beretta. And it's nearly dark!" With this Mrs. Pollifax left again, this time with her purse, to return to the guardroom and strip it. With the major's keys she found a Beretta pistol and a second Nambu, and she double-checked both to be perfectly sure that her stolen gun clips fitted. Then she decided to load up on cartridges for them and reached down to the drawer beneath. This time it did not budge to her fingers. The drawer that for a week had held a key in its lock was now firmly closed and not a one of the major's keys fitted. "What a pity," she murmured, and turned back to the hall.

But first she had something else to do, something that had occupied her thoughts quite tantalizingly from time to time. This was her curiosity about their next-door neighbor who had rapped upon the wall. Mrs. Pollifax tiptoed past her own cell and down the hall, not at all sure that Farrell would approve of this side excursion. She inserted keys into the lock and opened the door upon a dark closet of a room. She stood there uncertainly, peering inside.

From the farthest corner there came a rustling sound, and Mrs. Pollifax's instincts told her that something was moving. Suddenly the darkness expelled a form, a wraith, a gray genie of a man in flowing gray robes who began a repeated bowing of his head as he chattered to her eagerly in a melodic, singsong voice.

Mrs. Pollifax interrupted him. "Not now, please. We are going to try to escape. Escape," she told him. "Would you like to come along with us?"

He stopped speaking and regarded her with great interest. His face was surprisingly long and Gothic for an Oriental;

the mouth was thin and turned up at the corners into a fixed, sweet smile; his eyes were large and bright and childlike, with only a faint suggestion of an Oriental pouch above the lids. Between the pursed lips and the twinkling eyes he looked—well, not quite responsible, thought Mrs. Pollifax; rather like a happy child in the guise of a man, all twinkles, smiles and curiosity.

"Come," she said, as if to a child, and pulled him by the sleeve. He followed without protest, his eyes lively and curious. When they reached the cell Mrs. Pollifax said in a voice whose confidence was spurious, "Look what I found."

"Good heavens," said Farrell, staring at the little man beside her. "Who on earth is this birdlike creature?"

"The man next door. Colonel Nexdhet can tell us who he is, I'm sure." They both glanced at the colonel and saw that he was straining at his gag and ropes. Farrell bent over and slipped the gag from his mouth.

"No," said Nexdhet harshly. "No, I will not tell you who he is. No, you must not take him, absolutely not."

"Take him!" Comprehension was dawning upon Farrell, leaving him inarticulate. "You can't possibly—you're not thinking—?"

"Why not?" asked Mrs. Pollifax.

"But who is he? You don't know a damn thing about him. For heaven's sake, Duchess, he may be a Commie worse than General Perdido."

"Then why would he be in jail?"

"Who knows? He may have seduced somebody's mistress or tried to organize a *coup d'état*. He's Chinese, isn't he? He had to *be* somebody to get here."

"I refuse to listen to you," Mrs. Pollifax said indignantly.

"Trusting, always trusting," pointed out Colonel Nexdhet from the floor. "Now you are crazy."

Farrell's lips thinned in exasperation. "There's another point, Duchess. If he doesn't speak English he doesn't understand that we're escaping. When he does realize it he's likely to let out one long bloody yell at the wrong moment. He may not *want* to escape."

"Nonsense, everybody wants to escape," said Mrs. Pollifax scornfully.

"Have you explained the odds to him? He just may not want to end up in front of a firing squad," pointed out Farrell.

"Defeatist."

"Her conscience again," Farrell explained wearily to Nexdhet.

"You must put him back in his cell at once," warned Nexdhet. "And remember, I know who he is."

"You won't tell us?"

"Absolutely not." On this matter Nexdhet sounded unequivocal.

Both regarded him thoughtfully until Farrell, rousing, said, "Oh, to hell with it, Duchess, this whole thing is insane, anyway. Bring him along, damn it, we haven't all the time in the world."

Mrs. Pollifax wordlessly handed him the two pistols and helped him tie the last knot and stuff the gag in the colonel's mouth. "Okay, let's go," Farrell said crisply, and they moved out into the hall with Mrs. Pollifax hanging onto the sleeve of her genie. Carefully Farrell locked the door of the cell behind them and restored the keys to Mrs. Pollifax's purse. "Get rid of them later," he told her, and limped into the guardroom. "What do we call this—this lamentable mistake of yours?"

"Our Genie," said Mrs. Pollifax at once. "He reminds me of the one in Aladdin. Smaller, of course."

"Our Genie with the light-brown hair," quipped Farrell and ignored her cross glance. Leaning on his crutch he unlocked and pulled open the door to the outside. "Only two lights shining in the big building," he said. "Shall we go?"

With charming gallantry he held open the door for Mrs. Pollifax and her charge, and they walked past him into the sultry night air. "We're outside, we're free, we're no longer prisoners," thought Mrs. Pollifax, and she drew a long deep breath. She was in the process of expelling it when a voice to her right said unpleasantly, "Well, well, my three prisoners, and no guard in sight! It seems that I have returned from Peking just in time."

General Perdido had come back.

Seventeen

"Back—into the guardroom!" barked General Perdido, drawing the gun from his belt holster. "I'll have Vassovic's head for this. Lulash, see what they've done with Vassovic. At once."

As the general shouted orders, his attention distracted for a second, Mrs. Pollifax lifted her arm and threw the cell keys far into the night. She thought somewhat hysterically, "I shot an arrow into the air, it fell to earth I know not where," and she tried not to wince as she heard the sound of metal against rock. But neither her gesture nor the noise appeared to have been noticed by anyone, and Mrs. Pollifax began to feel more confident. She could not have said exactly why her courage revived except that two such unusual occurrences really ought to have been noticed by the general, and somehow this proved that he was not superhuman. A man who barked and shouted and popped up out of the dark could easily acquire such a reputation, she reflected; but these particular keys to the cells he would not get, and if there were duplicate keys they would require time to find.

And so, quite ignominiously, they were back in the guard-room, the three of them standing like naughty children before the desk at which the general had seated himself. Desperately Mrs. Pollifax tried to think: the electricity was primitive—only one line, the major had told her; it would be marvelous if she could hurl herself at the one power line and plunge the building into darkness. Unfortunately she was again without a knife, and totally without knowledge of power lines.

"What fools you are," hissed the general. "I would never have believed it of you. I will take great delight, Mr. Farrell, in punishing you for this. As for you, Mrs. Pollifax—yes, what is it, Lulash?"

Lulash appeared in the hall, his eyes anxious as they encountered Mrs. Pollifax's glance. "I can't get in," he said. "The doors to the cells are locked."

The general muttered an oath and irritably opened one desk drawer after another. "They're not here, one of these three must have them. Search them!"

Mrs. Pollifax's heart sank, because a search of their persons would reveal two pistols. She said defiantly, "I was carrying the keys, but I threw them away. Outside, in the dark."

The general stood up and walked around the desk to Mrs. Pollifax. He slowly lifted one arm and with precision struck her across the cheekbone.

Lulash looked stricken. Farrell cried angrily, "Hey!"

Mrs. Pollifax, reeling and a little faint, heard the general promise that this was only the beginning of what lay in store for them. The Genie spoke then, too, his eyes darting with interest from Mrs. Pollifax to the general. The general answered him in fluent Chinese, the Genie appeared satisfied and nodded.

"Go ahead, Private Lulash—search them," said General Perdido harshly.

Lulash exchanged a long glance with Mrs. Pollifax, but she could not tell whether she read apology or a plea in that glance. He moved carefully to Farrell and stood before him. "Turn to the wall, please, and place your hands against the wall."

It took a second before Mrs. Pollifax realized that Lulash stood squarely in front of Farrell, concealing him from General Perdido as well as protecting him from the general's gun. There was a curious smile on Lulash's lips as he looked into Farrell's eyes. "Faster," he said, "or I will shoot you."

Farrell understood. One hand moved swiftly to his pocket, the other seized Lulash. Over Lulash's shoulder he fired his pistol at the general, and then lightly tapped the guard on the head with the butt. The sound of the pistol's discharge in the small room was deafening. Both Lulash and the general had fallen to the floor.

"Let's go," said Farrell, and headed for the door on his crutch. But the Genie reached it first and the three of them fled into the night. Or perhaps fled was not precisely the word, thought Mrs. Pollifax, as Farrell stumbled and tripped over the uneven rocks, muttering a variety of oaths at his clumsiness. She went back and took his arm and they struggled toward the fir trees. "I'm afraid I only winged him," Farrell said furiously through his teeth. "I meant to kill him, but damn it I think I only got his shoulder or his arm."

"He fell to the floor," Mrs. Pollifax reminded him. "He disappeared behind the desk."

"Pure instinct. Self-preservation. Give him a few minutes to stop the bleeding and catch his breath and he'll be after us."

"Yes," Mrs. Pollifax said grimly, and realized that without Farrell to deter them they would already have reached the sanctuary of the fir trees. She took a long glance at this thought, examined it with brutal honesty, measured the difference this would make in both their small chance of escape and in their lives, and allowed herself one brief pang at being who and what she was. Then she put aside the thought forever. "Here we are," she said with relief as they reached the thin cover of firs.

"My God, the donkeys," gasped Farrell. "Look!"

Now that her eyes had adjusted themselves to the darkness Mrs. Pollifax could see at what he pointed: two donkeys were tied to a tree and were nibbling at the slender thread of green that separated the rocks from the forest of boulders beyond. "Luck," she whispered.

"Plain bloody miracle," growled Farrell, hobbling toward the animals. "Except of course with the general just arriving the donkeys had to be somewhere."

"But we don't have a knife to untie them," wailed Mrs. Pollifax.

"Feels like a square knot," murmured Farrell, working at it. "Tackle the center."

The Genie stood back, not helping. When the donkeys were freed he stepped forward and put out his hand for the two ropes, gesturing to Mrs. Pollifax and Farrell to mount. At the same moment Mrs. Pollifax heard the sound of a gunshot behind them and she froze. "They're after us!"

"Don't panic, it could be someone signaling for help from the main building. For God's sake jump on and let's go."

Mrs. Pollifax unfroze. She heard herself say calmly, "No, I will not mount one of these dreadful beasts again, I refuse. I believe the path or whatever it is lies to our right so we mustn't go that way and how could I ever make the Genie understand this? *He* must climb on, I'll do the leading. We have to find the edge of the cliff and follow it—it's our only hope." She was already tugging at the ropes and telling the Genie in frenzied sign language that he was to take her place. He climbed on at last, and with the two lead ropes in her hand Mrs. Pollifax set out to find the cliff and orient herself. There was now very little time left them—she could already hear shouts being exchanged behind them. The donkeys moved with maddening slowness. Without a flashlight Mrs. Pollifax could distinguish only the larger boulders, and her feet kept stumbling over those half buried in the earth. There was no moon; the stars covering the sky did no more than give her the ability to distinguish between a rock and a tree. Mrs. Pollifax was painfully aware of this, and of the fact that behind them a chase was being efficiently organized. The precipice, which they certainly ought to have reached by now, failed to materialize, and the rocks proved so abortive, so inconveniently placed, that Mrs. Pollifax soon wondered if in skirting the large boulders she might have begun circling back toward their starting point. It was not a happy thought.

No one spoke. At best they were only a few thousand yards from the main building and recklessly moving at right angles to it instead of away from it. "Where *was* that damn edge," thought Mrs. Pollifax, and was appalled at her choice of language. She tugged mercilessly on the donkeys' halters and quickened her step. It proved an ill-timed moment to increase her speed. Mrs. Pollifax's right foot moved out into space, sought reassurance, came down in anticipation of solid earth or rock and found neither. With a startled gasp Mrs. Pollifax pitched forward, guide ropes still in her hand, and meeting no resistance that would save her she catapulted into space, the men and donkeys dragged with her.

It was not a long fall. Just as she assumed that the end had come, her jacket was seized by something knifelike, her fall suddenly broken and Mrs. Pollifax discovered that she was ignominiously straddling a creaking, groaning tree branch that threatened to break at any moment. Mrs. Pollifax had found her cliff and walked over it. Mercifully she had also found a stunted tree branch that had grown perpendicular to the sides of the precipice. But where she was to go from here, and where Farrell, the Genie and the donkeys had gone, she had no idea.

"*Well!*" exclaimed a voice nearby.

"F-F-Farrell?" gasped Mrs. Pollifax in astonishment.

"Good God, you're here too?"

At the same moment she heard both the melodious voice of the Genie, a trifle reproachful, and the faint, anguished bray of a donkey. "But where are we?" cried Mrs. Pollifax.

"I don't think we should try to find out," Farrell told her fervently. "And I think the first thing you'd better do is join us. There's rock under me but what's under you?"

Mrs. Pollifax said nervously, "A tree branch and—and really I don't think there's anything else. Only air."

"Keep talking. Let me find you—this damn darkness—and I'll see what I can do."

Mrs. Pollifax began reciting poetry, first Wordsworth's "Daffodils" and then "The Rhyme of the Ancient Mariner," and tried not to consider her predicament if the branch broke or Farrell could not rescue her. When she felt a hand clutch her ankle a little sob of relief escaped her.

"You're lying straight out on a branch," he told her, as if she didn't already know this. "I want you to very carefully, very gingerly, start shinnying in the direction of my voice. Don't try to sit up and don't move hastily. I'm going to keep my hands on your ankles and very gently pull. If the branch starts to go I think I can still hang on to you."

"Think?" repeated Mrs. Pollifax, and felt like laughing hysterically because, of course, if the branch went, taking her with it, her brains would be dashed against the rock below no matter how tightly her ankles were held. But she obeyed, and thereby learned how subtly and sinuously a person could lift and move his hips if life depended upon it. After what seemed like hours her toes met the solid rock platform on which Farrell was kneeling. When at last she knelt beside him she allowed herself the luxury of feeling faint.

"It *seems* to be a small ledge we fell onto," Farrell explained.

"You didn't hurt your leg again?" she dared ask.

"I fell on one of the donkeys. The Genie wasn't so lucky, he fell on the first donkey and then the second donkey fell on *him*, but he's all right. Crazy. But from the feel of our fall I'd say we fell only about twenty feet or so."

"Only that," marveled Mrs. Pollifax, and then stiffened as she heard voices above.

"Back," whispered Farrell urgently. "There's a shallow overhang, and a hollow in the cliff. Find one of the donkeys and hold his mouth together, or whatever donkeys bray with. I'll take the other."

"The Genie?"

"Blast him, he doesn't understand English so he can't help. If we could see him I'm sure we'd find him bowing and scraping again."

Mrs. Pollifax found a donkey and by the touch system managed also to find its lips and encircle them with both hands. The two donkeys had crawled into the shallow indentation of rock, leaving no room for humans; Mrs. Pollifax did all but climb on top of them for shelter as she heard the general's voice querulously shouting orders. So Perdido was still alive—Farrell had been right about that. A powerful searchlight was turned on from above and directed downward, and Mrs. Pollifax closed her eyes, hoping this would make her even smaller as she pressed against the donkeys. Then the light moved farther along the cliff's edge and the voices of the men diminished as they moved away. Mrs. Pollifax relaxed, and presently fell sound asleep.

It was the Genie who awakened her with a tap on the

shoulder. Her head had been pillowed on the abdomen of a donkey, and when she lifted it she was startled to discover that she had slept through the whole night—the sky was perceptibly lightening in the east. In this first light of dawn she could see the appalling smallness of the ledge upon which they had fallen: it was no more than a lip on the side of the precipice, extending a bare seven feet from side to side. Below her, virtually at the edge of her shoes, lay a drop into the valley that turned her blood cold. Even the tree branch that had caught her looked no sturdier than an arm, and Farrell, noting her face, grinned. "The gods were with us, eh?"

Mrs. Pollifax replied with a shudder.

"The Genie donated his sleeves to tie up the donkeys' mouths," he pointed out. "Voices were heard now and then until about an hour ago. They're probably wirelessing the news of our escape all over Albania now. We'd better move in a hurry, before it gets light and the search begins again."

"Move!" repeated Mrs. Pollifax incredulously. "Move? Move *where?*"

He said mockingly, "Well, we absolutely can't move *up.* Did you really plan to spend the rest of your life here? Besides, I'm getting hungry."

"Hungry?" Mrs. Pollifax automatically groped for her purse, but stopped when she saw Farrell shaking his head.

"Your purse wasn't so lucky," he told her. "I've already looked, it's gone. Down *there,* presumably."

"I wish I could brush my teeth," Mrs. Pollifax said suddenly and fretfully, thereby expressing her complete dissatisfaction with the situation. She leaned forward just a trifle— heights always made her dizzy—and looked down into the valley. Her first thought was that Farrell was feeling suicidal to believe they could ever negotiate such a cliff, but her resistance to the idea was inevitably overcome by curiosity and then interest. The cliff did not drop to the valley like a plumb line; it slanted almost imperceptibly, with avalanchelike beds of gravel and rock, then short drops, then more beds of stone gravel until it reached a green terrace below, the same pasture where on her walks she had seen goats grazing. "But you couldn't make it with your leg," she protested. "Absolutely not."

Farrell smiled. "Look, you've forgotten something. Walking's hard for me, but nobody walks down a cliff. One slides down backward, using arms and hands, not legs. Come on, let's go."

"Oh, these happy morning people," thought Mrs. Pollifax, and then she realized that it was not simply a matter of temperament but of age; Farrell was younger and more flexible; Mrs. Pollifax at this moment felt unutterably weary and ancient. To be shot by a firing squad appeared absolute luxury compared to crawling down a precipice, even if it did slant. She had left a cell which from this distance appeared a haven of safety, had stumbled into space from the top of a cliff, been mercifully caught by good luck and a slender tree branch, and had endured the suspense of creeping inch by inch to this cliff ledge. What she wanted now was a great deal of reassurance, a hot bath, clean clothes and sleep. What Farrell wanted of her was more.

Very coldly she said, "All right, who leads the way, you or the Genie?"

Farrell said casually, "Neither, which brings up another subject. I don't trust the Genie."

"Oh, for heaven's sake!"

Farrell shook his head. "He jolly well may have come along as a spy, and I won't have you trusting him, either. I don't speak his language, I don't know what he said to General Perdido back there in the guardroom, I don't know anything about him. All I know is, he's here and we're stuck with him. You go first, then the Genie, and I'll go last because I still have the gun."

Preposterous, absurd, decided Mrs. Pollifax furiously. Gritting her teeth she inched her body forward and dangled her feet over the edge of the cliff.

"Not that way, backward," Farrell told her just as coldly. "Hang from the tree branch with your face to the cliff and reach with your feet for a toehold on the jut below."

She said bitterly, "Great—I can join the circus when I get home."

"If you get home," Farrell pointed out curtly, and this had a galvanizing effect. She told herself that scarcely anyone died as dramatically as they wished and that her being shot by a firing squad had been no more than a wistful dream after all. Her anger gave her the recklessness to place both hands around the tree branch and to anxiously let her body swing in space—and there was a great deal of space. There she hung for a sickening moment, with Farrell hissing directions to her from the ledge. "There—now you've got it," he said.

What she had gotten, as Farrell put it, was one foot on an

outcropping of rock below her, but she could not share his jubilance over this. She glanced under her at the rock, then below to the valley, thought of depending upon that rock for her life and clung harder to the tree branch. "No, no, you've got to let go," he told her.

"That rock will *not* support me," she said furiously.

"It will if you move your hands to that stubby little root growing out of the rock over there."

"I prefer staying with this tree branch, thank you."

Farrell said nastily, "For how many years, Duchess?"

She saw his point; she had to go up or she had to go down, and since either course could bring about her violent demise she might as well try going down. She felt for the root with one hand, the other still grasping the branch, and closed her eyes. "One for the money," she whispered, "two for the show, three to make ready and four to. . . ." She dropped her left hand from the branch, stoically endured that ghastly second when her weight was neither here nor there, and then she was clinging with both hands to the root, her feet braced on the rock jut below. Cautiously she opened her eyes to discover that she was still safe. What was more, her position had vastly improved, for instead of hanging from the branch, with nothing below her but ugly space, her body was now pressed tightly against the face of the cliff wall, which was just diagonal enough to give her some reassurance. She was even able to note a small hole in the cliff into which her hands could fit for the next move. Mrs. Pollifax was beginning to understand the mechanics of cliff-scaling.

In this manner the three of them descended inch by inch toward the valley, their cliff gradually changing in color from the luminous gray of dawn to a tawny gold as the sun discovered them. It was growing embarrassingly light when they reached the last slope, a charming easy hill of pebbles. They stopped here to catch their breath and to take stock of their surroundings.

This was the rocky pasture, usually alive with goats, that Mrs. Pollifax had seen on her walks along the top of the cliff. It lay just above another pasture, and then another, each terrace tipping a little drunkenly toward the floor of the flat dry valley. There were no goats now, and Mrs. Pollifax's gaze moved westward, to the right, and she saw what had gone unnoticed before, the home of the man who tended the goats. She recalled from Lulash's book that in this country a hovel like this was called a *han*. It was a small, primitive building built of rocks taken from the hillside; there were no windows. Then she drew in her breath sharply, for a woman stood in the doorway of the *han* watching them, her figure almost lost in the shadows cast by the cliff.

"What is it?" demanded Farrell.

Wordlessly Mrs. Pollifax pointed.

Farrell leaned on his crutch and slipped one hand into his pocket.

"No," Mrs. Pollifax said slowly, "you mustn't shoot her. Anyway, she can't be alone at this hour, there must be others inside."

"She's seen us," growled Farrell. "It's her or us, Duchess."

"At least let's be sure she's alone," begged Mrs. Pollifax. "Then we could just tie and gag her if she's by herself, couldn't we? A gunshot would be heard for miles." Her sympathy for the woman staring at them was instinctive and, in these circumstances, irrational. Still she could not help herself.

Farrell's hand left his pocket and he sighed. "Woman to woman, eh? Have it your way, Duchess—in for a penny, in for a pound."

Nervously Mrs. Pollifax led the way toward the *han.*

Eighteen

The woman looked as ageless and stoic as the rocks around her, nothing but her eyes alive in a watchful, sunburned face. When she was perhaps two feet from the doorway Mrs. Pollifax stopped, smiled wanly and pointed to the top of the precipice. Then she pointed to herself and to Farrell. *"Inglese,"* she said.

The woman's impassive glance moved to the cliff above, returned to Mrs. Pollifax to examine her torn dress and Guatemalan jacket, roamed briefly over Farrell's crutch and the Genie's flowing garments. She made a sudden turn back into the *han* and Mrs. Pollifax's heart constricted. Then the woman paused, holding back the goatskin at the door, and gestured to them to follow. Again Mrs. Pollifax led the way, aware that Farrell's hand had slipped back into the pocket that held his pistol. It was like twilight inside, with a small

fire burning in the center of the earthen floor. The first object
that caught Mrs. Pollifax's eye was her purse lying on the
ground beside the fire, and she realized that their progress
down the cliff must have been observed for some time. The
woman spoke to the two men squatting near the fire: the
younger was a boy of fifteen or so, the elder a tall, well-
built man with a fierce-looking moustache and smoldering
eyes. The three spoke together for several minutes, not heat-
edly, but in disjointed sentences interspersed with reflective
pauses. Mrs. Pollifax wondered if Farrell and the Genie felt
as edgy as she did standing there and being discussed with no
knowledge of what was being said. There were no chains
holding them here and yet the fact that they had been seen
by the woman gave her the power of life or death over them.
Were they going to have to kill the woman and her family?
"I'm too old and too soft for all this," she thought.

Suddenly the man of the *han* stood up and went to the
door, pushed aside the goatskin and went out, causing Mrs.
Pollifax and Farrell to exchange alarmed glances. The boy
also jumped to his feet and brought stools from the shadows,
gesturing to them to sit. "What do you think?" asked Mrs.
Pollifax in a low voice.

"I don't know," Farrell said, and limped to the door and
glanced outside.

The woman had gathered up three wooden bowls and was
dishing into them something that resembled lumpy oatmeal
drowned in oil. With a polite smile Mrs. Pollifax accepted
hers and sat down. Farrell, too, came back and sat down
beside the Genie. "I don't know," he repeated.

Mrs. Pollifax nodded, spooning up the honeyed grain but
scarcely aware of its taste as her mind worried over the
man's disappearance. He had consulted and then left. Where
had he gone? What had been decided by these three people?
She felt again that her fate was no more than a slender
thread loosely held by indifferent strangers, yet there was
nothing to do but wait. She sat and waited, having no idea
what to expect. It was the woman who made the next move.
She walked to a chest in the corner of the room and began
pulling from it an assortment of clothes. Astonished, Mrs.
Pollifax wondered if possibly these people were going to help
them. She turned to Farrell and saw the same look reflected in
his face: the confusion of a suspicious and desperate man
confronted by hope. The woman had taken out a shabby,
cone-shaped felt hat that she now clapped on the Genie's

head; then she held against Farrell the loose-flowing clothes
and sash of an Albanian mountain man. To Mrs. Pollifax
she handed two petticoats and a voluminous woolen dress
with inserts of handmade lace. She gestured toward the blanket hung across one corner of the room.

"Well!" exclaimed Mrs. Pollifax, beaming at Farrell.

"Could still be a trap," Farrell said.

"I refuse to think so," she told him loftily, and retired behind the blanket to wrestle with the voluminous skirts.

A few minutes later they reassembled around the fire,
their appearances strikingly changed. Because of his un-
shaven jaw, Farrell was clearly the most authentic of the
three, looking as fierce and dangerous as a bandit. The Genie
appeared much the same: small, birdlike, somehow tran-
scending the absurdity of his costume. Mrs. Pollifax had no
idea how she looked but she knew she felt very warm indeed
under so many layers.

The woman held out Mrs. Pollifax's purse to her, her fingers stroking the soft dark-blue calfskin. On impulse Mrs.
Pollifax opened it, extracted the pistol and its clips, the compass, the map, the food and her pack of playing cards, and
gave the purse back to the woman. "Keep it," she said,
smiling. "It doesn't go with these new clothes. I'll use the
pockets instead, there are so many of them. One in each
petticoat," she told Farrell in an aside. She showed the woman
how to zip and unzip the purse, a feat that brought surprise
and then delight to the woman's face. Her smile was beautiful and Mrs. Pollifax realized that in years she was still only
a young woman. She also pressed the Guatemalan jacket on
her, hoping she would not wear it outside the *han* for a good
many months.

Now it was the boy who flung back the goatskin at the
door, and Mrs. Pollifax saw that his father had not gone to
report them but to assemble his goats for the day. He had
driven them to the door, where they were milling about
bleating rudely and with no sense of direction or intelligence.
With his shepherd's crook the man prodded them even closer
to the door. The boy turned to the three of them and with an
eager face began explaining in pantomime what the family
had decided. First he pointed to the cliff and crossed himself, grimacing, so that Mrs. Pollifax understood that General
Perdido's mountain eyrie was known and disliked in the
neighborhood. Then he pointed to the sun and appeared to
be emphasizing the need for them to go quickly, before men

came to the *han*. In their new clothes—he pointed to them and rubbed a piece of Mrs. Pollifax's skirt between his fingers to prove he meant clothes—they might be able to reach the road unaccosted.

"Road?" said Farrell, startled.

Mrs. Pollifax nodded. "It can't be seen from here but I've spotted it from the cliff. It runs across the plain from south to north about five miles from here, I'd say."

The problem was in getting unobserved to the floor of the valley but the boy had not finished. The pastures around them could all be seen very clearly from the buildings above —a fact to which Mrs. Pollifax could testify—and someone might be watching, perhaps even with binoculars. Here the boy made circles with his fingers and squinted through them. Today his father had decided to drive his goats beyond this pasture and down to the one nearest the valley. If Mrs. Pollifax and the Genie would become goats they could move with the herd and not be seen from above.

"Become goats," said Mrs. Pollifax dazedly—obviously she had misunderstood his gestures. But again he dropped to his hands and knees, this time crawling into the center of the thickly clustered herd.

"Good heavens," said Mrs. Pollifax faintly.

Scrambling to his feet again the boy pointed to Farrell's leg and shook his head, seized his father's crook and placed it in Farrell's hand. The father in reply got down on his hands and knees.

"Well, I never," breathed Mrs. Pollifax.

Farrell was grinning. "You really ought to see your face, Duchess. Do you get the same message I do? From the cliff above it will appear that Mac here and his son are taking their herd of goats out, as they do every morning at this hour. One man and a boy going out, one man and a boy coming home. But going out I will be the goatherder while he joins you and the Genie and the goats—pretty damn noble of him, I have to add—and in some convenient place we are left behind."

Mrs. Pollifax found herself wishing she were back on the ledge. On the ledge she had wished herself back in her cell. What, she wondered crossly, must she endure next? She made only one comment and it was succinct. She said clearly and irritably, "Damn."

"Acquiring some downright bad habits, Duchess," grinned Farrell. "They'll be blackballing you at the Garden Club this winter, won't they? Hurry now, I think they're waiting for you."

The Genie was already crouched down among the goats, apparently undismayed by this new development; he glanced once over his shoulder, his eyes bright, twinkling and as interested as usual. Gingerly Mrs. Pollifax sank to her knees and crawled in among the beasts. "For heaven's sake move them slowly," she cautioned.

Farrell grasped the shepherd's crook and the boy called out something in the high clear air and prodded the goats in the front. The herd, with Mrs. Pollifax, the Genie and the shepherd as its nucleus, began to move slowly out into the pasture.

The boy did most of the work, running backward and forward to keep the goats in a tight cluster. But it was the tightness of the cluster that soon became Mrs. Pollifax's major concern, for although she had not crawled on hands and knees since she was a child—and never for any distance —it was the goats that proved especially unnerving. They stepped on her, they bleated alarmingly in first her left ear and then her right ear, they playfully nipped her, and over and above these hardships there was their smell. She had never thought of goats as smelling; she had never thought of goats at all, but of course no one bathed goats and this was the dry season. They had a particularly obnoxious odor, and she was surrounded by, and distressingly intimate with, an entire herd of them. From time to time Farrell and the boy would halt the procession so that the three humans in their midst could catch their breath, but Mrs. Pollifax found that catching her breath was the very last thing she wished to do. It was during these resting intervals that the goats butted her, licked her and stumbled over her. Nor was this all, for as the ground slanted more and more perceptibly the soft grass became thinner, to be replaced by pebbles that cut her knees, and once they left the shadow of the cliffs the sun beat down on them mercilessly. To walk on all fours was difficult enough for a child, but for a woman of her age it was quite mad. Yet as their queer progress continued and the time spent on hands and knees grew longer and less bearable all early reactions faded, even thought faded as Mrs. Pollifax's mind fixed itself upon the next rest when she could throw herself full-length on the earth, indifferent at last to how many goats stepped on her. The slow, gradual descent into the valley must have taken them an hour, but after a long time Mrs. Pollifax became aware that the herd had come to a standstill and that she was being lightly touched by a shepherd's crook. She looked up to see Farrell standing over her. "You can stand up now, Duchess," he told her. "We're hidden from the top of the cliff, we've reached the valley."

He looked drained and white and Mrs. Pollifax realized that a shepherd's crook was not the same as a crutch; he must have had to place his weight on a leg broken in two places, poorly set and unmended yet, and all this on a rocky downhill terrain. Pity brought her to her feet. "Where's your crutch?"

"The man has it."

The Genie's head popped up from among the goats and he joined them looking so untouched and cheerful that Mrs. Pollifax began to feel almost hostile toward him. She took a step forward and almost fell, regained her balance and glanced furiously at her knees. But she had always been a gracious hostess; she tottered forward to wring the hand of the boy and his father who had helped them at so much risk to themselves.

"Det," the man kept saying over and over again, pointing westward.

Mrs. Pollifax recalled that this word meant sea, and nodded, smiling. Farrell also shook their hands and the Genie, odd little man that he was, went into his bowing and nodding routine. Then the man and the boy strolled away toward the goats that had fanned out across the pasture, and Mrs. Pollifax, Farrell and the Genie were alone.

They were standing in the center of a dried-up brook bed at the base of the last terrace. Behind them rose scallop after scallop of rocky pasture culminating in the towering cliff above. In front of them stretched the flat dry valley, already shimmering in the morning heat. To the south, barely visible, lay a cluster of objects that might be tall rocks or a village. There were almost no trees. "Well," said Mrs. Pollifax doubtfully, and then because it all seemed so overwhelming she suggested they sit down and rest.

"Not on your life," said Farrell flatly. "They must be combing the mountains for us, they'll be getting to the valley next."

She nodded wearily. There seemed nowhere to hide in this naked countryside and she was bone-tired but they had come this far and somewhere to the west lay a road. She glanced at the Genie and he vivaciously smiled at her. Farrell, following her glance, sighed heavily. "Not a brain in his head, is there? You certainly picked a lemon, Duchess."

She frowned. "I don't know, sometimes there seem to be flashes of intelligence there."

"An intelligent man would be tired or scared stiff. All this guy does is smile."

"But the Chinese are always polite, aren't they?" pointed out Mrs. Pollifax. "He may be just a little eccentric."

"Eccentric!" barked Farrell. "Well, we're stuck with him, anyway. Let's get moving."

They clung to the security of the creek bed, knowing without mentioning it that although they wore native clothes they were still three in number, and it was three for whom the general would be searching. The sun was searingly hot, for it was at least midmorning, and Mrs. Pollifax's knees did not grow any more reliable. She stumbled along in the prison of her woolen dress and two petticoats, the old numbness reasserting itself. She longed for water—they had none—and for something green to look at, anything but this tawny, rocky, dusty hot August landscape around them. She was aware, too, of Farrell's hobbling as she plodded. Only the Genie had the resilience to give the appearance of a man out for a morning stroll. She was beginning to feel very sorry that she had liberated this annoyingly tireless man.

They came in sight of the road very suddenly, so suddenly that Farrell, glancing up, gave a sibilant hiss through his teeth and dropped quickly to the ground behind a rock. The Genie promptly imitated him and Mrs. Pollifax gratefully sat down beside them. The road was still some distance away, perhaps half a mile, but it was overrun by men. These men, wearing the striped suits of prisoners, were spread out along the road for nearly a mile, listlessly splitting rocks and carrying them to the roadbed. What was most alarming was the number of guards posted near them; she could identify them because they were seated on the rocks with rifles across their knees, and several of them were sprawled in the shade of a large black car. The road ran in a straight line across their path, vanishing in the south against the horizon, while in the north it lifted gradually to begin a spiraling toward the cliffs from which they had escaped. This was the road by which the general had come from the airport, but with so many people rimming it the road might as well have been an unsurmountable wall. "What can we do?" whispered Mrs. Pollifax helplessly.

Farrell ran a dusty hand across his eyes. He was terrible to look at with his week's growth of beard, bloodshot eyes and a dreadful pallor that was new today. Mrs. Pollifax noted that his hand trembled and she shuddered at what he must be enduring. He said in a cracked, furious voice, "What rotten luck, we'll have to wait until dark to cross the road. Spend a whole bloody day here without water? God."

Dear Farrell, she thought, poor Farrell, and then she glanced beyond him and stiffened. Her look of horror caused both Farrell and the Genie to look too. Men—half a dozen of them—were crossing the plain behind them, clearly visible in the brilliant sun and less than a mile away. What had first caught her eye, however, was the flash of a mirror that was shortly answered from a tree-lined foothill up on their right. The search for them was underway, obviously a methodical daylight search leaving no margins for error, one group combing the cliffs, the pastures and the foothills, another group taking the valley. She wondered if they had already been seen, she wondered if the message flashed from the hill was in fact reporting three suspicious shapes crouched beside a rock.

The Genie suddenly stood up.

"Hey," yelped Farrell, reaching for him.

"Down—get down!" cried Mrs. Pollifax, forgetting that he couldn't understand.

But the Genie backed away from their groping hands, jumped over the rock and began running toward the road and the men there. "What on earth," faltered Mrs. Pollifax.

"I told you I didn't trust him," snarled Farrell. With an oath he fumbled in his pocket for the pistol and drew it out. His shaky hands fumbled with the safety catch and Mrs. Pollifax, befuddled by sun, thirst, exhaustion and panic, watched him steady the gun on the top of the rock. Dimly she realized that she ought to stop him; they were already trapped on three sides and it was senseless to take the man's life now. Yet she made no move to halt Farrell. The Genie was racing to betray them, he was running over to the enemy and because it had been her idea to bring the Genie with them it made his betrayal the more personal. She had no right to halt his execution; she could even share some of Farrell's rage and frustration that all their suffering came to nothing. All wasted.

Farrell swore again and dropped the pistol. "Too late," he groaned. "My hand shakes, damn it, damn it, damn it."

She thought from his voice that he might be crying, so she was careful not to look at him. Instead she stared out across the dust and the heat at the Genie, who had slowed to a walk as he approached the guards. He was in conversation with them now. "Of course—he's Chinese," she remembered bleakly. This was a country controlled by the Chinese, naturally the guards would treat him with respect; perhaps they were Chinese too. She glanced behind her and saw the men in the valley walking with more purpose now, a few of them running. Her eyes moved to the hillside and she could see the men who had flashed the message; they, too, were hurrying down the slope toward the valley. She realized that within a few minutes the two groups would converge upon them.

"Well?" said Farrell grimly, holding up the pistol in a meaningful way and lifting his brows at her.

She said steadily, "Yes—yes, it's really the only thing left to do, isn't it. Except—I'm sorry but I'm afraid I couldn't, you'll have to be the one to—the one to—"

He said harshly, "I understand. But for God's sake, Duchess, you realize it's only to spare you worse. Tell me you understand that."

"I do realize it, of course I do."

"Because I've grown damnably fond of you, you know."

"Thank you," she said gravely. The Genie and a guard with a rifle were climbing into the big dusty black car parked beside the road, the guard taking the driver's seat, the Genie sitting beside him. The car started with a jerk, turned and left the road to bounce over the dry earth toward the rock that sheltered them. "They're coming," she said quietly. "They're coming in the car, the Genie and another man. I think you'd better hurry."

Farrell nodded and ran his tongue over parched dry lips. With one hand he lifted his gun, trying to steady it as he aimed at Mrs. Pollifax's heart. "Is that really the best place?" she asked curiously. "Isn't the brain faster?"

"Oh for heaven's sake," groaned Farrell, the pistol wobbling. "Just don't talk, will you do me that favor please?"

Mrs. Pollifax sat up straight and primly folded her hands in her lap—as if she were about to be photographed, she thought—and waited patiently for oblivion. Again Farrell lifted the pistol and took aim. She did wish he would hurry because the car was racing toward them in a cloud of dust, but she feared reminding him of this lest she disconcert him again. Farrell carefully steadied his shaking hand and his lips thinned with the concentration this took. She could see the perspiration beading his nose and brow and watched a drop fall from his temple. Farrell lifted an elbow to clear his eyes and patiently took aim a third time.

But it was too late. The car was already upon them, and the Genie leaped from the opened door and knocked the pistol out of Farrell's grasp. It fell into the dust, to be retrieved in an instant by the Genie. With a low moan Farrell hid his face in his hands, utterly drained and exhausted. It was the Genie who brandished the pistol now, gesturing them both into the car.

Mrs. Pollifax sat and regarded him without expression, her mind sifting a thousand reproaches and a few epithets, but if he was Chinese he would understand none of them. And if he was Chinese he could not really be called a traitor either, nor could she call him a fool when she had proven the greater fool. Silently and wearily she climbed to her feet and bent over Farrell. "Come, they want us in the car," she said, and then in a whisper, "I still have the Beretta, you know." Without looking at the Genie she walked past him and climbed into the back seat. It was a Rolls, she noticed, looking over the accouterments that reminded her of childhood rides in the park with an aunt. "A very ancient one," she amended. "Highly appropriate for funerals."

Farrell sank down beside her in the rear seat and the guard slammed the door. This time the Genie slid behind the wheel of the car and started the engine while the guard climbed in beside him and propped his rifle between his legs. With the motor idling the Genie turned his head and smiled at the guard, his eyes bright and fathomless.

"Snake-in-the-grass," thought Mrs. Pollifax, watching him.

With one smooth and effortless movement the Genie lifted the pistol he had taken from Farrell and astonished Mrs. Pollifax by shooting the guard between the eyes. As the guard slumped in his seat the Genie leaned across him, opened the door and pushed the man's body into the dust. Slipping back behind the wheel he said over his shoulder in clipped, perfect English, "I think we'd better get the hell out of here, don't you?"

Nineteen

Their shock was so complete that for a moment neither Mrs. Pollifax nor Farrell could utter a word. Then something like a small gasp escaped Mrs. Pollifax, and from Farrell came a brief, violent grunt. The Genie abruptly backed and turned the car and the sudden movement brought them to life. "Who the devil are you?" demanded Farrell.

"And why didn't you tell us you speak English?" asked Mrs. Pollifax.

"Didn't dare trust you—sorry," the Genie said over his shoulder, and as the car regained the road he added, "I don't know how long we can stick with this car. There are only something like four hundred cars in the whole country but there are wirelesses and things like roadblocks. And I'm not very good at driving the bloody thing, had to watch what buttons the guard pushed to learn how it started. Whole dashboard is full of buttons."

He was leaning grimly over the wheel as he spoke, and noting the speedometer Mrs. Pollifax reached for Farrell's arm. "We're going one hundred miles an hour," she told him in horror.

"That's kilometers, not miles, Duchess. We're in Europe now."

It still felt alarmingly fast. Mrs. Pollifax turned to look out of the rear window, and the men who were scattered all over the landscape—guards, working prisoners and search party—were already receding into the distance.

Farrell said with his old briskness, "This road leads into Shkoder. Hell, we don't want to go there, do we?"

Mrs. Pollifax, surrounded by so much masculine profanity, said firmly, "Hell, no."

Farrell turned to stare at her and his old debonair smile crossed his face. Gently he said, "No, Duchess, absolutely no more swearing. Absolutely."

"All right," said Mrs. Pollifax meekly. To the Genie she said, "We have a map, you know. There look to be two villages between us and Shkoder, and to the west of us there's a huge lake called Lake Scutari. Shkoder lies at the southern tip of it. Would you like to see the map?"

"They're following us," interrupted Farrell savagely. "Damn it, they've found one of those four hundred cars the country owns." He had turned around to look through the rear window and Mrs. Pollifax turned too. It was all too true: she saw first the cloud of dust and then the small gray car racing in front of it.

"Three, maybe four miles behind us," said the Genie, his eyes on the rearview mirror. "No time for maps. I say we stick to the car as long as we can. A car moves faster than six legs, one of them broken."

"They must have wirelessed——"

"I know, I know." The Genie was peering at the panel in front of him. "There's plenty of gas, thank heaven." He shoved the accelerator to the floor and the car surged ahead in a burst of speed.

"One hundred kilometers an hour," thought Mrs. Pollifax in dismay, and wished that she dared close her eyes. The landscape moved past them like a projector that had run wild: olive trees, scattered farms and wells all blurred together. Ahead of them Mrs. Pollifax saw the outlines of a village and had no sooner seen it than they were upon it and the Genie was braking to avoid an oxcart plodding through its street. The next obstacle was a sheep that stood its ground in the center of the narrow road and baa-ed at them indignantly. They swerved around it and through a cobblestoned main street with stone houses on either side, and then the village was behind them and the Rolls resumed its breakneck speed. Mrs. Pollifax wondered how the Genie managed to hold tight to the wheel, for the ruts in the road, which could at best be called primitive, produced a strange undercurrent of jolts that not even the magnificent upholstery of a Rolls could overcome. At the same moment she heard a growing, indefinable noise and looked out and up in time to see a small plane zoom over them, bank and fly over them again at low altitude. Farrell said grimly, "They've heard about us in Shkoder, too."

"We'll have to ditch the car," the Genie said. "But where and how I don't know."

Mrs. Pollifax didn't know either, but her mind grasped at once that just ditching it wouldn't be enough, not with a car following behind them and their progress observed from the

air. They wouldn't have a chance of getting away, not with
Farrell unable to run. "An accident," she said suddenly.

"What?"

"An accident. Isn't there some way to tip over the car and
set it on fire? They would think for at least a few minutes
that we were still inside."

Both men were silent, fumbling with the idea, and then
the Genie said, "You haven't any matches, have you?"

"Two," said Farrell.

"You said there's a lake to the west of us, to the right?"

"Yes."

The Genie had seen a cart track branching from the road
into Shkoder and with a squeal of brakes the car slowed
enough to turn its wheels down the track and head west.
The car bounced hideously, and Mrs. Pollifax's head hit the
ceiling. "They'll see our dust, won't they?" she gasped. She
had no sooner spoken than they left the cart track to plunge
toward a copse of trees.

"In there looks the place," said the Genie. "The trees will
be cover for getting away. You'll have to have a head start,
Farrell—that's your name, isn't it? I doubt if any one of
us has the strength to tip the car over but I'll try to ram it into
a tree. Start running as soon as we stop."

As soon as they were in among the trees he braked the
Rolls and jerked open the door next to Farrell. "Out," he
said. "Out and hurry in a straight line that way." He pointed.
"Go as fast as you can."

"Me too?" asked Mrs. Pollifax.

The Genie shook his head. "Out, but wait for me. I'll need
your help."

They left the car, Mrs. Pollifax to stand uncertain and nervous as she watched Farrell hobble away for dear life. Dear
dear life, she reflected, and how tenaciously people held on
to it and what things they did to remain alive!—that is,
physically alive, she amended, for to remain alive inside was
far more intricate and difficult and defeating. Her thoughts
were interrupted by the roar of the Rolls engine as the Genie
pressed his foot to the accelerator. Aghast, she watched the
car pass her at top speed, the Genie leaning half out of the
door. Faster and faster it went, heading inexorably toward
the largest of trees, and then the tree and the Rolls met with
such force that the front of the Rolls crumpled like an ac-
cordian and the tree shuddered to its roots. Then Mrs. Pollifax saw the Genie, shaken but entirely whole. He had leaped

at the last minute and now was fumbling for the matches Farrell had given him. She ran to help. "How? Where?" she cried.

He was wrestling with the cover to the gas tank, his hands trembling. Mrs. Pollifax gave it a twist and lifted it off. "Start running," said the Genie as he lighted one of the matches.

Mrs. Pollifax obeyed, too numb to protest. She did not look back until she heard the explosion, and then it was only to see if the Genie was still alive. He was both alive and running, with more vitality than she possessed, and she envied him. Together they came out into the open country beyond the copse of trees, and there they discovered Farrell leaning on his crutch and looking very ill again. It was obvious that he could go no farther.

The landscape offered no hope of concealment, and when it was discovered that their bodies were not in the Rolls General Perdido would expect to find them nearby. Mrs. Pollifax could see the roof of a *han* some distance away, a good many rocks, another dried-up creek bed, and a pen of some kind where goats or sheep were kept at night. Her eyes moved over and then swerved back to an object in the corner of that pen: a two-wheeled primitive wooden cart filled to the brim with hay.

"Look," she whispered, and without a word they moved toward it, recognizing it as only a slim hope and not at all sure what to do with it. But it did have the advantage of being out of sight of the *han,* which presumably housed the owners of the farm, and it was the only object in sight that could possibly shield them. They stood and looked at it; rather stupidly, thought Mrs. Pollifax, until she realized that both Farrell and the Genie were exhausted and that as the senior member of the party—rather like a Scout leader, she thought with blurred, semihysterical humor—she was going to have to assume command whether she was exhausted or not. At that moment, as if to emphasize the need for decisiveness, she heard the plane returning. It was still some distance away but obviously it was flying back to scour the countryside for signs of life.

"Into the cart," she cried, pulling out tufts of hay. "Quickly, both of you." There was barely room for the two; both Farrell and the Genie had to curl up in womblike positions and she prodded them mercilessly.

"What about you?" demanded Farrell.

"They don't know I'm in peasant clothes," she pointed

out, devoutly hoping this was true. "And they're looking for
three people." She was recklessly piling the hay back on top
of them. "For heaven's sake don't move."

One of them replied by sneezing.

"And don't sneeze either," she added crossly. The plane
was circling now over the woods where they had abandoned
the car and she saw what she had not noticed before—a
plume of fading black smoke above the trees. The Rolls was
still burning then, or had been until a moment ago, and presently the remains of it would be cool enough to examine.
Hadn't she read somewhere that bodies, turned to char, still
held their shape until breathed upon or touched? She supposed it depended upon the heat of the fire. At any rate they
couldn't remain here indefinitely. The first time she was seen
from the air she might be mistaken for the farmer's wife
contemplating clouds or earth, but if she was seen a second
time in the same place such rootedness would be suspicious.
Mrs. Pollifax regarded the cart speculatively, glanced over
the terrain and then kicked the rock from under the wheels.
Bracing herself she picked up the tongue of the axle, moved
between its two shafts and tugged. Oddly enough the cart
moved quite easily, being high enough from the ground to
balance the weight of two grown men, and the earth sloped
conveniently downward to aid momentum. With a squeak of
wood against wood the cart began to make progress toward
the next copse of trees with Mrs. Pollifax feeling rather like a
ricksha boy. At any moment she expected to hear shouts
from the direction of the *han,* but none occurred. Without
any challenge, and having achieved a precarious speed, Mrs.
Pollifax marched sturdily on, the cart at times pushing her
in front of it. It was rough pastureland they crossed now, but
a wood lay less than half a mile away. The noon-hot sun
glared down but there was grass—green grass—in this pastureland and it led Mrs. Pollifax to hope that they were nearing the coast. She was in the middle of the pasture when
another plane passed overhead. Its presence ought to have
alarmed her, but as it roared over them and then headed
west Mrs. Pollifax saw its pontoons and her heart quickened.
"It's a seaplane, and where there are seaplanes," she thought
with a flicker of excitement, "there has to be water."

Water!

Twenty

After ten minutes of being pushed by the cart, and another ten minutes of pulling it, Mrs. Pollifax had to concede that she was neither an ox nor young enough to imitate one. The ground was rough, and after thoughtfully slanting downhill it had begun to slant uphill, but what was most discouraging was the field of maize that lay ahead directly in their path. She could not pull such a broad cart through narrow corn rows, and the field stretched from left to right almost as far as the eye could see: the thought of walking around it utterly dismayed her. Mrs. Pollifax stopped and laid down the shafts, wiped the sweat from her brow with a sleeve and said aloud, in an anguished voice, "I just can't pull you any more."

It was the Genie who emerged first from the straw. "Quite so," he said in his clipped British voice. "Farrell badly needs a rest too. I suggest we crawl into the corn and rest a few minutes."

It was a very bad idea. Mrs. Pollifax knew it and the Genie must have known it too, for if the burning Rolls had confused and diverted General Perdido it would not be for long. Ashes would be sifted: for rings—her wedding ring, for instance—or teeth or gold fillings or bone fragments. Even if the general remained in doubt he would be compelled to assume they had gotten away because he was not a man who could afford doubts; his reputation and his pride were too valuable and both would be at stake.

Yet Mrs. Pollifax conceded there was nothing else for them to do. Certainly she could not go on much longer in such an exhausted state, and what was worst of all her mind felt battered and senseless. It was a major effort even to weigh what the Genie was suggesting, and all of her instincts told her that a mind was needed to compete against the general's cunning. "Yes," she said simply, and stood back and let the Genie help Farrell out of the hay.

Farrell looked utterly ghastly but his mind at least was unaffected, for he took in the situation at a glance and said, "We'll have to be careful not to break off any stalks as we enter. And the cart can't be left here."

The Genie's eyes shone with their usual birdlike brightness, half mockery, half inquisitiveness. He bowed with his hands tucked into his sleeves and said, "I, too, have read your Leather-stocking tales. You go, I'll move the cart and cover your trail as I join you."

Together Farrell and Mrs. Pollifax tottered in among the cornstalks, each helping the other, but neither of them impressively secure. They did not stop until the rows of corn neared an end and then they fell apart and sank wordlessly to the ground. Here in the shade of the tall stalks there was at least shelter from the blazing sun and the illusion of a faint breeze as the stalks rustled and creaked and whispered. With a groan Farrell stretched out his damaged leg and studied it with bloodshot, menacing eyes. "Damn thing," he growled. "Never gave it a thought before, but damned if legs aren't pretty useful appendages. I'm hungry, by the way."

Mrs. Pollifax roused enough to explore the capacious pocket of her first petticoat. She drew out the pistol, the map, the compass, and then one slice of stale bread and a small amount of cheese. "There isn't much and we have to save some for later," she reminded him.

"Later," mused Farrell. "I can't imagine anything more distant than 'later.'"

They could hear the Genie looking for them, his footsteps stopping and then starting again as he peered into each aisle of corn without finding them. Mrs. Pollifax carefully put aside his portion of food, returned the remaining cheese and bread to her pocket, picked up the pistol to put it away, and hearing the Genie's footsteps virtually at their door she glanced up smiling.

But it was not the Genie standing there and looking down at them, it was the guard Stefan who had accompanied General Perdido. He was staring at them with his mouth half open, his eyes incredulous and a look of blank stupidity on his face. For just the fraction of a second Mrs. Pollifax shared his stupidity, and then she realized that she was holding the pistol in her hand and without thinking she lifted the pistol, aimed it as her cousin John had taught her years ago and squeezed the trigger. The noise was deafening in the stillness of that hot, quiet, summer afternoon. The look of stupidity on Stefan's face increased and Mrs. Pollifax realized with a feeling of nausea that she was going to have to shoot him again. She lifted the pistol but Farrell rolled over and clasped her wrist with his hand, deterring her, and that was when she saw the blood slowly spreading across Stefan's chest. She watched with horrified fascination as he began to crumple, his knees carrying him steadily downward until they struck the earth and his hips and shoulders following. Farrell was already reaching for his crutch and struggling to get to his feet. Mrs. Pollifax said blankly, "I've killed him. I've killed a man."

"He'd have gladly killed both of us in another minute," gasped Farrell, standing upright. "For heaven's sake, don't just sit there, Duchess, they must have heard that shot for miles."

Certainly the Genie had heard it. Mrs. Pollifax became aware that he was with them again; he was kneeling beside the dead guard removing his pistol and checking his pockets. She stuffed pistol, map and compass away and stood up, curious as to whether her knees would hold her or if she would slowly sink to the ground as Stefan had done; Stefan, the man she had killed—*she,* Emily Pollifax of New Brunswick, New Jersey. "Madness," she muttered under her breath. "Madness, every bit of this."

"They certainly know we're alive now," Farrell was saying grimly. "God how I wish I could run."

"I saw him and had to hide," the Genie said in a stunned voice. "There wasn't a chance of warning you." He was tugging at Mrs. Pollifax's arm to get her moving, and Mrs. Pollifax automatically took a few steps, then turned to look back at the dead man, but Farrell reached over and forced her face to the west. "Don't ever look back," he told her harshly.

So he understood in his rough, compassionate way. With an effort Mrs. Pollifax pulled herself together, lightheaded enough by now to see the three of them, blood-smeared, exhausted and harassed, as absurdities pitted against the whims of fate. They entered the forest of pines that lay beyond the cornfield but the shadows brought only meager relief and this was from the sun rather than the heat. Yet it was lovely among the pines, the earth soft and springy with layer after layer of pine needles, some old and brown, others freshly green. It seemed very peaceful and Mrs. Pollifax yearned to forget General Perdido and sink to the ground to rest.

The Genie said suddenly, "I smell water," and he began hobbling stiffly ahead, leaving Mrs. Pollifax to wonder how anybody could smell water. She stayed with Farrell, whose pallor alarmed her; he looked already dead, she thought, like someone embalmed and strung up on wires by a fiendish mortician. Then she realized that she, too, smelled water, except that smell was not quite the word, it was a change in the air, a freshness new to her nostrils. "Something's ahead," she gasped to Farrell, but he only grunted, not lifting his head. If it was the lake—and it could be nothing else from the look of the map—they must be very near Yugoslavia and very near to freedom. "Bless Tito and foreign aid," she thought reverently, hope rising in her. The Genie was ahead of them waving his arms, but it seemed an eternity before they reached him. "Look," he said.

Mrs. Pollifax lifted her head to see water glittering in the sunshine, water to bathe in, water to drink, water to cool overheated flesh and relax parched dry throats. Water—she wanted to stumble through the scrub to the shore and bury herself in it, but as she started forward the Genie clutched her arm and she heard the sound of the plane again. "This way," he said, and led them back in among the pines to head north along the shore of the lake.

Lake Scutari, she remembered from the book . . . two hundred square miles in size, a large lake, half of it in Yugoslavia. . . . The plane roared over the lake at low altitude and it gave her a queer sense of panic to realize that it must be looking for them. Of course—she had shot a guard and advertised their aliveness. In this quiet, pastoral countryside the sound of a gunshot would be heard for miles. Not many natives would own guns, the country was too poor, too barren of life to supply money for such a luxury. There would be no explaining away such a provocative noise.

The plane disappeared to the north and the Genie stopped, one finger on his lips, one hand on Mrs. Pollifax's arm. She and Farrell halted. The floor of the forest had been sloping upward so that it was higher than the water on their left, causing a drop that made it less accessible from land. Apparently the Genie had thought of something, for removing his shoes and tying them around his neck he began retracing their steps. Mrs. Pollifax waited. She wanted to sit, she wanted to fall to the ground, but she knew instinctively that Farrell couldn't sit down—mustn't, in fact, lest he never get up again—and an innate courtesy kept her upright. Presently, much to her surprise, she saw the Genie wading toward them along the shallows of the lake. He appeared to be searching for something and she looked away without interest, all curiosity deadened by the stupor of her body. Minutes or hours later the Genie was touching her arm, and she and Farrell followed him to the bank. He gestured toward the water, directing them to sit down on the bank and them jump into the shallows. Mrs. Pollifax did so, obediently and humbly. Then he was guiding them back a few yards toward an old tree that hung over the lake, its roots exposed and rotting. There was no beach here; the water lapped the eroded banking and over the years had brought to it an accumulation of debris. The Genie parted the branches of a sumac that had grown from the gnarled roots and said in a low voice, "It's not particularly dry but there's room here for three people."

"There is?" and then, "Will they think of it too?" Mrs. Pollifax asked anxiously, and then was sorry she had said this, for there was no safety anywhere in life, except as illusion, and she was surprised at herself for wanting a guarantee from the Genie. Perhaps it was her American blood, Americans were so very security-minded, or perhaps she was just too tired and stiff and afraid. But the Genie did not reply and she was grateful that he didn't. Instead he pushed aside a stout log that had been caught in the flotsam and helped Farrell to kneel and crawl into the tiny cave under the bank. She followed, and the Genie squeezed in after her, taking care to bend back the branches of the sumac and to pull the log back to its original position.

The little cave was not dry. The earth was wet but at least there were no puddles. The ceiling was too low for sitting; they had to lie on their stomachs, Farrell pressed against the earth, Mrs. Pollifax in the middle and the Genie nearest the outside. It was a curiously womblike place: dark, quiet and blessed cool. Mrs. Pollifax felt her eyes closing. She knew there were questions unasked and things undone and yet her eyes simply would not remain open. Fatigue won and Mrs. Pollifax slept, not deeply and certainly not comfortably, but with a fitful, twitching, feverish need from exhaustion.

She was awakened not so much by sound as by the awareness of danger that emanated from Farrell and the Genie, a stiffening of their bodies and a lifting of heads. She, too, stiffened and lifted her head from her arms to hear the roar of a motor nearby. Straining, she realized it wasn't a plane but a motorboat, and running so near to the shore that it was a wonder its propeller cleared the bottom. She lay inert, terrified that at any moment some trace of them be seen. The boat drew level with their hiding place, passed them by and in its wake came the waves. Mrs. Pollifax had not thought of waves and in any case would not have considered them a threat. All motorboats caused waves, some large, some small. Waves rippled charmingly as they swept toward shore, and always they made lovely sounds as they met the beach. She had forgotten that here there was no beach.

The water came with a rush, lifting the debris outside their hole and flinging twigs and leaves aside to sweep inside their tiny earthen cave. One moment Mrs. Pollifax was gazing at the entrance and the next moment she was totally submerged and without hope of escape as the water filled their cave from floor to ceiling. "This at last is the end," she thought as she fought to hold her breath. As her lungs gasped for air she drew in the first water through her nostrils, found no sustenance in it and during the brief moment of panic that precedes drowning she arched her body for one last fight. The struggle brought her head up, and suddenly there came the near alien sensation of air entering her lungs again. Sputtering, choking and gasping she realized that the water had receded. She had just time enough to fill her lungs before the next wave entered. All in all there were six waves, three of them that filled the cave and three that came only to her shoulders before retiring. Then the surge of water desisted.

They were still alive. Farrell lay on his side, with only a weak smile to show that he survived. The Genie was vomiting water, his shoulders heaving, and she brought up one arm —it was difficult in so confined a space—and patted his shoulder in commiseration. The Genie gagged once and rolled over on his back, an arm across his face.

"Close," said Mrs. Pollifax.

The Genie only nodded.

From far away came the sound of the airplane, its noise steadily increasing, and from above they heard the sound of men's voices shouting, and Mrs. Pollifax conceded that the chase was on in earnest. Men called unintelligible orders above their heads, the launch came back, slowed for an exchange of shouts, then sped away sending fresh waves to torture them in their cave. The men along the shore moved away, their voices growing distant as they shouted back and forth in the forest, and as Mrs. Pollifax lifted a tired and dripping head a small lull occurred.

"I'm hungry," said the Genie.

Slowly and stupidly Mrs. Pollifax realized that he had not shared in the small meal that she and Farrell had divided in the cornfield and she fumbled in her petticoats for food.

Sadly she drew out a sodden piece of cheese and handed it to the Genie—the bread had completely disintegrated and not a crumb of it was found. The pistol, too, was wet, and drearily she remembered that pistols did not usually function after being submerged in water. She turned her head and watched the Genie munch his cheese, very slowly, to make it last, and then her attention was distracted by the sound of gunshots from far away. This confused her tired mind; she wondered if only a part of herself and of Farrell and the Genie had hidden here in the cave while their physical selves had gone on and on through the pines and if somewhere along the shores of the lake the general was capturing them now. She pinched herself experimentally and it hurt, and this reassured her that she had not become disembodied after all.

"Must have caught some other poor devil in hiding," Farrell said in a low voice.

Mentally Mrs. Pollifax thanked him for reassuring her.

The plane was returning, and the launch with it, and for the next ten minutes each of them fought mutely and individually to keep from drowning. Nor were there any lulls following, for it became obvious that a number of police launches had begun to patrol the shores of the lake. Whole centuries passed—what time had they crawled in here, wondered Mrs. Pollifax, at one o'clock in the afternoon, two o'clock?—and each century left her colder and wetter. In what other world had she yearned for cool water to drink and bathe in? Now she was sated with it, and she kept recalling an old saying that one should never wish too hard for something lest the gods bestow it.

"Rubbish," she thought with a sniff, and wondered if next she might become delirious.

Then where patches of sunshine had illuminated the log outside and filtered through to the cave there was a deepening twilight. Farrell leaned across her and said to the Genie, "We have to leave soon."

She could no longer see the Genie's face but his voice said blankly, "Leave?"

Mrs. Pollifax turned her head back to Farrell. He said flatly, "Absolutely. I suggest we float that log that's outside, and hang on to it all the way across Lake Scutari. If we're lucky, if the wind isn't against us, if we have enough strength, we might land in Yugoslavia."

Mrs. Pollifax marveled at his resilience, that he could make plans after being so nearly embalmed, and then she realized that ever since this journey had begun there had been one of them to carry them a step farther when the other two could manage nothing more. How very surprising this was, she reflected, and again she pulled herself together to help and heard herself say, "Yes, of course, that's what we must do." Eight words and each of them labored, but at least she had said them.

"Police boats," pointed out the Genie wanly.

"We'll have to watch out for them, that's all. And if they have powerful searchlights—can you swim, Duchess?"

"Feebly."

"The same here," contributed the Genie.

"Then we either hide behind the log, or under it, or—"

Or be seen and captured, finished Mrs. Pollifax silently, and asked, "How far?"

"Who knows?"

Mrs. Pollifax turned to the Genie. "We still know nothing at all about you, you haven't told us even your name."

"Smith will do nicely if you'd like a name."

Mrs. Pollifax found herself reviving and bristling at such an insult. She said coldly, "I don't think it will do at all unless your name really is Smith."

"Nobody's named Smith," growled Farrell. "Not in my circle."

"Much, *much* better if you don't know my name," replied the Genie. "Better for you if you meet General Perdido again. Safer. He'd never appreciate your knowing."

"Can't think why," Farrell retorted.

"I was thinking of next of kin," Mrs. Pollifax told the Genie reproachfully.

Something like a chuckle came from the Genie. "Bless you, they would have held the funeral for me two years ago. I've been dead a long, long time, Mrs.—Pollifax, is it?"

"Yes," she said, thoroughly puzzled by now. "Well, no point in arguing."

"Right, it's time we go," Farrell reminded them. "You want to stick your head out?"

The Genie began pushing at the twigs and branches and dead leaves that had returned to the bank after the last wave, and presently he crawled out. Mrs. Pollifax knew when he left because he kicked her in the face as he went. She heard him stand up outside, dripping only a little, and a few minutes later he reached in to place an icy hand on her shoulder. "All clear," he whispered. "There are a few lights on the opposite shore but that's a distance of miles. No police boats to be heard or seen at the moment."

Mrs. Pollifax grimly began the job of moving a body that had lain on its stomach for half a day, and after considerable manipulation and experimentation she managed to climb to her knees and then to squeeze through the opening under the bank. Farrell followed slowly, pushing his damaged leg and homemade crutch ahead of him. The darkness they met was dark and opaque, broken only by a scattering of stars in the sky and half a dozen lights shining across the lake. The air was soft as velvet. The faintly abrasive murmur of a motorboat came to them from a great distance and as they stood there, listening, a fish jumped in the lake and drops of water scattered behind it. There were no other sounds.

The Genie was wrestling with the log. It had the advantage of being large enough and high enough out of the water to give them sufficient cover, but on the other hand this had the disadvantage of making it harder for them to cling to it from the water. "Straddle if for now," suggested the Genie. "We can paddle with our hands or feet and if a boat comes we can slip off and hide behind it."

But for three exhausted people to mount a wet, round log proved not only difficult but nearly impossible; Mrs. Pollifax began to understand the problems of the logroller. No sooner had one of them climbed on than the others fell off, and they finally brought it back to shallow water and climbed on at the same moment.

"Everybody ready to set sail?" asked the Genie.

"As ready as we'll ever be," sighed Mrs. Pollifax, thinking how hungry she was, how sleepy, how cold and bone-tired.

"Damn it, let's go," Farrell said fiercely.

Gingerly they paddled the log out from the shadows and into the breeze that had sprung up from the north, their destination Yugoslavia.

Twenty-one

In Washington, D.C., on the morning of that same day, Peattie notified Carstairs that he had received information from Peking concerning General Perdido. He would bring in the messages personally whenever Carstairs had the time to see him.

"Come along now," said Carstairs, and hung up. As he sat back and lit a cigarette his eyes fell on the calendar and he realized it was now eight days since what he called the "Pollifax Affair" had erupted. Eight days was a long, long time in the life of his department, and he reviewed the facts. They did not cheer him and when Peattie was ushered in he had to forcibly remove the frown from his brow in order to appear civilized. "Good to see you," he murmured, half rising to shake his hand. "Dropping in doesn't inconvenience you, I hope."

"Lord, no. The Operations Department always fascinates me. I suppose I'm hoping you'll drop a few clues about how this is turning out."

"Badly," said Carstairs dryly. "What have you come up with?"

"Yes. Well." Peattie put on his reading glasses. "It seems that General Perdido has been in Peking, yes, but he did not arrive there until August 24, five days after the kidnapping of your Mrs. Pollifax and Mr. Farrell."

"Five days after," mused Carstairs, frowning. "Was anyone with him?"

"No one, he arrived quite alone."

"Hmmm. So presumably Mrs. Pollifax and Farrell were not taken to Cuba and not taken to China, either."

"Also, and this you may find interesting," went on Peattie, "he arrived in China on a jet that collected him in Athens."

"Athens!" exclaimed Carstairs, visibly electrified. "Athens?" He leaned forward and briefly swore. "The Mediterranean—the Balkans—I never thought of Albania, although why on earth he'd take them so far—"

Peattie nodded and went on. "He remained in Peking until the middle of the week, leaving yesterday in a private plane, destination unknown except that a very reliable informant tells us the plane was heading for—care to guess?"

"Albania?"

"Right. But your friends were not with him, and have apparently not been in Peking at all."

Carstairs stubbed out his cigarette. "No, obviously not. Albania . . ." he repeated with a shake of his head. "Anything else?"

Peattie smiled with the pleasure of someone holding a very interesting card up his sleeve. "Yes, a little something more. I took the liberty of—well, after all, since Albania has become the prodigy of the Chinese Reds it has naturally fallen into my province and so I went ahead, that is—"

"That is, what?"

"I made inquiries. General Perdido *did* land in Albania last night, his plane came in at Shkoder, whereupon the car that met him took off immediately for the mountains."

"Very interesting indeed," said Carstairs. "So on the twenty-fourth, five days after the kidnaping, the general flies from Athens to Peking, remains a few days and then flies to Albania." He frowned. "It could mean a great deal, it could mean nothing."

Peattie nodded. "We know frustratingly little about Albania since the Red Chinese moved in, but there have been rumors that somewhere in the North Albanian Alps there is a building, a very primitive stone fortress originally built by bandits, where a few very top-secret political prisoners are kept. The countryside is almost inaccessible: cliffs, gorges, crags, landslides, you name it, and the mountain people are a clannish bunch. Still, the rumor persists that such a place exists, and it was into these same mountains that the general disappeared."

"Who's the informant?" asked Carstairs idly. "Reliable?"

"An Orthodox Christian priest," said Peattie. "You may or may not know that the churches have been closed and desecrated in Albania. Our friend's mosque, for instance, has been turned into a bar and his own existence is precarious. Not too long ago he was put to work for a month on a road gang that repairs and builds roads in the north, and it's there he heard stories about this place."

"Any chance of pinpointing its whereabouts?" Carstairs was already out of his chair and crossing the room to the wall map.

With a shrug Peattie joined him. "Anywhere from here to there," he said, tracing the line of the mountains in the north. "We know the road ends about *here*," he added, "but of course that doesn't mean anything, the roads are constantly coming to a crashing halt in these countries and life still goes on, by mule, donkey, bicycle, oxcart, et cetera, et cetera."

Carstairs shook his head. "There's not a chance in the world they could still be alive, not a chance, but is there any way of confirming the fact that they were taken there? That they were killed there?"

"Very difficult making inquiries," Peattie said. "Take weeks, I'm afraid. Foreigners, of course, are immediately suspect and the few allowed into the country as tourists see very little. A good many Albanians are connected with the secret police, by membership, through relatives or marriage —the usual trick, you know, to keep the citizenry terrorized. I'm not sure . . ." He hesitated and then said firmly, "I'm *very* sure the agents we have over there wouldn't be allowed to endanger themselves for the sake of—"

Carstairs bluntly completed the thought. "For the sake of two agents who have been at the mercy of General Perdido for more than a week. Quite right, I wouldn't allow it myself."

Peattie very pointedly looked away and added, "I think I should tell you that this mountain eyrie has a most unsavory reputation. My informant tells us that those who are Catholics cross themselves when it's mentioned. It's spoken of in whispers, and said that no one has ever left it alive."

"I get the point," Carstairs told him harshly, and then, more gently, "I wonder . . ."

"Wonder what?"

"I'm curious about that mountain fortress." He got up, excusing himself, and went out to confer with Bishop. He returned a few minutes later. "I had an idea," he explained. "I've asked for a private seaplane to get lost over the Albanian Alps. They should have it there in an hour."

"Reconnaissance?"

Carstairs nodded. "Strictly unofficial, of course—we'll share any information we get with you people, but if Perdido's going to go on snatching Americans we'd jolly well better find out if he's tucking them in there for the night."

Peattie stood up. "You'll keep me posted then. Good."

Carstairs also stood. "And thank you for stopping in. Let's get together for a drink one of these days."

"Yes, let's," said Peattie with his wry smile. "One of these days or years . . ."

When he had gone Carstairs went back to his paper work, made a few telephone calls, went to lunch and conferred for an hour with his chief upstairs. It was after two o'clock when he returned to his office to be handed a radiogram by Bishop. It was a report from the pilot of the seaplane that had made a sortie over the Albanian Alps. No building of Carstairs' description had been seen with the naked eye but the reconnaissance photographs would be dispatched as soon as they were developed. What had intrigued the pilot, however, was the activity going on in the area bounded by the Alps in the east, Shkoder in the south and Lake Scutari in the west. He had seen a large number of men scouring the area on foot, a stream of very black smoke rising from a wood—obviously something containing oil or gasoline had been set afire—and an unusual concentration of police launches patrolling Lake Scutari.

Carstairs frowned, wondering what the devil this would mean, if anything. He wished he knew more about Albania, he wondered if Peattie would have knowledge of whether this type of activity was normal or irregular for that country and he was about to pick up the phone when Peattie himself was ushered in again.

"This just came through," Peattie said without preamble. "Something's up all right in the north of Albania. One of our agents broke silence to send it—damned risky of him. Here, read it yourself, it's fresh from the decoding room."

Carstairs picked up the sheet and scanned it. It read:

GENERAL PERDIDO ARRIVED ALBANIA YESTERDAY, MYSTERIOUSLY SHOT AND WOUNDED DURING NIGHT, TODAY DIRECTING LARGE SEARCH PARTY FOR ENEMIES OF STATE ESCAPED MOUNTAIN HIDEAWAY IN CAR, NUMBER IN PARTY UNCERTAIN STOP TWO GUARDS DEAD, ONE ESCAPEE RUMORED AMERICAN, GROUP ASSUMED STILL ALIVE AND HEADING WEST OR NORTHWEST TO COAST STOP

Carstairs leaped to his feet to look at the map. "Whoever these people are we've got to give them every possible help," he sputtered. "If one of them's rumored to be American there's always a chance it could be Farrell, but even if it isn't these people can give us valuable information. Look at this map, see how damn close they are to Yugoslavia, that's where they'll head, it's their only chance. Bishop," he bellowed into the intercom, "get me Fiersted in the State Department." To Peattie he said, "If Fiersted will clear the way for us with the Yugoslavian Government we can scatter a few of our men along their border to watch for them. We can have men there by midnight—by midnight at the very *latest*," he vowed.

By midnight Mrs. Pollifax, Farrell and the Genie were no longer adrift upon the waters of Lake Scutari. They were not in Yugoslavia, either. They had been blown by an ill wind in the opposite direction—south, and deeper into Albania— and at the stroke of midnight they were huddled behind a stone wall in the city of Shkoder at the southern tip of Lake Scutari. High above their heads stood the walls of a grim-looking, medieval castle. A fuzzy, heat-stricken pink moon shed a faint light on the scraps of wet paper that had once been their map, and by this light Mrs. Pollifax was trying to make some sense of the lines that had not been obliterated.

"The damn thing looks like a river," the Genie was saying, regarding the water in front of them angrily. "It can't belong to Lake Scutari. There's a current, we felt it, and anything but a real river would have dried up in this heat a month ago."

It had felt like a real river, too; in fact if the moon had not emerged from wisps of cloud their log would have sailed right out of Lake Scutari, past the castle on the hill and down this unidentifiable body of water. They had barely managed to propel the log toward land, and they were now hiding in the shadows of an ancient, cobbled alley while they desperately tried to think what to do. Their log had been lost in the darkness and they were back in the city where they had first met Albania. It was difficult to decide whether they had made progress or not.

"There *is* a line," said Mrs. Pollifax, peering nearsightedly at the map. "The line goes from Shkoder to the Adriatic Sea but it has no label, nothing *says* it's a river."

"I copied every single word there was," Farrell informed her stiffly.

"Of course you did, it's just such a small map. But there *is* a line, see?" She passed the scrap of paper around, and the two men took turns squinting at the line and pondering its significance. Mrs. Pollifax added hopefully, "The only other lines like that on the map are rivers. It even says they're rivers."

"And this does appear to be a river," the Genie said, nodding. "Even if we didn't expect a river here."

"A very good river, too," put in Farrell.

"But nameless, unknown and confusing," said the Genie.

Mrs. Pollifax took back the wet piece of paper to study again. "There's this to be considered," she told them softly. "To go by land from Lake Scutari to the coast looks quite a distance, between ten and twenty miles, I'd say, and all of it to be done on foot. This funny line meanders a bit, but this line, if it really is a river, ends at the Adriatic. If one had a boat—"

"If one had a boat, and if this truly is a river, and if it should empty into the Adriatic—"

The Genie broke off without finishing his sentence and they were all silent, contemplating the succession of hazards. "So many *ifs*," sighed Mrs. Pollifax at last. "A gamble in the most terrifying sense of the word."

The Genie said soberly, "But that is precisely what life is, wouldn't you agree? Everything is a matter of choice, and when we choose are we not gambling on the unknown and its being a wise choice? And isn't it free choice that makes individuals of us? We are eternally free to choose ourselves and our futures. I believe myself that life is quite comparable to a map like this, a constant choice of direction and route." He was silent a moment. "Stay here," he added, standing up. "I will try to find a boat for us."

Mrs. Pollifax nodded, feeling a very deep relief that someone had told her to remain sitting. It was bliss not to move, and even greater bliss to be ordered not to move since this immediately eliminated all sense of guilt and responsibility. She closed her eyes, then opened them to see that Farrell was already asleep and with a sigh she forced her eyelids to remain open, knowing that someone had to remain on guard or all their previous efforts would come to nothing. To occupy herself she began figuring how many hours ago they had escaped. They had left their prison around nine o'clock Thursday night, hadn't they? It had been roughly dusk, or nine of this day, when they had set their log afloat on Lake Scutari. This meant they had escaped only a little more than twenty-four hours ago, which was incredible because it already seemed a lifetime of nightmares. She then began figuring when they or she had last slept and when they had last eaten, but this was even more arduous and numbers kept slipping from her mind and her lids were just closing, her will power diminishing, when she heard the quiet drip-drip of an oar or paddle in the water nearby. She put out a hand to waken Farrell and when his eyes jerked open she placed a warning finger across her lips. They both turned to watch the silhouette of a long boat move across the path of weak moonlight. The boat looked a little like a Venetian gondola, its prow and stern sharp-pointed and high out of the water. A man stood in the center facing the bow, an oar in each hand, but Mrs. Pollifax couldn't be sure it was the Genie until the boat drew in to the shore. She and Farrell went to meet it.

"Come aboard," said the Genie, bowing as had been his custom, and Mrs. Pollifax could even see his old twinkle in the moonlight. The Genie was feeling pleased with himself, and quite rightly, she thought, wondering how he had found the *londra* and hoping he hadn't been forced to kill for it. She moved to help Farrell—it was necessary for him to sit on the side of the boat and tumble in backward because of his bad leg. She, too, half fell into the boat and lay on the floor too exhausted to move or speak. It was the Genie who was taking over now, it had become his turn, and she lay on her back and stared up at the clouded moon and hoped her turn would never come. The Genie was at work with the oars again, giving the water quick, short jabs. Mrs. Pollifax said in a low, dreamy voice, "You found a boat."

"Tied up, not far away," the Genie whispered over his shoulder. "Sleep a little, the current helps. With this moon I'll keep close to the shore."

Mrs. Pollifax's gaze traveled from him to the shape of Shkoder's castle set high above them, its sides almost perpendicular, the lines of its buildings outlined black against the deep-blue night sky. There was a solitary star, and with her eyes upon it Mrs. Pollifax fell softly asleep. When she awoke both the castle and the star had disappeared and she thought the sky looked a shade lighter. Then she realized that what had awakened her was the sharp crack of a pistol shot from somewhere along the shore. She sat up at once.

"Down," whispered the Genie violently.

Farrell, too, fell back, his eyes alarmed. "But what was it, who is it?"

"Someone on the shore. I think he wants us to stop."

"Are we going to?" asked Mrs. Pollifax weakly.

"I haven't seen him, it's too dark," the Genie said, speaking without moving his lips. "I heard something and glanced toward the shore. I could dimly make out a man waving his arms but I looked away. I am still looking away, I see nothing."

"He may fire again and hit you the next time," Farrell pointed out.

The Genie said pleasantly, "Yes, I know. But we are moving faster now, can you feel it? You mustn't look but the river has been growing wider in the last ten minutes, and the earth flatter. These are rice paddies we are passing now. There is a definite change in the air, too—smell it?"

Both Farrell and Mrs. Pollifax sniffed. "Salt," said Farrell wonderingly. "Salt? Am I right?"

"Yes."

The pistol was fired again and something plunked against the sides of the boat. "Above water line, I hope," said Farrell. "He's a damn good shot in this light."

"He's running away now," the Genie said casually. "He has begun thinking."

"Thinking?"

"That he can't question a man going toward the sea in a boat if the man in the boat refuses to stop. He will either find a boat himself or find a telephone and talk to people on the coast who will stop us."

"May I sit up now?" asked Mrs. Pollifax.

"Yes, he's gone."

She sat up and looked around her. The darkness was rolling back to uncover a very charming scene of springlike tender green, flat to the eye and stretching as far as the horizon. Ahead—Mrs. Pollifax wondered what lay ahead and beyond. From the boat she could see only a floor of water, a huge ceiling of brightening sky, and a number of birds. "But those are sea gulls!" cried Mrs. Pollifax.

"We've got to know what to do," Farrell said in a brooding, nearly desperate voice. "Where we're going, what we're going to do. My God, to keep playing it by ear—"

"Yugoslavia is north," Mrs. Pollifax reminded him. "We know that."

"But we don't even have a gun that's dry!"

The Genie said, "Yes, we have." The two turned to stare at him and he said, "The guard Stefan, do you remember my taking his pistol? His holster was the waterproof type. Remove it from my pocket and check it. There may be time, too, to clean the others. Know how?"

"No, damn it," said Farrell. "You?"

The Genie shook his head. "Not my cup of tea, I'm afraid. Got the gun?"

Farrell was holding it and breaking it open. "Five cartridges."

The Genie nodded. "And you?" he asked of Mrs. Pollifax.

She began emptying the various pockets in her petticoats. Out came the playing cards and Farrell exclaimed, "Not those! My God, Duchess, I won't be able to see a deck of

cards for the rest of my life—if I have a life—without thinking of you."

"Well, that's one form of immortality," she retorted, and
drew out the pistol, the magazine clip, the dried shreds of
map, the compass. "And if I'm captured again perhaps
they'll spare me a few minutes for a game of solitaire instead
of the usual last meal or cigarette. That's all I have," she
added, gesturing toward the small pile. "No food. Not a
crumb."

"That damn lake," sighed Farrell.

"Actually I've stopped feeling weak," said Mrs. Pollifax.
"Rather like catching one's second wind, I suppose, except of
course we've had drinking water to sustain us."

"The kind that will bring on dysentery in a week," contributed Farrell gloomily. "It's getting lighter."

"Too light," said the Genie.

Mrs. Pollifax roused herself again. She said to the Genie,
"You've been standing there all night, would you like me to
take a turn? The current's so strong now there's really no
need to row, is there?"

"There's still need for steering," he pointed out dryly. "And
I think we're very near the Adriatic, near enough to walk to
it if this river decides to turn and go elsewhere."

Farrell said thoughtfully, "If they should know by now
there's a boat on this river, and be waiting to stop it, perhaps
we *should* walk to the Adriatic."

The Genie shrugged. "Maybe."

Mrs. Pollifax said gently, "No, Farrell. I mean, your leg.
I mean—"

"Then let me take my chances with the boat and *you*
walk," he said, and Mrs. Pollifax knew by the suppressed
fury in his voice that his pride was quivering. On the other
hand her amateur work in hospitals had taught her when a
patient was on the verge of collapse, and Farrell's nerves
had reached a breaking point, gone beyond and returned. He
had more stamina than most men, but even a Hercules would
have had to admit that the past thirty-six hours were ener-
vating.

Suddenly the gaudy, blood-red sun cleared the high cliffs
behind them and the misty landscape lost its oriental quality
and Mrs. Pollifax thought, "Why, this is the dawn I was sure
I'd never see!" For a moment she was caught by the magic
of life, its brevity and unpredictability, and she stared at
this world as if just born into it. The distant mountains were

snow-capped, the nearer cliffs tawny with deep-purple shadows. Around her the ground mist that only a few minutes ago had been gray and tattered was transformed by light into silky clouds of pearl-white and palest pink. The air was cool, and smelled of damp earth and wet grass, and the river flowing around and past them contained in it mosaic patterns of sky and sun and shore. Mrs. Pollifax felt a stirring in her that was almost mystical; an exhilarating sense of freedom that she had never known before, as if in this moment all the rules and habits of a lifetime fell from her and she stood at the very core of life and felt its heartbeat. It came of experiencing dawn in this strange country a continent away from her own, it came of being still alive when she ought to have been dead; it was compounded of surprise, appreciation, exhaustion, hunger, the effects of danger and an unquenchability of the human spirit.

She heard Farrell say, "You all right, Duchess?"

She started. "Yes. Yes, I'm fine, thank you."

At that moment ahead of them the ground mist rolled away and they saw the sun shining on the clear, sparkling water of the Adriatic. Almost simultaneously Farrell cried, "Oh, God—look!" and Mrs. Pollifax glanced to the shore of the river on their right and saw a police boat setting out to intercept them, flags flying from its bow and stern, the spray rising majestically in an arc behind it.

Twenty-two

There were two men in the boat, each of them faceless silhouettes from this distance, but it could be assumed they were well armed—police usually were—and each man was leaning forward with an intensity that suggested fixity of purpose. Their boat was too old and too broad in the beam to move with speed, but it took the waves like a sedate and experienced old dowager, and even a motor that kept missing and cutting out would make progress against a *londra* with one man at its oars. Mrs. Pollifax said anxiously, "They can't possibly know who we are, they know only that we came down the river."

"They'll find out who we are soon enough," pointed out

Farrell dryly, and he began to swear quietly and thoroughly at their impotence while the Genie frantically churned the water with the oars, his face grim.

Mrs. Pollifax glanced around, hoping for some wild improvisation or concealment to present itself but behind them the river was empty, and ahead of them the sea was open and boundless, furnished only with buoys noting the river's entrance. Buoys . . . no, nothing could be done with buoys . . . Mrs. Pollifax's gaze swerved to the left bank of the river and she gave an exclamation. "Look! There's a wharf and a boat—a sailboat!"

"So?" growled Farrell, snapping the safety on the gun.

"But sailboats go fast!" Mrs. Pollifax leaned forward and clutched the Genie's arm. "Do look," she begged. "The man's getting ready to take the boat out, the sail's already up, we have that gun and we can make him sail us out to sea, it's our only chance!" She found herself standing and helping the Genie push and pull at the oars. "Faster," she whispered. "Faster, faster, faster." The Genie had backed one oar to change their direction but they were rowing against the current now and the police launch, coughing and sputtering, was nevertheless gaining on them with shocking speed. The wharf was a small one, a float, really, with a narrow catwalk leading over the water to it. The boat moored beside it looked heavy but certainly seaworthy; it was roughly twenty-five feet in length, with a sunlit white sail flapping gently in the wind as the man secured the halyards. Behind them the asthmatic whine of the motor launch grew louder, and now Mrs. Pollifax could see the two men clearly, one thin and dark-faced, the other fleshy and bald. Mrs. Pollifax began to tremble.

"Faster," Farrell was saying sharply. "For God's sake faster, we're almost there and so are they."

The fisherman wore a red jersey and a pair of tattered trousers. He seemed completely oblivious to the race being run nearby. In a leisurely fashion he reached from his boat to the dock, picked up a bucket and stowed it away, walked forward to untie the mooring lines, returned aft and pulled in the stern lines. Grasping the tiller he gave it a thrust, the sails filled with wind and the boat swung free of the wharf. The Genie had been aiming for the wharf; now he swerved to follow the sailboat out to sea, and both he and Mrs. Pollifax began shouting to the man at the helm. "Wait—wait for us," cried Mrs. Pollifax, and the startled fisherman turned to look at them. They were very close to him now, and the motorboat was even closer behind them. "Wait," shouted Mrs. Pollifax, waving violently. The fisherman scowled. Undecided, watchful, he gave the tiller a jerk and brought his boat about into the wind, sails luffing, bow pointed directly at them as he regarded them with suspicious curiosity. The Genie viciously thrust one oar back through the water and the *londra* shot across the bow of the fishing boat. Dropping both oars the Genie leaped over Mrs. Pollifax and jumped aboard the sailboat.

"*Zott*," gasped the fisherman. He stood up and roared his indignation but the Genie ignored him and leaned over the water to pull the *londra* against the sailboat.

To Farrell the Genie shouted, "For heaven's sake aim your gun at this man! And climb aboard before he kills me with his bare hands!" His voice mingled with shouts from the policemen behind them. Their launch was heading straight for the sailboat to ram it, but the Genie had now pulled the *londra* between the two boats as a buffer. "Hurry," he told Mrs. Pollifax, and she stumbled toward Farrell to help him drag his useless leg over the side.

The fisherman had stopped bawling his indignation. He stood watching them with opened mouth, his stare moving ponderously from the gun in Farrell's hand to Mrs. Pollifax. He glowered briefly at the Genie and then his eyes came to rest on the men in the launch and narrowed as he recognized their uniforms. Startled, confused, he glanced back at Farrell climbing aboard, looked again at the policemen and then decided that he was caught in an insoluble situation, and very sensibly chose a prudent course. He jumped overboard and began swimming toward the wharf.

"No, no, come back," implored Mrs. Pollifax, seeing him slip through their fingers.

The tiller that he had deserted moved idly to one side and hung there a moment, then abruptly, savagely, the sails filled with a wind that sent the boom crashing, lifted one side of the boat and sent buckets skidding across the deck.

"Grab the tiller!" screamed Farrell from the bow.

"What's a tiller?" screamed back Mrs. Pollifax hysterically.

"That thing—for God's sake hold it steady!"

Mrs. Pollifax retrieved the long arm of smooth wood that jutted from the deck and clung to it, the boom nearly decapitating the Genie before it settled, the sails flapping erratically, the boat threatening to turn over on its side before it steadied. What saved them was the *londra*, which the Genie held captive with both hands, and which the two policemen also held captive, having attached themselves to the other side of it like barnacles. Only a second earlier the bald man had started to climb across it to reach the sailboat—he was caught with one foot in the *londra* and one still in the police boat; jerking upright he waved both arms wildly in a fight for balance, lost the fight and fell ignobly to the floor of the *londra*.

At once the thin man behind the wheel of the launch pulled out a revolver and fired across the boat at the Genie. Farrell returned the fire and the policeman slumped over the wheel. Mrs. Pollifax screamed, not because Farrell had shot the thin man but because the bald one in the bottom of the *londra* had climbed to his knees and was aiming a gun at Farrell. "Shoot," she screamed at Farrell, pointing, and Farrell and the bald policeman exchanged shots simultaneously.

But the Genie's clutch on the *londra* had weakened during the melee and it was the *londra* that had acted as a sea anchor. With nothing to hold them now the rigging tightened, the sails went taut and the wind carried them zooming off across the water with an abruptness that sent Farrell sprawling across the Genie on the deck. Mrs. Pollifax, holding tightly to the tiller, screamed for help.

"Let the tiller go! Drop it!" shouted Farrell, thereby totally confusing Mrs. Pollifax because earlier he had insisted that she grab it. She was further mystified when she let it go and the boat came about into the wind and ceased its reckless caroming. She said with interest, "Why does it . . ." and then stopped because Farrell had lifted himself from the Genie and was staring at him in horror. "Oh no," she whispered, and both hands flew to her mouth to keep her lips from trembling. She understood now why the Genie had stopped holding the *londra*. Creeping over the coils of line she knelt beside him. "Is he dead?"

Farrell very gently placed the Genie's head in his lap. "Not dead but very *very* badly hurt."

"Oh God, you're hurt too," she told him, seeing blood well out of Farrell's sleeve at the shoulder.

He nodded. "Not badly but I can't risk moving and I don't think it would be very healthy for the Genie, either. Duchess, you're going to have to sail this boat."

"I?" gasped Mrs. Pollifax in a shocked voice. "Me?"

"I can tell you what to do," he pointed out. "Duchess, you've got to, you can't fall apart now, you realize how far we've come, don't you?"

She thought back to the night on the precipice, to the goats and the wild chase in the Rolls Royce and the guard shot in the cornfield, to the day spent in being periodically submerged by motorboat waves, and the night floating across Scutari on a log. She nodded wearily. There came a time when a person wanted desperately to give up; she supposed it was as good a time as any to rally; surely there must be a few ounces of overlooked iron in her soul. "I'll try," she said, and wiped a tear from what must be a very raddled cheek by now. "I can't help crying," she told Farrell. "I'm tired."

"Can't imagine why," he said dryly. As she crawled drearily back toward the tiller he added casually, "Have any idea whether I winged that bald chap in the *londra?*"

Mrs. Pollifax looked back. "The boats are still there, bobbing around at some distance from each other. No head showing in the *londra.* You must have hit him a *little.*"

Farrell nodded. "There may not be much time before they're discovered, and two boats, each with a wounded or dead policeman in them, will set off a merry chase. Duchess, before you take the tiller, do three things."

"Yes?"

"Look for fresh water. Hand me that tarp over there so I can make a tent to keep the sun off the Genie. See if the fisherman packed a lunch."

"Lunch?" said Mrs. Pollifax, brightening. "You mean *food?*"

"Naturally I mean food—the stuff we haven't had since heaven knows when."

Mrs. Pollifax, foraging around, was staggered by her success. She could not remember any triumph in her life that could possibly equal what she felt as she carried to Farrell the goatskin bag containing the fisherman's noon meal. She brought from it a slab of cornbread, six olives and a square of cheese. From a smaller goatskin bag she poured a cup of goat's milk. When she crept back to the tiller it was with her mouth full of flaky, exquisitely flavored cornbread and her heart filled with a faint hope that if the gods were smiling on them now their smiles might linger just a little longer.

"Okay, Duchess, full speed ahead."

"But speed is what I'm afraid of," admitted Mrs. Pollifax ruefully.

He paid this no attention. "Wind from the north. We can't risk heading north to Yugoslavia, we might run into more police launches. We'll have to head straight out to sea."

Mrs. Pollifax gaped at him. "Out to sea!"

Farrell grinned weakly. "We've been doing everything else the hard way, Duchess, why stop now? Give me that compass and turn the tiller to starboard—the right, I mean. And brace yourself first," he added.

Mrs. Pollifax tossed him the compass and turned the tiller to the right. At once the boat came to life; the wind seized them like a gigantic hand, the sail tightened, the rigging creaked and Mrs. Pollifax was overwhelmed by a feeling of total helplessness as wind, sail and boat combined to send them skimming the waves. "But how do you *stop* this thing!" she wailed. She had the feeling of being on a roller coaster, idle one moment, the next moment hurtling at breath-taking speed.

"Easy does it," Farrell shouted to her over the wind. "Keep the tiller in the center. You're broad-reaching now, the wind on your starboard side."

"Like this?"

"Excellent."

"Yes—oh *yes*," gasped Mrs. Pollifax. She had just felt the boat steady itself in response to a subtle turn of the tiller, had felt the boat under her become disciplined, the sails taut but not under strain, and she was delighted.

"Keep it that way," Farrell told her. "If you hit a squall and get scared let the tiller go, the boat'll come about by itself. If the wind increases but you're not scared then move the tiller slightly left or slightly right—you'll be tacking then. The important thing for now, though, is to get the hell out of sight of land as fast as possible." With his one useful arm he was pulling the tarp over his head and shrugging it into position so that it would shade the Genie.

Mrs. Pollifax, tiller in hand, dedicated herself to getting them the hell out of sight of Albania as fast as possible.

Toward five o'clock that afternoon the *Persephone*, a sea-going tug returning to its home port of Otranto from Port of Venice, was making its way southward when the first mate sighted a sailboat with someone waving what looked to be a white petticoat. "Another damned tourist," he growled, mentally and savagely condemning those pleasure-loving hordes that descended upon the Adriatic believing anybody could sail a boat. He reported it to the captain, who ordered their course slowed, and presently the small boat drew alongside the *Persephone*.

The first mate looked down into the boat and gasped. *"Mon Dieu,"* he whispered, for seated at the tiller was one of the wildest-looking women he had ever seen, white hair in shreds, face filthy and blistering from the hot sun. Yards of voluminous skirt surrounded her, but although he recognized the clothes as Greek or Albanian the woman's features did not match them. Then he saw the tarpaulin lift and his eyes widened, his memory flashing back to the war years and to lifeboats found in the Mediterranean. Both men looked as if they'd had it but the bearded one at least was in motion; he was grinning broadly and waving an arm, although it was plain from the blood-stained cloth strapped around his other arm that he badly needed a doctor. The first mate gave a brief thought to the type of gunfighters they might be escaping, and hurried to report to the captain.

Mrs. Pollifax, gazing up at the ship from below, wondered why on earth the sailors along the rail were staring at her with horrified fascination. She had naïvely pictured them being welcomed back to civilization with delighted smiles and shouts of joy. Now it occurred to her that in the eyes of civilization she and Farrell and the Genie might just as well be returning from a trip to the moon: their experiences of the past fortnight were too exotic, too melodramatic for a prosaic world to digest. It was the three of them who must adapt now; it was they whom violence had made foreign, and for the first time she conceded how tattered and bizarre they must appear to these well-scrubbed sailors just finished with their tea.

"We're curiosities," she realized.

Then the spell broke; a sailor shouted, *"Inglese!* Welcome!" Cheering broke out along the deck rail, and Mrs. Pollifax had to look away to conceal the tears in her eyes.

"Well, Duchess," said Farrell, smiling at her.

"Well, Farrell," she said, smiling back at him, and lifted a petticoat to wipe her eyes.

"You look like hell, Duchess," he said fondly, "but you're safe."

"Safe," repeated Mrs. Pollifax, tasting the word on her tongue as if it was a rare wine.

A rope ladder was flung over the side and an officer with a medical kit descended hand over hand to their boat. He went at once to the Genie and bent over him. Two sailors followed down the ladder and in broken English instructed Mrs. Pollifax in the rudiments of rope climbing. With their help she began the ascent, a dozen men shouting words of encouragement from the rail. She would have preferred waiting for Farrell but an officer in a starched, white uniform insisted upon escorting her at once to the captain.

"I must request identification," said the captain, and then, unbending a little at sight of her face he added, "There must be people you would like to notify?"

Mrs. Pollifax thought of her son and daughter and reluctantly put them aside. "If you would be so kind as to contact Mr. Carstairs at the Central Intelligence Agency in Washington," she said.

The captain's eyes flickered. "It's that way, is it?" He looked at her with open curiosity. "Suppose you write the message. I ask only that it not be in code and that I see it before it is sent."

Mrs. Pollifax sat down gratefully at his desk and tried to pull her thoughts together. After chewing on her pencil for a moment she wrote the following:

SIR: RESCUED FROM ADRIATIC SEA THIS AFTERNOON BY . . .

She looked up. "What ship is this, and where are you going?"

"The *Persephone*, due to land at Otranto in two hours, or at 1900 hours."

Mrs. Pollifax began again:

SIR: RESCUED FROM ADRIATIC SEA THIS AFTERNOON BY S.S. PERSEPHONE ARRIVING OTRANTO AT 1900 HOURS. FARRELL AND SECOND COMPANION IN NEED OF MEDICAL ATTENTION. HAVE NO PASSPORT OR MONEY AND MUST REQUEST SOME HELP OTHERWISE IT HAS BEEN A MOST INTERESTING TRIP. SINCERELY YOURS, EMILY POLLIFAX.

The captain read it through and nodded. "It will be sent immediately," he said. "I will also send word to Otranto that a doctor will be urgently needed. We do not have one aboard, unfortunately." He looked at her and smiled faintly. "And you," he added, "you would perhaps like to wash a little and comb the hair?"

Mrs. Pollifax's eyes widened. "Wash a little," she repeated. "Wash a little? Yes, that would be very nice," she said politely, and suddenly began to laugh.

The boat had not yet docked when a harbor launch drew up beside the *Persephone* and requested permission for two passengers to come aboard. Both men wore business suits; one carried an attaché case up the rope ladder and the other a medical bag. They were escorted at once to the cabin where Mrs. Pollifax, Farrell and the Genie were resting, and without a word the doctor hurried to the berth where the Genie lay. The second man stood and looked appraisingly at Farrell and Mrs. Pollifax. Completing his scrutiny he said, "Ben Halstead's my name, I believe we have a mutual friend named Carstairs."

Mrs. Pollifax brightened. "Yes indeed," she said, rising from her chair. "I am Emily Pollifax and this is Mr. Farrell, who has a broken leg and a fresh bullet wound in his shoulder and an old one in his arm; and this man . . ." She glanced toward the Genie, whose eyes were open now but vacant as he gazed at the doctor. "We don't know who he is but we brought him along anyway. He's a very peculiar but resourceful Chinese man who speaks English, except that he preferred keeping it a secret for quite a long time."

"Oh? That's interesting." Halstead moved to the berth and over the doctor's shoulder looked down at the Genie. "He dropped no clues at all, you don't know anything at all about him?"

"Actually I didn't trust him at first," put in Farrell. "Nor did he trust us, which is provocative. But he's not a Red, and he rescued us from a very sticky situation."

Mrs. Pollifax said slowly, "Yes, and when I asked him yesterday about next of kin, in case anything happened, he gave a little chuckle and said nobody would miss him, they would have held his funeral two years ago. He'd been dead a long time, he said."

Halstead frowned. "There's something damn familiar about the look of him. What's his condition, Bill, can he be questioned?"

The doctor removed the stethoscope from his ears. "Not for a day or two, sorry. He needs immediate attention and the best of care, but he can be moved. Stretchers, an ambulance, then blood transfusions and straight to the operating room."

"Will he survive?" asked Mrs. Pollifax anxiously.

"The vital thing is removing the bullet and that'll be a bit tricky. After that I could answer with more certainty. Some signs of malnutrition, of course; considerable patchwork needed after removal of the bullet, but the odds are in his favor. Barring anything unforeseen—yes, he'll survive."

"I'm so glad," Mrs. Pollifax said warmly.

The doctor, standing erect, only nodded. "From the sound of it we're docking now." He pulled the blanket from the top berth and tucked it around the Genie. "The ambulance is waiting at the pier, I'll send them word to hurry along with a stretcher and then I'll take a look at you, Mr.—Farrell, is it?"

Farrell said cheerfully, "That's me, but no need to hurry. I simply wouldn't feel comfortable without a bullet in me somewhere." He was watching Halstead, who kept staring at the Genie. "You recognize him, don't you." It was a statement, not a question.

"Very astute of you," said Halstead, not turning. "Except recognize isn't precisely the word; it's more a feeling of familiarity. If I could only—good grief!" He exclaimed, snapping his fingers. "Dr. Lee Tsung Howell!"

"I beg your pardon?" faltered Mrs. Pollifax.

"Considerably thinner, of course, that's what fooled me. Good heavens, and it was exactly two years ago that he disappeared—that ties in—and a memorial service really was held for him. Every bit of evidence pointed to his murder by the Red Chinese. There were even two reputable witnesses to testify he was killed and his body carried off by his assassins."

Mrs. Pollifax and Farrell glanced in astonishment at the Genie. "*Who* is he?" asked Mrs. Pollifax.

"And *what?*" asked Farrell.

"Dr. Howell, the scientist. Brilliant man. Born in China; father English, mother Chinese. English citizen. Made the mistake of traveling to Hong Kong two years ago. That's when they murdered—except they didn't murder him, did they? Snatched him."

Farrell said incredulously, "You mean he's *the* Dr. Howell? The protein man?"

"Please," said Mrs. Pollifax despairingly, "please can someone tell me what we're talking about, and why on earth a protein man would be locked up in a cell in Albania for two years?"

"Food," said Halstead. "Can you think of anything China needs more desperately for her underfed millions? She needs food more than communism, guns, armies, factories. If I tell you that at the time of his disappearance Dr. Howell was at work on a method for extracting protein from a common weed—a protein that would feed hundreds of people for only a few pennies—does that explain Red China's interest in him?"

Farrell whistled.

"Except," added Halstead, glancing at the Genie, "except they did a fantastic job of covering their tracks. We knew they tried to kidnap him but we believed he fought for his life and was killed."

"Except there was no body," pointed out Farrell.

"No, two witnesses instead, each highly placed and of impeccable reputation."

"Not so impeccable now," said Mrs. Pollifax.

"No indeed."

"Do you think they tortured him?"

"Possibly at first, but he'd be no good to them dead. They probably settled for solitary confinement, or slow starvation." He shook his head. "What a break for the world that you found him! The presses will be humming all night long."

"Will they hum for us, too?" inquired Mrs. Pollifax.

Both men turned to look at her. "Good God, no," said Farrell. "The Genie—that is, Dr. Howell—will have escaped by himself against impossible odds. As for Emily Pollifax of New Brunswick, New Jersey, who on earth is she?"

"But I feel like *such* a heroine," confessed Mrs. Pollifax sadly.

"And so you are, Duchess, so you are. But you have never left Mexico City, remember? As for Albania, where is it? You haven't even read about it in *Time* magazine, let alone visited it."

"Oh," said Mrs. Pollifax.

Farrell grinned. "Cheer up, Duchess. Do you recall—and it pains me to do so—my suggesting that the Genie was mentally retarded?"

She smiled back. "Yes I do remember, and I believe I said there were flashes of intelligence now and then."

Halstead laughed. "Just to be charitable I might add that he's known as quite an eccentric. Would that help?" The stretcher was brought in by two orderlies and they were silent as the Genie was lifted very gently onto it. As he was carried out of the stateroom Mrs. Pollifax said suddenly, "Will I be able to send him get-well cards? I should like to very much if you'll give me the name of the hospital here."

Halstead said, "Actually you can learn the hospital's name simply by reading your newspaper tomorrow morning in Washington, D.C."

"Washington!" exclaimed Mrs. Pollifax.

"My orders are to fly you at once, nonstop, to Washington." Seeing their stunned faces he added, "Sorry. You can eat and sleep on the plane, you know, but Carstairs has to see for himself that you're alive." He gave them a crooked half-smile. "Apparently he can't believe it. At any rate immediate questioning is in order. We leave as soon as Bill has taken a look at that arm and pumped Farrell full of anti-infection and anti-pain shots."

Mrs. Pollifax groaned. "But I'm still wearing the clothes of a goatherder's wife and I still haven't had a bath—only a facewash—and the lice are back and I think they've multiplied. Is there no rest at all for the weary?"

"Never. Not in this job, anyway." He added with a grin, "You may never be in the newspapers, but it isn't everybody who has a jet plane specially commandeered for them." He glanced at his watch. "It's seven o'clock now, European time. There's a car and a plane waiting, you'll be in the air within the hour and land in America shortly before midnight—losing a few hours on the ocean, of course. Looks like Walter Reed Hospital for you, old chap."

Farrell nodded. "Afraid so, yes."

"America," repeated Mrs. Pollifax nostalgically. "I feel like singing the national anthem."

"Better not," suggested Farrell mildly, and visibly braced himself as the doctor joined them.

Twenty-three

They sat in Carstairs' office, each of them facing him across his broad desk. The lights had been turned low and there were cigarettes for Farrell and hot soup and coffee for them both. Farrell's arm was in a sling and he had been given four injections and seven hours of drugged sleep on the plane, but still he looked white and frail. After one glance at him Carstairs said flatly, "I won't keep you long. The important thing is to put the frame of this on tape before you forget; it will surprise you how unreal your adventures will seem to you once you reach a fairly normal state of recovery. At the moment it is only too fresh to you. We need that freshness. You've seen General Perdido—he's important to us. You've been in Albania—you've experienced a country we know too little about." His face softened. "And may I congratulate you both on rescuing Dr. Lee Tsung Howell?"

"You may," said Farrell with a grin.

"And on coming back yourselves," added Carstairs. "I don't mind telling you that I gave you both up long ago."

"Did you really!" exclaimed Mrs. Pollifax in a pleased voice.

"I'm going to call in Bishop now," went on Carstairs. "He'll take a few notes but the bulk of it will be put on tape tonight, the rest of the picture can be filled in tomorrow. I hope a tape recorder doesn't make you self-conscious?"

"Too tired," said Mrs. Pollifax.

He nodded. "I think we might give Johnny the rest he needs by letting you do most of the talking, Mrs. Pollifax. Johnny, you join in when it suits you, agreed?"

Bishop had come in, and Mrs. Pollifax noticed that his nostrils looked pinched during the introductions. "It's the goats," she told him forgivingly. "Just don't sit too near me." Half a day in the waters of Lake Scutari had subdued the smell but it was obvious that only a complete change of clothes and a vast amount of hot water and soap would ever make her acceptable to society again.

"*Goats?*" said Carstairs, startled.

She nodded. "Goats. Where would you like me to begin?"

"With your abduction—the rest can be filled in later," said Carstairs. "Begin with your meeting Johnny. That would be the nineteenth of August?"

She nodded. "*They* gave us soup and coffee too—the men in the shack." Awkwardly, and then with increasing absorption, she told of their flight to Albania and their subsequent days there, Farrell joining in occasionally to emphasize a point. Carstairs did not interrupt until Mrs. Pollifax mentioned the missile site.

"Missile site!" he exploded. "Missile site?"

"You didn't already know about this?" asked Mrs. Pollifax demurely.

"Albania is not a country where the CIA is given much scope," he said dryly. "No, we did not know about this, Mrs. Pollifax. Are you *sure* it was a missile site?"

"No," she said, "but Colonel Nexdhet was."

"Who . . . ?"

Farrell grinned. "Let her go on, it gets more and more interesting."

Mrs. Pollifax continued, eventually concluding, ". . . and we think the two men were left dead in their boats so we sailed west, straight out to sea, and by that time the Genie—that is, Dr. Howell—was more unconscious than conscious. At first we avoided any boats we saw in the distance but when we finally decided it was safe to be rescued nobody paid the slightest attention to us. We'd wave at them and they'd just wave back."

"Thought we were out for pleasure," added Farrell wryly.

Carstairs smiled and flicked off the switch of the tape recorder. "Quite a story. . . . Let's let it rest there for the moment. It's a good place to stop. There'll be many more details to clear up, more information on General Perdido, for instance, and I'd like that missile site pinpointed on a map if humanly possible. Those stone buildings, too. All this can wait, though. The important item—and after hearing what's happened to you the most surprising item—is that you're both alive."

Farrell said soberly, "You've very carefully avoided the beginning of all this, haven't you? Mexico City, I mean. I take it the whole thing blew up like a bomb and turned into a disaster area for us. They got DeGamez?"

Carstairs sighed. "I'm sorry you ask." He bent over a cigarette and a lighter, carefully avoiding Farrell's eye. "One thing lost, one thing found," he said. "Let's not underestimate what you accomplished in getting Dr. Lee Tsung Howell back, as well as yourselves." He put down the lighter and looked directly at Farrell. "Yes, Johnny, DeGamez is dead. He was murdered on the seventeenth of August."

"Damn," said Farrell savagely.

Mrs. Pollifax felt a tremor of shock run through her. She said quietly, "I'm terribly, terribly sorry. General Perdido did this?"

Carstairs nodded. "Fortunes of war, Mrs. Pollifax. All our agents know the risk."

She shivered. "Yes, but he was so kind, he was such a good man, he was such a *gentleman.*"

Carstairs suddenly became very still. Slowly he turned his head to stare at Mrs. Pollifax and his silence had a stunned quality. He said at last, very softly, "But how could you possibly know that, Mrs. Pollifax, when you never met the real Senor DeGamez?"

"Oh, but you see I did," she told him eagerly. "Not on the nineteenth, of course, but a few days after arriving in Mexico City—well, I had to be sure I could locate the shop, don't you see? And after finding it I passed it nearly every day. I really grew to think of it as *my* shop," she confessed with a rueful laugh. "And that's why—well, after passing it so many times and seeing him there I thought I would stop in one morning and browse around a little. I didn't think it would hurt," she added anxiously, suddenly noticing the intensity of Carstairs' gaze.

"Go on," he said in a stifled voice.

"So I went inside and we had a lovely chat, Senor DeGamez and I."

"When? What date?" The voice had urgency behind it.

"When? Why, it must have been—let's see, it was four days before the nineteenth, I believe. That would make it August 15 when I stopped in. Yes, it was definitely the fifteenth."

"What exactly did you 'chat' about?" demanded Carstairs, and so harshly that Farrell gave him a second glance and narrowed his eyes.

"Why, mostly about traveling alone, and the grandchildren we had, and did I play solitaire. He gave me a book called *77 Ways to Play Solitaire,* and although at the time I didn't warm to the idea—"

"Mrs. Pollifax," interrupted Carstairs in a strangled voice.

"Yes?"

"Mrs. Pollifax, DeGamez was given your photograph on the ninth of August."

"My *what?*"

"Mrs. Pollifax, when you walked into the Parrot Bookstore on August 15 DeGamez knew who you were. Do you understand, *he knew who you were?*"

A small gasp escaped Mrs. Pollifax.

"He must also have had very strong suspicions by that date that he was being closely watched. Mrs. Pollifax, I want you to tell me every word he said, and just where I can find that book."

"Oh, but there was nothing in the book," she assured him. "They thought there was, I forgot to tell you that, but General Perdido spent days somewhere having it tested. They found nothing."

Carstairs sat back and looked at her. He said carefully, "If DeGamez had received the microfilms, Mrs. Pollifax, I know that he would have found some way to give them to you on the fifteenth. I want you to think. I want you to go back and reconstruct that visit as closely as possible."

Very soberly Mrs. Pollifax sent her thoughts back to that morning.

"Describe it, tell me everything that happened."

Patiently and carefully Mrs. Pollifax began speaking of the morning when she first entered the shop. The book of memoirs. The parrot's shout. The conversation about Olé, about traveling alone, about American geese, and the presentation of the book on solitaire. "He wrapped both books together in white paper," she added, frowning. "But by that time two other customers had come in and so I left."

"Try again," said Carstairs.

Again Mrs. Pollifax described her visit, and once again uncovered nothing. "The two other customers had walked in, and he said something to me—in a more public voice, you understand—about wishing me a beautiful visit in his country. And then I—*oh*," she cried, "the *cards!*"

"Cards," repeated Carstairs, and leaned forward.

"Yes, of course," she said in a stunned voice. "How on earth could I have forgotten! It was just as I reached the door. He called out, 'But how can you play solitaire without the cards, senora'—yes, those were his words—and he threw them to me. Just threw them to me across the store. And he said, 'How do you Americans call it, on the house?' and I caught them. I held up two hands and caught them like a ball and tucked them into my purse. But surely he wouldn't throw anything of value like that, so casually, so impulsively, you don't think . . .?"

Carstairs' voice was filled with suppressed excitement. "That is precisely the way a man who is under surveillance would dispose of something dangerous. Mrs. Pollifax, what happened to those playing cards?"

Farrell said incredulously, "Duchess, that deck you played with in Albania, that's surely not—?"

"But of course," she told Farrell. To Carstairs she said, "I have them right here in my pocket."

Carstairs stared at her in astonishment. "You mean you carried them *with* you? You mean they're with you *now?* You still *have* them?"

Farrell began to laugh. "Have them! Carstairs, the Duchess here played solitaire with those playing cards day in and day out, endlessly, right under the guards' noses, and in front of General Perdido, too. Have them! She drove everybody nearly crazy with them."

Mrs. Pollifax gave him a reproachful glance. Reaching

down to her second petticoat she brought out the deck of cards and placed them on the desk. For a long moment Carstairs stared at them as if he could not quite believe they were there. Then he reached out and picked them up and ran his fingers over them. "Plasticized," he said softly. "They're enclosed in plastic. Bishop," he said in a strange voice, "Bishop, take these to the lab on the double. On the double, Bishop—it's microfilms we're after."

"Yes sir," gasped Bishop, and the door closed behind him.

Carstairs sat back and stared at Mrs. Pollifax with a look of incredulity.

"I know just how you feel," said Farrell, grinning. "She's full of surprises, what?"

"Rather, yes." Carstairs shook his head, a little smile tugging at the corner of his lips. "And ten days ago I believed I had sent an innocent lamb into a den of wolves. You seem to have great resources, Mrs. Pollifax."

"It's my age," said Mrs. Pollifax modestly.

"And if those cards should turn out to be . . ." Again Carstairs shook his head. "Why, then, nothing would have blown up in Mexico at all. It's incredible, absolutely incredible."

"But I simply can't think why I didn't remember about those cards," said Mrs. Pollifax. "In my mind I always identified them with Senor DeGamez, yet I completely overlooked his tossing them to me like that. Is this what's called a mental block?"

The phone buzzed and Carstairs picked it up. "Carstairs." He listened and grinned. "Right. Thanks, Bishop." Hanging up, he smiled at both Farrell and Mrs. Pollifax. "They've found the first microfilm. Tirpak used two packs of very thin playing cards. He cemented the back of one card to the front of another, with the film between, and enclosed each in special plastic." He added fervently, "If that was a mental block, Mrs. Pollifax, then bless it. Perdido would have sensed at once that you were concealing something—if you had consciously recalled how you received those cards. It very definitely saved your life when you were questioned, and it's certainly recovered for this country a great amount of invaluable information." He shook his head. "Mrs. Pollifax, we are in your debt."

She smiled and said gently, "If I could just have a bath and a change of clothes . . . I can't think of anything I'd enjoy more."

Carstairs laughed. "I'll make certain you have both within

the hour. And for you, Johnny—a bevy of beautiful nurses."

Farrell stumbled to his feet and walked to Mrs. Pollifax. He bent over and kissed her. "I won't say good-bye, Duchess, I couldn't. Just don't you dare leave town without coming to see me on my bed of pain."

Mrs. Pollifax looked up at him and beamed. "I'll bring roses, I promise you, my dear Farrell, and just to prove how opinionated and shortsighted you've been I'll also bring a deck of playing cards and teach you one or two games of solitaire."

He didn't smile. He said gravely, "A very small price to pay for my life, Duchess. . . . God bless you and have a *wonderful* bath."

Mrs. Pollifax put down her suitcase in front of the door to apartment 4-A and groped in her purse for the key. It seemed a long, long time since she had last stood here, and it filled her with a sense of awe that the externals of life could remain so unchanged when she felt so different. Like a kaleidoscope, she thought, her imagination captured by the simile: one swift turn of the cylinder and all the little bits and pieces of colored glass fell into a different pattern. As she inserted her key into the lock a door across the hall flew open, spilling sunlight across the black and white tiles of the floor. "Mrs. Pollifax, you're back at last!" cried Miss Hartshorne.

Mrs. Pollifax stiffened. She said, turning, "Yes, I'm home again, and how have you been, Miss Hartshorne?"

"As well as can be expected, thank you. You must have had a marvelous trip to stay so long."

"Yes, marvelous," agreed Mrs. Pollifax with a faint smile.

"I've a package for you, it came this morning and I signed for it." Miss Hartshorne held up one hand dramatically. "Don't go away, don't even move, I'll be right back."

Mrs. Pollifax waited, and presently her neighbor reappeared carrying a box wrapped in brown paper and covered with seals. "It came special delivery all the way from Mexico City! I'm giving you last night's newspaper, too, so you can catch up on our news here."

"How very kind of you," said Mrs. Pollifax. "Won't you come in and have a cup of tea with me?"

Miss Hartshorne looked shocked. "Oh, I wouldn't dream of bothering you now. As an experienced traveler myself I know how utterly exhausted you must be. But I hope you'll invite me in soon to see your slides. I trust you don't mind, I took it upon myself to tell the Lukes and Mrs. Ohrbach that they could see them too. We're all looking forward to them so much."

Mrs. Pollifax said quietly, "I'm afraid there'll be no slides, Miss Hartshorne."

Her neighbor's jaw dropped. "No slides? You mean your pictures didn't come out?" Her glance was stern. "Didn't you study the lighting charts I gave you?"

You've forgotten pi again, Emily. . . . Mrs. Pollifax smiled and said gently, "I didn't take any snapshots, I was too busy."

"Too busy?" Miss Hartshorne looked horrified.

"Yes, too busy. In fact it might surprise you how busy I really was, Miss Hartshorne." She added firmly, "I believe I'll insist that you come in for a cup of tea now if you have the time. I don't believe we've ever had a cup of tea together, have we?"

Miss Hartshorne looked shaken. "Why—why, no," she said in an astonished voice. "No, I don't believe we have."

Mrs. Pollifax pushed wide the door and walked inside. "Do sit down, I'll put some water on to boil and then I'll join you." Leaving package and newspaper on the couch she hurried out to the kitchen to fill the tea kettle. "There," she said, returning, "that won't take but a minute." From where she sat she could see the headline on the newspaper that Miss Hartshorne had given her: RESCUED SCIENTIST GAINS STRENGTH, DR. HOWELL TO MEET PRESS TOMORROW. Mrs. Pollifax smiled contentedly.

"Your package," pointed out Miss Hartshorne.

"I beg your pardon?"

"The package. Aren't you dying of curiosity or is it something you ordered from Mexico?"

Startled, Mrs. Pollifax turned to eye the box beside her. "No, I didn't order it and yes, I *am* curious. Would you hand me the scissors on the table beside you, Miss Hartshorne? I'll attack this right now."

Scissors in hand she cut the strings. The box inside bore the label of a very expensive shop near the Hotel Reforma Intercontinental. "What on earth," she murmured, and eagerly tore it open. "Serapes!" she gasped.

"How beautiful," said Miss Hartshorne in a hushed voice. "A gift? How many friends you must have made, Mrs. Pollifax."

Mrs. Pollifax lifted out first one and then another until the couch was aflame with their brilliant colors.

"Six!" cried Miss Hartshorne.

"Why so there are," beamed Mrs. Pollifax. "One for each grandchild, one for Roger, one for Jane and one for myself. Isn't that lovely?" Then she saw the card that had been slipped between the folds of the last serape. It read very simply, "With mingled gratitude and apologies, Carstairs."

Carstairs. . . . A great warmth filled Mrs. Pollifax at the thoughtfulness of such a busy man. She glanced around her apartment at the familiar furniture, the sunshine striping the rugs, the atmosphere of quiet security, and just for a moment a procession of unusual people trouped through her thoughts: a goatherder and his wife, a Genie who talked of life's choices being like intersections on a road map, Colonel Nexdhet of the walrus moustache, Lulash, Major Vassovic and a man named John Sebastian Farrell who faced pain with gaiety. She said with a smile, "I met a great many unforgettable people on my trip, Miss Hartshorne. Somewhat eccentric people, perhaps, but extremely unforgettable, all of them."

Simultaneously the tea kettle began to sing and the telephone rang. Mrs. Pollifax said hastily, "Oh, Miss Hartshorne, would you pour the tea? The tea bags are in the cupboard over the stove and so are the cups. Do you mind?"

Miss Hartshorne laughed. It was the first time that Mrs. Pollifax had ever heard her laugh. "How casually you live, Mrs. Pollifax. This takes me back to my college days. No, of course I don't mind, this is really quite fun." Over her shoulder she called, "Call me Grace, won't you?"

But Mrs. Pollifax had already picked up the telephone. "Why Roger!" she exclaimed with pleasure. "How wonderful to hear from you, dear. Yes, I got in only a moment ago." She listened attentively to her son. "Worried?" she repeated. "You worried about me when I telegraphed I was staying longer? Yes, I fully intended to write but I was so busy." Mrs. Pollifax laughed suddenly and delightedly. "Roger dear, what possible trouble could I have gotten into at my age and in Mexico of all places. . . ." Her gaze fell to the serapes lying on the couch. With a small, very private smile Mrs. Pollifax picked up the card that had arrived with them and slipped it into her pocket.